GOING NOWHERE SIDEWAYS

Going Nowhere Sideways

a novel

Leigh Curran

FITHIAN PRESS · SANTA BARBARA · 1999

Copyright © 1998 by Leigh Curran
Printed in the United States of America

Published by Fithian Press
A division of Daniel and Daniel, Publishers, Inc.
Post Office Box 1525
Santa Barbara, CA 93102

Book design: Eric Larson

LIBRARY OF CONGRESS CATALOGING-IN-PUBLICATION DATA
Curran, Leigh.
    Going nowhere sideways : a novel / by Leigh Curran.
      p.   cm.
    ISBN 1-56474-289-X (alk. paper)
    I. Title.
    PS3553.U664G65   1999
    813'.54—dc21
                                                    98-34547
                                                        CIP

For all the people who told me I was too tall to act.

Without their discouragement,
I never would have written a word.

ACKNOWLEDGMENTS

Special thanks to my mother, Barbara Griggs, for her wisdom, curiosity and proofreading skills; to Montine Hansl and Kendis Marcotte for their absolute faith; to Sherry Sonnett for her editorial expertise; and to Kate Corisand, Paul Benedict, David Greenan, Sloane Shelton, Patricia O'Connell and Mary Petrie for feedback that stuck.

GOING NOWHERE SIDEWAYS

I had never smoked dope and I had certainly never done acid so
when I began to see people's faces melting and the sky raining
blood I closed my eyes, which I had been warned not to do, and fell
into the void. Joan Baez sang something meaningful and Janis
Joplin did more damage to her throat. Jimi Hendrix threatened to
pull me back with the Star Spangled Banner...even opened my eyes
which closed with a scream when his crotch burst into flame. In the
void there were monsters of my own making and the guy I had
come with was swimming nude in a muddy pond with his best
friend's old lady.

If I hadn't been so depressed I might not have gone. Might not
have wandered over to Washington Square and seen the crudely written letters on a piece of paper bag: Woodstock. Might not have started
a conversation with a stringy-haired stranger and gotten into a van
with him and a couple of other people and headed north pretending
I had lived as long and hard as they had when, in fact, I hadn't which
is probably why I was feeling so depressed to begin with.

A few nights before in an alcoholic rage my boyfriend, Davis,
called me an arrogant fuck because I appeared shocked when I
stumbled on him necking with his roommate at a table for two in
the back of a restaurant in Greenwich Village. As soon as I retrieved
my jaw from the floor, I fled, locked the door to my apartment,
turned off the phone, opened this journal and burst into tears. Determined not to let the apparent end of my "relationship" with
Davis get the better of me, I collected myself, turned on the radio
and switched from WQXR to parts unknown. And as "This is the
Dawning of the Age of Aquarius" unsettled the stuffy air in my

modest walk-up, I stood before my bathroom mirror, parted my hair in the middle and searched my tear-stained face for the hippy who would free me from older men, the *New York Times* and classical music.

The next day, on my way to work, this scrap of paper attached itself to something on the bottom of my shoe:

TOFU, RICE CAKES, ORGANIC CARROTS
NOW IS ALL THERE EVER IS.
PEANUT BUTTER, MUNG BEANS, SPROUTS, GOAT'S MILK
THERE ARE NO—

And I decided since Now is all there ever is I would go with the first thing that came into my mind that would complete the second sentence and that was: There are no good reasons to go to work. So I didn't. Didn't even call in. Just began walking. Taking in the day and the city. When I came to a corner I went in the direction that felt right at that moment. And the moment began to so absorb me that I found a euphoria replacing the anguish I thought I should be feeling and wondered if what I'd been in with Davis was Love...or some sort of idea of it. And suddenly there I was in Washington Square on a glorious day and there was this guy with stringy hair holding a sign that said Woodstock and that reminded me of the scrap of paper so the first thing I said to him was: Finish this sentence. There are no— And he said: Accidents.

At that moment a psychedelic van pulled up in front of us and it was pretty clear the only place to be was on it.

Inside the van I took my first look at a joint. A young woman whose name I can't remember...a sort of earthy, flowing thing with scattered hair and understanding eyes, took the joint to her lips, licked it, lit it...and sucked it deep into her lungs. Then she held it out to me.

Acapulco gold...she said readjusting a generous breast so her baby could keep on nursing.

I considered taking a toke but was afraid since I didn't smoke I'd start coughing and give myself away. The woman whose name I can't remember, instantly hip to my ambivalence, motioned for the joint and discreetly gave me a demonstration.

You haven't lived until you've made love stoned...she said.

God...she was probably right. I took the joint. I looked at the guy with stringy hair. Dirty skin. Beads. Barefeet. I tried to imagine us "in the sack." Then, as if our thoughts had actually comingled, his skinny arm crept along the top of the back seat. I handed him the joint in an effort to divert his intentions. He took a hit and, as the joint dangled from his mingy lips, he let his arm fall casually over my shoulder. I looked at the woman whose name...whatever. She rolled her large, soulful eyes.

You got an old man, Molly?...she asked.

Well...I stammered.

She nodded her head as if 'yes' was the only answer.

Sure...I said. Then added: Over thirty...(which was true)...and for good measure tossed out: Republican.

Pretty soon the arm found its way back to the top of the seat where it remained until the proper amount of time had passed and it could be returned, without embarrassment, into the lap of its owner.

What's his name?...asked the woman.

Davis...I said and found myself awash in a wave of nausea.

I'm hip...she said...my old man, awwww...it is so fucking complicated. Why is it always so fucking complicated? Like... where's the joy? Except I got you, Babe...she said nuzzling the bald head having its way with her breast. All they're really good for is making babies. What do you think about that, assholes?...she said raising her voice to the entire van.

Time to cop a few zzzzzzs...said the guy with stringy hair.

And that's pretty much what he did in spite of several shabby choruses of Cum Baya which eventually segued into I Can't Get No Satisfaction.

On the 10-mile walk from the car to the concert the woman whose name I can't remember lit another joint and I took (yes, it's true) my first puff of marijuana. The rush was so liberating that I began a conversation about rock music as if I were an authority. Mainly I thought fans should start a protest against rock groups who mumble their lyrics. The driver of the van said: They don't make any sense anyway. The woman said: Who? The lyrics or the fans? And the guy with stringy hair said: Your thing is your thing.

And I suddenly felt pompous and exacting like Davis who is (no, WAS) obsessed with saving the English language from extinction which is why I'm sure he gave me this journal. He said it was so I'd have a place to put the secrets of my soul…but I know he meant abandon my fondness for ellipses…employ the King's English and, above all, USE QUOTATION MARKS! Electrical wires hissed and spit in the pit of my stomach. Somebody passed me the joint again and after burning my newly cut bangs trying to relight it…I asked the question: When you know you don't belong where you are and you stay anyway…are you in the moment? The guy with stringy hair said: Bummer, man. The earthy, flowing thing with no name gave me an understanding pat on the back and I started flashing like a neon sign on my last year with Davis. The mood swings, the nervous excuses and the tearful confusion that accompanied Davis's attempts to, let's just say it: Get It Up! And the sudden shock of recognition opened my mouth and to the hills of Woodstock and long, spaced-out lines of my generation I shouted: You were never impotent! You were fucking your fucking boyfriend!

And I began to laugh and cry at the same time. The woman whose name I can't remember had gotten swallowed, along with her baby, in a wave of Birkenstocks that was crashing on a fallow cornfield and nobody else was paying much attention. I was, evidently, doing my own thing. I grabbed onto a serious, square-looking woman in front of me who had most likely exchanged her dress for a pair of jeans and a sweatshirt the day "The Female Eunuch" came out and never taken them off.

Men are assholes…she said unsympathetically.

That was the second time in one day a woman had called a man an asshole. And both times I'd secretly wanted to agree with them. And the realization that my mind was actually responsible for such a shameful thought—

Take me home. Somebody please take me home! I'm not supposed to be here!

I held out my thumb and worked my way to the back of the line.

We're never going to get out of here…I cried. As soon as the concert is over this line will reverse itself and an entire generation will be stranded in rural America.

A big burly guy with a bandana on his head put his arm around my shoulders and taught me the meaning of the word: Paranoia. Then he gave me a Valium which turned out to be acid and anyone or anything that might have been familiar was lost to me.

Johnson said I was carried into the medical emergency tent kicking and screaming. I know when I looked into his almond eyes and his shiny, black hair fell between us, I buried myself in it as if I were burying myself in Jesus.

He said the first thing I wanted him to know was that I didn't smoke or drink and that included caffeine and I wasn't particularly political so would he please not ask me how I felt about draft dodgers hiding out in Canada. When he asked me what I'd taken I said: Nothing. Then I started to cry and braid the lock of hair that was draped over his shoulder.

There's some bad acid going around…he said.

No one wants to take me home.

Where's home?

I don't knooooow!

And he put his arms around me and rocked me back to reality as if he had all the time in the world. Later I learned he also had a car.

Chapter One

Molly's wide fingers drift across the cover of her journal. She doesn't think she'll keep on reading. It makes her feel prickly and stifled. Pinned like a butterfly to the indifferent pages of an unremarkable life.

She pulls at the oversized sweatshirt that has become her nightgown and shifts her weight on the floor of the closet in the Manhattan walk-up she moved into shortly before Woodstock and, until recently, thought she had left behind.

The voices of children collect on the stoop underneath her window as Molly leans against the closet wall and stares at the jungle animal sheets that lie damp and twisted on the history of her bed. For the past month they have held her agony and been her place of peace. Then two days ago she curled in the fetal position and put down roots. They spread into her box spring and on down to the place beneath. And this morning when she opened her eyes she was actually sucking her thumb.

'It is definitely time to get up,' she thought as her upstairs neighbor flushed the toilet. 'Time to put on my coat, pay my bills and get some food. Time to quit stewing and start DOING!'

It took every fading particle of determination, every flickering sliver of hope for Molly to lift her chest and maneuver her hips to the side of her bed. For a while she sat in the startled breath of a new position and wondered how a spirited girl who passionately believed there were no accidents could end up a thumbsucking bag of bones whose entire life felt like a train wreck. Then, in case she was tempted to put

down roots, she moved her right hip off the edge of her bed and
reached for her winter coat with her toes. She was swatting at the hem
when she heard something slide under the door in the living room.

'Perfect,' she thought, 'an eviction notice.'

And as she summoned the energy to stand, her winter coat slid to
the floor of her closet and landed on top of an unmarked box. Molly
meant to pay her rent, she really did…but the lump on her closet floor
was far more compelling and as she moved her coat to one side, the
chatter returned in full force.

'Molly, leave the box where it is and pay the rent. You are such a
panic artist. Fuck you. Asshole. This is constructive. What if he calls
the police? What if he does? You don't mean that. Try me. Molly, get off
your knees. We are through looking back. That's why we got out of the
bed. Thank you for sharing. Close the box. You read this shit you won't
get out alive! Good! Good? You heard me…good!'

Molly's upstairs neighbor turned on the shower. Molly could hear
the water running through the pipes inside her closet as she opened the
journal Davis had given her and started to read. Almost eighteen years
had passed since she'd taken refuge in its cool, blue-lined pages. Eighteen
years of telling the truth, then tucking it away in an unmarked box.

'That's nice. Now, let's get up. I might as well be on my way to
Woodstock. Molly, don't go there. But nothing's changed. That's why
we're going to pay the rent and press on. Molly?'

Later

On the long, slow voyage from Woodstock to our former lives I
learned about Matilda, Johnson's live-in old lady…and about the
baby they are expecting and the commune they are getting ready to
leave New York City for. I said babies made me nervous. I thought it
was best to come out with it. Johnson laughed a gentle laugh and
said: They make me nervous, too. I said: Then why are you doing it?
And he said: 'Pain is the breaking of the shell that encloses understanding.'

Then there was this silence. I can't explain it. It was as if we
both stopped breathing. As if we sensed, deep in our bones, the next
step was levitation. Then some jerk tooted at us because we had neglected to move forward the half inch we were allotted every fifteen
minutes and all Johnson said was: Kahlil Gibran. I nodded like I

knew what he was talking about. Then he smiled because he knew I didn't and I blushed because I knew he knew and very gently he said: The Prophet. And that was the first time I felt helpless. And probably because he could tell, he started talking about how "The Prophet" changed his life. How it taught him all about Unconditional Love.

By then I didn't know whether to laugh or cry or jump out the window. Every time he opened his mouth he took me someplace I hadn't been but had been secretly trying to go! It was much more liberating than acid! But the body part.... And the last year of waiting for Davis to get it up.... I swear to God, if J.'s old lady hadn't've been pregnant...or, for that matter, if she'd hadn't've been...I would have taken him right there on the front seat of his VW bug. Well, assuming it was mutual.

Anyway, by the time he got around to asking me about Davis, he was so beside the point (Davis), all I could do was laugh and admit how totally relieved I felt to be finally FREE!

Free to do what?...asked Johnson.

I don't know. There is so much going on! Protests, riots, assassinations, demonstrations...the entire Age of Aquarius...and, it's like...where have I been?! Who have I been? WHY have I been?

Johnson looked out the driver's window at green trees and pockets of poverty. He seemed suddenly sad. As if he'd turned a corner that was all his own. A persistent breeze tugged at a strand of his hair gradually lifting it until it slithered like a small snake across his high forehead. I felt suddenly responsible. As if I'd hurt his feelings. Said something careless and unthinking about children when I asked him why he and his old lady were going to have their baby...especially if it made him nervous.

There was this woman I met on the way up here...I babbled. I can't remember her name. Anyway, she couldn't have been more than nineteen and she was already a mother...but, she was in her life. You could tell. Her love was...what you were talking about.... Unconditional. You could see it in her eyes. When I said babies scare me...it's like...I don't want to have them because I'm supposed to...that's all. Or because I don't know what else to do with my life. When I turn forty I want to be proud of the choices I've made.

Johnson sighed and brushed the snake off his forehead.

I want to be proud of how I've handled the unexpected...he said softly.

And I hoped, however stupidly, that he was referring in his own elliptical way to US.

By the time we hit the New York Thruway we had abandoned the meaning of life for the science of astrology and the stories of our birth. I went first. I was an induced baby who managed to arrive a day late, nonetheless. My mother said (still says) it was a sure sign I would always insist on having My Own Way (which is the polite way of calling me Selfish). I say I was a day late because I wanted my stars to be in the right position because I didn't see the point of taking up space on earth if I wasn't going to live a useful life.

Johnson's birth was normal except for the fact that his mother only spoke Chinese. His father was away on some secret mission for the Air Force and somehow his mother got herself to the hospital and when the nurse approached her with the birth certificate asking what she was going to name her baby she said the only English word she knew which was the name of her doctor...Dr. Johnson. J. was lucky. My doctor's name is Snelling.

Anyway, when J. was eight his parents separated because his mother insisted on treating him with acupuncture instead of taking him to a doctor for Western medicine. But his father was a Fundamentalist and the only needles he'd seen stuck in anything were in Voodoo dolls. When Johnson caught pneumonia from his best friend in grammar school his mother reassured his father that his fever was a good thing...he was releasing toxins. But when the fever didn't break Johnson's father pirated him, in the middle of the night, to the emergency room of the local hospital where Johnson proceeded to get worse. His father, who (in Johnson's words) "meant to be patient but saw to it that he failed"...blamed his Chinese wife and she blamed the chemicals in Western medicine and the wound grew and festered until the truth, which had never been entirely clear, had been successfully buried.

When I told J. my life was drab by comparison, he asked me why I felt I had to apologize. I had never thought of it quite that way...which is what I mean about him and why it's so sad he's got this other life.... But, anyway, I told him how my parents are still married and living in the house where I grew up in Connecticut.

And how my sister, Heather, is getting ready to go to Barnard and how my brother, Conrad, graduated from dental school in June and is now in practice in Greenwich with my father. And that while they are all nice people I can't honestly say I feel close to any of them...except for my brother's wife, Nancy...and how sometimes she and I go for walks in the woods and tell each other the whole truth and nothing but the truth. Or, anyway, as much of it as we can decipher.

Then, in the middle of the Palisades Parkway, some idiot threw a container of junk food out the window as if, in J.'s words: The world was his toilet. And that got us into a discussion of the environment. Words like Nuclear Waste and Carbon Monoxide jangled in the air waiting to be considered. I struggled to keep up. The depth of his commitment sent my heart soaring. His knowledge drew my brain inside his head. His love for his work filled me with the courage to define my own and when we parted outside of my apartment on 31st between Second and Third I had been reborn. Refocused. And I saw what was good about the movement and I felt the pride I'd always been leery of feeling at being born a member of the Peace and Love generation. He said: Good luck. And I said: Thanks. And he said: Stay conscious! It's not only your life...it's your planet!

Yesterday I was fired from my "job" at the reception desk in the ad agency, for disappearing without proper notice...and today I received a note from Davis on purple paper and stuck it in the back of this journal. I thought about opening it but something in me went completely cold...like when my baby brother died and I heard my mother say: He's been sick for a long time. He would want us to go on. So that's what we did. That's what we always do. I can't even remember the last time we talked about him (Timmy). Time will do the same thing to Davis.

PS: Am LOVING "The Prophet." Keep thinking about Unconditional Love and the woman whose name I can't remember. Have decided to call her Chloe.

October
Guess what? I got the job in that New Age bookstore on St. Mark's
Place! I start tomorrow. I get to read about tofu and biorhythms
and the power of thought. This is my new thing. The Power of
Thought. It's right up there with Unconditional Love. In fact, when
you really think about it, you can't have one without the other. Well,
maybe if you're evil and SELFISH and only care about your own ad-
vancement. Anyway, I told this to Nancy. I said: It isn't up to politi-
cians anymore…it's up to us! Nancy nodded her head but I could
tell she wasn't listening so I took her hand and said: Let's sit down
right now and love Washington, D.C., unconditionally. Then, I'm
sorry, she looked at me like I was deluded or pathetic and I told her
to go fuck herself. And she said she had a lot on her mind and I told
her it was time for her to hire a nanny so her life wasn't all about
kids, kids, kids.

April, 1970
Nancy's gone. Left Conrad with all three kids. Just like that. Heather
read the note. It said something like: Dear Conrad.… I'm not who
you think I am or who I wish I was. She didn't even sign it Love.

Later
I don't know why, but I keep expecting Nancy to call. Or at least
show up at the bookstore. I surround her with white light (but I
don't tell anybody). Mother is in a total snit. First I break up with
Davis who we all know was the "perfect gentleman"…and now
Nancy, the "perfect mother," leaves Conrad. Maybe I shouldn't say
this, but I can see leaving Conrad. He is so committed to being
solid. But the kids…I mean, I never thought I'd hear myself agree
with Mother, but talk about Selfish.… It's like there should be a law.
People shouldn't be allowed to get pregnant until they know who
they are. There should be a test. For individuals and couples. And it
should be rigorous. I started to say as much (in semi-jest) and my
father got off into this whole thing about Gloria Steinem and how
she is the one who is really responsible. I said: But, Father, she
doesn't have kids. And he said: My point exactly. Thank God
Heather was on a break from Barnard. We went to the Yacht Club
(because we could charge it to my parents) and had a good, stiff

drink. Come on, Nancy! Get it together. Call! I won't hold it against you...I promise.

July, 1970

Started reading a great book today. That Jamaican woman told me about it. The one with the long, skinny face who came in on her lunch break to talk to Devon about becoming the new assistant manager. Hatia (sp?). It's called "Future Shock" and it's all about what will happen to the planet if we don't begin to DO something instead of talk, talk, talk. I invited her to that consciousness raiser on Saturday in Brooklyn. The one about nuclear waste. She picked my brain about Devon. I told her he's really laid back...especially for a boss.

Still think about Johnson. Wonder how he's doing in his commune in Pennsylvania with his new baby. I hope he's miserable. But I'm better about it.

Sunday

Finished "Future Shock." Can't quit shaking. Hatia said I should start "The Findhorn Garden" right away so I don't collapse in total despair. Met this Armenian guy at a lecture on carcinogens at the New School, instead. He smelled like Patchouli so I slept with him. All I could think about was Johnson. So much for casual sex.

Still no Nancy. Hope she wasn't murdered. But I guess there's not much we can do if she was.

DON'T FORGET!: NEXT SATURDAY, 10AM—THE GEORGE MCGOVERN RALLY. BRING APPLES, WATER AND THE STAPLE GUN!

Chapter Two

Molly rests her head on the back of her closet as Davis's unopened letter in the purple envelope falls to the floor. She has forgotten the names of half the people she marched with, brainstormed with, wrote slogans with and hoped to convert. She rarely thinks about the regulars who crowded the back of the bookstore after hours for her Talk-a-thons. Their faces have merged with the faces from Woodstock. Except for Chloe, the mountain of motherhood, the blossoming bosom of Unconditional Love. She looms and dangles and refuses to be erased by the recent realization that true understanding or connection or whateverthefuckitis, is a myth because human beings can only perceive each other through Thought and therefore will never be, CAN never be, anything more to each other than shimmering figments of lonely imaginations. And as for Unconditional Love....

Molly closes the journal Davis gave her and decides to crawl back into bed like an aging animal to slink into the heart of forty to decompose.

'See, I told you all this reading would only fuck you up. Let's get some food. Let's get under the covers. No, no, not the covers. We'll get stuck. Then let's take a hot bath. Get out the razor. Will you stop with the razor? There has to be one somewhere. Behind something. The radiator. The rollaway. Or what about the mat knife that fell down the airshaft? Are you kidding? Go outside? She can't get her butt off the floor of her closet.'

Molly puts her arms over her head and rests her forehead on her knees. She is as disturbed by her thoughts of mat knives and razors as she is by her thumb. Why can't she think of herself with fondness? Why can't she feel something other than a bitter combination of shame and pity for the tall, loud, slightly horsy young woman who asked too many questions and assumed too many answers but who became a fixture, nonetheless, in the bookstore on St. Mark's Place by the sheer dint of her passion for true and honest change? Why can't she admire herself for standing alone in the face of the infighting, the mindfucking, the powerplays and the endless experimentation with drugs, drugs, drugs?

"Guys, I don't know how else to say this but Peace doesn't come to the Unconscious. It also doesn't come to the Pissed Off. Peace comes because we take responsibility for our actions. And that includes our Rage. And Rage is energy, pure and simple. And energy can be transformed. And I know, I know…I came into the movement late and you're all sick of the word Love…but, guys, the older generation…they aren't the ones who are going to change. They don't have the tools or the time. We do. We're young. We're curious. And we've got brains. Remember your brains? We can't go unconscious because George McGovern was defeated."

"Annihilated is more like it."

"It's time to quit stewing and start DOING!"

"Get a life!"

"This is my life!"

"This is your sex."

"Back off, Douche Bag. He didn't mean it, Molly."

"Fucking Richard fucking Nixon!?"

"It's a sign."

"It's not a sign. It's an opportunity!"

"If you're going to start with that 'Pain is the breaking of the shell' bullshit."

Molly puts the journal Davis gave her on top of his purple letter as a shaft of sunlight penetrates the years of soot that cling to the window over her bed, illuminating frenetic particles of dust and creating a warm glow in the sanctity of her cave. She looks at the composition book that lies on her bedside table and considers writing something…anything, but her pen has run out of ink and, finally, there is nothing left to say. And that leads her, once again to the single-edged razor. She'd bought a box of them when she'd first moved into

the apartment, drunk on potential and riddled with hope. She'd in-
tended to clean her landlord's lackluster paint job off the living room
window so she'd have a clear view of the airshaft. She remembers a ra-
zor falling behind something. The radiator? The rollaway…or maybe
the stove. Or no! The refrigerator! Her heart begins to race.

'It will still be there. Come on! Let's go. It will be rusty but it'll be
there. Hatia never cleaned behind anything. She was too superstitious.
And she had all kinds of stories about the troubled well that housed the
refrigerator.'

The last ray of sunlight flickers then falls off the wall and dies.
Molly shivers and realizes she has arrived at the fork in a deeply
twisted road. If she leaves the closet she will retrieve the razor and
bleed to death in a hot pink bath. If she gets back in bed she'll revert to
infancy and die of neglect.

Molly pulls the hem of her coat over her shoulders.

'Mommy, I want Mommy! Get lost. I'm scared. Well, I'm bored.
Well, I want to see how far we can go.'

Molly digs her fingernails into her scalp and decides to make her-
self a deal. If the street lamp comes on by the count of ten she will read
the journal with the flower decals on it. If not she will move the refrig-
erator. 1-2-3-4-5-6-7-8-9-

December, 1972

This is so weird! Just when I'm losing faith in the power of thought
(to say nothing of my "friends") who should walk into the bookstore but JOHNSON!!! I kid you not! I did this totally major double
take right there in Eastern Philosophy. I saw the back of his head
first. That silky, black hair. And before I could say: Get a grip!…my
heart, which has been on hold for what is probably a world record,
leapt out of my chest and threw itself around his long, graceful and
unmistakable neck.

Johnson?

Molly?

(Oh, my god…he remembered my name!)

What a surprise!…I stammered. What are you doing here?

Christmas shopping. What about you?

This is where I work.

Lucky you. Oh, sorry…this is my son, Ethan.

Hi, Ethan...I said extending my hand as Ethan pulled back, turned into the knees of a person in black leather and burst into tears.

Johnson picked him up. Said he was tired (Ethan). We kind of had to cut to the chase. Johnson said he was going to Columbia to become an environmental lawyer. <u>DOING!!</u> not stewing! Then the man in black leather asked me to help him with a special order. Why did it have to be so busy? And J. asked me if I wanted to go for coffee on my break but I'd already forfeited it so Hatia could go home early because she has some sort of Asian flu or maybe German...I don't know. Anyway, I tried not to babble but I was afraid Johnson was going to tell me he and Matilda were blissfully happy. When he said the commune had fallen into disarray I gave him my card. He smiled and put it in his wallet. Then I sold him a copy of "Mastering the Art of Meditation" and as soon as he walked out the door I felt soooo LONELY! I can't begin to tell you. I'm glad things suck on the farm. I know it isn't very metaphysical of me...or, for that matter, Unconditional...Heeeeelp! I don't want to think about him anymore!! It's like what's the POOOOOOOINT?????!!!!!

Tuesday! 1973!!

Johnson called!!! He needs a babysitter for Ethan. Matilda is having what sounds like a nervous breakdown (yes!) and he has some big exam. I called in sick. Thank God Hatia answered the phone. I didn't want to lie to Devon because he's been so nice about the Talk-a-thons. Hatia knew what I was up to immediately. I told her if she breathed a word to anybody I'd unleash my unconverted rage at all the assholes who are destroying the ozone layer, beam it toward St. Mark's Place and wipe her totally O-U-T. She said: You go, Girl! And I could see her lips coming together...sort of pooching the way they do in what has got to be the world's softest, sexiest kiss. Will you listen to me? Johnson doesn't have a chance! Is that good or bad? Fuck it. (Only if it's mutual) Oh, God...it feels as if he is (they are) never going to get here! Please, please, please...I'll do anything You wan— The buzzer! Heeeeellllllppp!

Later

Ethan is finally asleep and I'm quietly praying he stays that way until Johnson gets back and takes me (us) out to dinner because Lord knows, I've earned it. Not that this experience hasn't been good for me. I mean, Ethan's definitely his own person. But what are you supposed to do with an eighteen-month-old for five hours? And he's so frail. Kind of exotic looking, actually, with auburn hair and almond eyes and a sprinkling of freckles on this almost translucent skin.

Anyway, after Johnson left, I sat beside him. Nancy always said the best thing to be with your kids is yourself…especially when they're scared. So, since I'm a talker, I thought I'd engage him in conversation. When that failed I gave him a copy of something by Alan Watts to chew on and put the toys that Johnson had brought on the floor. But Ethan remained rooted to his spot determined not to respond so I turned on the TV and we watched the news.

Ever notice how when Richard Nixon is through talking there's this little smirk of a smile that crosses his face that just reeks of "Don't trust me," I said. My parents voted for that man. You can be proud of your father. He has a social conscience. Did you know he acquainted me with mine? Quite accidentally on the Palisades Parkway somewhere around Nyack. He has probably acquainted you with yours, too. See, here we are…total strangers and already we have something in common.

Ethan's eyes filled with tears.

Do you like apple cider?…I asked hopefully. It's organic.

Ethan began rocking his body. Tears fell onto his cheeks. I reached for his hand but it was withdrawn. I sat awkwardly. I imagined J. coming through the door alarmed by my inadequacy. I wondered what Chloe would do. Ethan banged his head on the back of the couch.

Ethan, stop! You'll hurt yourself. Why do you want to hurt yourself? Ethan, please!

And I found his squirming body in my arms as afraid to be held as I was to let go.

Ethan shhhhhh…I'll put you down but you mustn't bang your head. Come on…please. Why are you so afraid of me?

The struggle continued to escalate…tears falling out of my eyes, now.

Look, I'm sorry...I said as Ethan's attention turned to the on-off button on the television. I don't know a whole lot about kids, okay? Being a mother is sort of out there somewhere along with whoever it is I'm supposed to marry if I'm supposed to marry any-body which I may not...be supposed to. Because, let's face it...I like my life. And you guys take over...I know. My brother has three of you and he can't hear himself think. I can take it for about an hour then my muscles bulge and my knees get stiff and I turn into—

And I walked around the room snarling and growling like Fran-kenstein. Ethan ran into the bathroom and hid behind the door. I knocked gently. No response.

So how old were you when you lost your sense of humor?...I said.

The toilet flushed. I waited uncertainly. It flushed again. Then it became too quiet. When I opened the door I discovered Ethan had removed his rubber pants and some of his diaper and was peeing on the floor. I washed him off...or tried to. I wrapped him in a bath towel and laid him on my bed. He watched me try to remember how to fold a cloth diaper. His eyes are like Johnson's...they look through you into parts unknown. I turned his attention toward the baby powder. I figured something out and moved the diaper under-neath him. He insisted on shaking the powder on himself, on me, then on the bed. Then he jumped on it and a white dust settled on the room. The third and final time I repinned his diaper he became fascinated with my lower lip...pulling on it like a rubber band. This turned into a game where he approached my face with his hand and I tried to kiss it before he pulled it away. Laughter followed (whew!) and eventually I was able to read him "Pat the Bunny" and he was able to fall asleep in my lap and I was able to hold him as if it had always been that way with us. And that was nice.

God, I wish Johnson would get back. Isn't that terrible?

Thursday
Canceled the Talk-a-thon tonight. Only one person showed up. It was just as well. Ethan's babysitter had somewhere to go. When I asked Hatia if I could go home an hour early to relieve her Hatia got into a rap about Equality and how Johnson should pay me for babysitting since I do it more than the regular babysitter. God! It's not like J. hasn't offered.

Later
I'm getting better with Ethan. I'm not taking his outbursts so personally. I imagine I'm Chloe. I take a deep breath and wait for her
wisdom. She's begun to respond. Last night she told me to give him
something special to play with. Something that is special to me and
he knows it. So I gave him my journal. He looked at me with the
most delightful combination of bewilderment and delight. It's
amazing with kids...how fast their feelings change. Like the sun
breaking through my bedroom window. Anyway, I gave him a pencil and let him scribble (see previous page) and when he started to
jab and rip I took his hand and stroked it gently across the pages.

Nice journal. Nice journal.

Ethan isn't here today and he won't be here tomorrow. I wish I
missed him...but I don't. They say when they aren't yours it takes
time.

This year
Hatia got on my case again today...in a teasing sort of way. Made
like Butterfly McQueen and said I'm only one step away from sur-
rendering to my oppressor. God! Johnson spends a couple of nights
and Hatia goes on a mission to save my life. How many times do I
have to tell her...we aren't lovers! We Aren't Lovers! WE AREN'T
LOVERS!

Not yet...she says with that wicked look that makes me
blush...but why else would a girl let a man take over her apartment?

What's Johnson supposed to do? His wife is falling apart in
Pennsylvania and he's trying to raise his son and get a law degree in
New York. Why can't I help him out without her telling me I'm be-
coming like my mother? She doesn't even know my mother!

Hatia and my sister, Heather...I swear. They should start another country. FEMINISTS! Give me a break!

Today, 1973
Last night Johnson and Ethan and I went for Chinese food and
Johnson asked me, again, if he could pay me for looking after Ethan
and I told him again I thought it was good for me so would he
please shut up and let me be his friend. When the won ton soup arrived he offered to rent the rollaway in my living room while

Matilda has what's sounding like a nervous breakdown and he has midterms. He said he's grown fond of sleeping with his head in an airshaft. I told him I found all this talk about money insulting. He helped me out when I needed it. What about Woodstock? Then he said he couldn't allow himself to stay here without an agreement of some sort. It went against his manly grain. So I pushed my Kung Pao Chicken with no MSG to one side and we wrote the following: (see placemat)

> I, Molly Adair Williams, accept you, Johnson Stillwater, as the sole tenant (except when you bring Ethan) of my rollaway in the living room on the second floor of 226 East 31st Street on the island of Manhattan in New York City, New York, for a sum of $5.00 a night. This amount is to include gas and electricity. Diapers, baby bottles, law books and Legos may be stored in the trunk that serves as a coffee table at no extra charge. Signed on this day, May 3rd, 1973. Molly Adair Williams and Johnson Stillwater.

I was in the kitchen washing my red sweater when J. reached over my shoulder and opened the cupboard to get a glass, playfully making a point of not being able to decide which one he wanted and casually allowing his upper arm to whisper to my cheek. I thought: Oh, so now that we have a contract it's safe to flirt. I don't know where thoughts like that come from. Probably Hatia. Anyway, as soon as Ethan was asleep we had an earnest conversation about fidelity (in my bedroom) and how J. doesn't want to end up blind to what he already has like his father. I told him I thought Matilda was a lucky woman. This morning he asked me what I write about in my journal then said: Don't tell me! And took a cold shower. I know it was cold because there was no steam on the windows when it was my turn and because I could hear him yelping and telling Ethan to join him...that it would put hair on his chest which I am pretty sure Johnson doesn't have.

Labor Day, 1973
Took Johnson and Ethan to Connecticut to meet my family and celebrate the final days of summer...a family tradition having to do

with the end of fresh tomatoes and corn in the work of art we call My Mother's Garden.

I don't know how many times I have told my parents that Johnson is half Chinese...but, as usual, they attach themselves to words like Lawyer and forget the rest. You should have seen the look on my mother's face when she saw J.'s "slanted eyes" and long, black hair. She started to flutter as if the rape of her village was just around the corner. Ethan, who has become very talkative, reverted to shyness. Conrad's kids had been assigned to play with him while the adults had cocktails and cooked lobster. They took one look at him, decided to play war and locked him in my parent's bedroom accused of spying for the Viet Cong. My father and brother ignored the dilemma by involving themselves in a discussion of porcelain caps and difficult teeth. Johnson climbed a tree and found his way into the bedroom through a window where he remained for some time in contemplation with his son. My brother left with his children shortly thereafter, when they reminded him that three weeks ago he'd promised to take them swimming. I turned off the water that was about to reach a rolling boil and freed the squirming lobsters. I told my mother that lobsters were living creatures and all living creatures needed to be taken into consideration in this family.

You didn't tell me he was married...she said as if J. had a social disease.

You didn't ask...I said removing the pegs from the lobsters' claws.

My mother wiped her hands on her apron (hostess panic) and opened the kitchen door.

Dear, would you come in here and control your daughter?

Control me...that's right...control me!...I said jabbing the air with a pinching lobster.

Clack, struggle, clack. The rest of the group made their way across the linoleum floor.

I will not stand by and watch you torture these poor helpless creatures...said my mother nervously.

And boiling them is kinder?

Clack, struggle...clunk. My father opened the kitchen door. Three lobsters found themselves propelled like pinballs toward the refrigerator while another tried to escape into the dining room only to be retrieved by my sister, Heather, who is never far behind my father.

What is all this?…he asked.

Molly wants to have a Talk…said my mother.

A TALK?…shouted my father cupping his right hand around his ear.

About her Young MAN…said my mother raising her voice and looking nervously at the floor.

I could kill for his hair…said my sister, fascinated.

Why don't we talk about what's really going on?…I challenged. Why don't we talk about the color of his skin and the shape of his eyes?!

Dear, if I don't cook the corn right away it gets starchy and you know how you hate starchy corn.

Mother…what is important to you? Is anything important to you?

I don't have to answer that.

You have treated two people who mean a great deal to me as if they don't exist.

Give your mother the lobsters…said my father…and let her cook the corn.

He's just a friend. God…the way you're carrying on you'd think he'd proposed marriage.

Well, it's not hard to wonder if he isn't taking advantage of you, Moll…said my father. Eating your food. Using your electricity. And not even sleeping in your bed.

We have an agreement, alright?

He's not a poofter like Davis, is he?

Dad…Poofter is a derogatory word. As are Nigger, Wop, Dago and Chink and I will thank you to—

Molly…said my mother with that politely pained expression that makes me think she pities me…you're raising your voice.

So what does that make me…a Freak?

I will not stand here and let you talk down to your mother.

Well, I will not stand here and let you talk down to me. Just because I have a more expanded view of the universe—

House rules! No politics!…said my father throwing open the kitchen door and making a beeline for the den.

I picked up the phone to call a cab. My mother came toward me looking genuinely hurt and artificially concerned.

This whole visit was your idea...I stammered bursting into tears.

You're right...she said touching me gently on the shoulder. We're just concerned. Can't we be concerned without it being a Federal offense?

Mother, Johnson is a good man. He treats me with respect.

I know, Darling.

I love when my mother calls me Darling. She doesn't do it a lot but when she does it feels deep and unconditional and I always go slightly weak at the knees. It is also when she puts her arms around me. I never quite know what to do. Normally, my mother loves me from afar. Not that she's a bad mother...or, for that matter, person. Just the victim of antiquated thought forms and thirty years with a slightly deaf dentist.

The Day After the Infamous Day Before

Dear J.,

I know you don't like me to apologize for my parents but in light of yesterday's visit, I feel I have to say something because they're not unenlightened people... just tired of fighting with me about what's wrong with the world...especially when they feel they gave me such a good one. I know you feel it would have been better if we'd stayed but I just felt so sad and ashamed and on the verge of becoming strident and didactic (which I would have if they had even looked at you or Ethan cross-eyed at the dinner table). I've been thinking a lot about what you said on the way home...that we missed an opportunity. I'm trying to write them a letter...but I've written them so many I'm sure they see my return address and throw them unopened into the garbage. I think it's our living arrangement more than your ethnicity. They don't know how to explain the rollaway to their friends. Anyway, next time, and there will be a next time, if you want to stay and hash it out we will because I know we should have this time and I'm glad you told me what you did. Your friend in the other room, M.

PS—I'll pick up the granola.

Dear Friend in the Other Room,

Thanks for your note. And for taking our conversation on the train to heart. I don't know how I'd feel if Ethan brought home an Arab girl. I hope it wouldn't bother me, but it probably would if I was to be totally honest. Especially in light of the games that are currently being played with the earth's oil. Your father has the Japanese (let's face it, we all look alike) in his memory bank and the Second World War. I'm not saying it's right, but it's real.

Your friend in the airshaft,

J.

PPS—About the granola, I already did.

Mid-October, 1973

I don't know how J. does it! Last week, Matilda wandered in the nude onto the neighboring farm which happens to be Amish. J. is so tired of having to bail her out. He actually said as much. Hung his head in that sweet way he has and confessed that he is finding it harder and harder to justify staying with her when half the time she doesn't even know who Ethan is. The last time he took Matilda for help he said that was absolutely it. Today she fled her doctors and her medication, and gave her life and sizable inheritance to a guru. When Johnson called to persuade her to return to her doctors she threatened to sell the farm. This freaked J. out. Evidently Matilda and Johnson included the farm in their wedding vows. Promised to preserve and protect it as long as they both shall live. Evidently also…Matilda owns the farm outright. When she reminded J. of this unfortunate fact, his retreat was so immediate and so complete I had the feeling that even in the black fog of her madness she was able to discern the nature of her hold on him.

Still Mid-October

I'm feeling really depressed and Johnson isn't much better. He's becoming impatient with Ethan when he wants to know what things mean. Yesterday he asked if he could leave Ethan alone with me for the night so he could return to Pennsylvania and settle the guru thing. He explained to Ethan that his mother was sick again. Today Ethan fingerpainted a playmate's hair during day care. When J. got back I told him and he hit the roof.

Mommy, I want Mommy!...cried Ethan.

You can't have her!...said Johnson. How many times do I have to tell you...you can't have her! Not when she's sick. I know that's hard to understand. But you have to try. Please, Ethan...when Mommy is sick...you have to help Pop. You have to be good and you have to...help!

It was pointless pretending I couldn't hear them so I opened my bedroom door. Ethan looked at me...his eyes wide with confusion.

Sometimes it's fun to help...I said, somewhat uncertain of my place in the proceedings.

Ethan rocked his body.

Can I write in your secret book?...he asked.

Sure. In fact, we'll make a list of things we can do to make Pop's life...your pop's life easier. How does that sound? We'll make a list in my secret book.

Ethan twisted his hair, sucked his thumb and considered my of-fer. Then got down off the rollaway and ran into my bedroom. Johnson pulled on his neck and looked out the window into the airshaft.

You want some hot milk and honey?...I ventured.

The way you make it...yes...he said.

With nutmeg?

He nodded vaguely and I started for the kitchen. The air hung heavy. I wondered what the point was in leaving him to pull on his skin and wrestle stoically with imperfection.

What I love is that you talk to Ethan like a human being...I said leaning against the door jamb. I'd never been around people who did that with their kids until you came here and...well...I've learned a lot just...I mean about relating...because maybe you think you're...but when you're not...well, here...I...I...well, I...anyway...

Me, too...said Johnson as Ethan returned with my journal.

I don't know, Ethan...you must be pretty special. I've never been inside her secret writing book. I don't even know where she keeps it.

Under her covers...he said proudly.

It's true. I sleep with it, I'm afraid.

Well, there are worse things to sleep with...said Johnson softly.

Like Asian men with troubled eyes?

I said that!! I did! I actually said that! I thought for sure he'd look at me the way my mother does, kind of ashamed and embarrassed like I'm a poor needy thing, but instead, he turned his eyes to the floor and very gently said: Probably. And if it hadn't've been for Ethan jumping up and down with my journal and carrying on about the list, the list, the list, my heart would have melted, right then and there, to…no, through the floor. Talk about your basic cheap date! Anyway, in our excitement, Ethan and I went into a huddle and agreed it would be more fun to read the poem thing we'd written on the way back from day care (see piece of paper bag) than make a list. But first, Ethan had to get Johnson to lie down on the rollaway: Quick, Pop, quick! Then he jammed the covers under J.'s shoulders and when he was satisfied his father was all tucked in, he took my hand and I opened my journal and read the paper bag:

I walk along the street, the same tired street
How old is the sky?
I watch the traffic light frozen in monotony
How much is Christmas?
I wait at the corner I no longer see because I have waited at it
so often
How high does rain fall?
I feel a hand, small and questioning
Why do frogs burp?
Frogs don't burp…they croak
How much do you know about forever?

That's really good…said Johnson with a bewildered appreciation in his eyes. Sort of haiku-ish.

Ethan started jumping up and down again.

We're going to give it for you to Christmas!…he cried.

Johnson looked far into me. I never know what to do when he looks far into me. I always feel he can see things I can't and I'm not sure if what he's seeing is any of his business, since I obviously haven't made it any of mine. So to compensate, I babble: It's just a poem. It's not even a poem. It just sort of happened. I made up answers and Ethan made up questions.

Now can we write one about the moon?...asked Ethan jumping up and down. I want to write one about the moon, okay? About this boy and a big...not a monster...bigger than a monster...this big, Pop...look and oh, and maybe we could go there forever and ever and ever.

What about Mom?...asked Johnson.

Mom...maybe Mom...we wouldn't...because if she found out...only we go to the moon, okay?...so Mom...she can take a nap.

Sounds good to me!

Johnson and I said that simultaneously. And for the first time in weeks laughter filled the apartment and for the first time ever we felt like a family.

Chapter Three

Molly stares at the word Family and feels she's had enough of the journal with the flower decals on it. She considers diving into the next one but all this looking back is making her bladder full. She puts her arms in the sleeves of her overcoat and shuttles along the closet floor as the children on the front stoop move inside, taking the stairs two at a time. She can hear her landlord telling them to slow down and as their giggles fade, his broom clacks and shuffles among the banisters. Molly is sure her landlord is setting up camp on the landing outside her living room door knowing full well she will emerge once she runs out of whatever sustenance Hatia left behind.

Molly reaches for the flashlight beside her composition book on the bedside table. She is positive her landlord never liked Hatia. Positive he saw the words Illegal Sublet brandished across her quirky face like an angry scar. She bangs the flashlight a few times on the palm of her hand then turns it on. This is her second night without electricity, the first resulting in that unnerving business with her thumb. The flashlight flickers. She bangs it one more time and takes a few steps toward the bathroom. Then, in case she puts down roots when she's on the toilet, she grabs another journal. The one Ethan got hold of on an off night and ripped…well, not exactly to shreds, but chronology was no longer an option.

April 17, 1973

Nixon announces "major developments" stemming from his OWN investigation into Watergate. What can they be? J. and I are hopelessly addicted. We have invented a character, a right wing redneck named Lyle White. We have written letters to Tricky Dick, Dow Chemical, MacDonald's, RJ Reynolds…you name it, proclaiming Nixon's innocence. We signed each letter: God Bless America. Now we wait for their responses, morbidly fascinated by their powers of rationalization. J. and I work well together. He is the idea man and I put it all into words.

August

I have this recurring dream about Matilda. She is looking at my hand which is full of hallucinogens. Every time she takes one she is seized with the urge to fly. So far she has always been rescued at the last moment but when I wake up there is comfort in knowing I can kill her off any time I want.

Monday

Possible Slogans for the Roe vs. Wade Rally:

My body is my business!
It takes a whole woman to raise a child!
Life is for the living!
Women are human beings, too!
If you don't respect the mother how can you respect the child?

Don't know. Don't care.

Had a fight with Ethan who has become enamored with throwing his food. Was on the phone where I always seem to be these days, trying to get an idea of who is actually GOING to D.C. for the rally so I could charter a bus. Asked Ethan to please stop. Asked him nicely. He started throwing food at me. I didn't raise my voice. Didn't throw food back at him. Didn't put my fingers around his neck and slowly start to squeeze. I told him calmly if he didn't stop I'd put him on the next train to Pennsylvania and let him figure out how to get back to the farm by himself. Am trying to read everything ever written by Dr. Spock and Krishnamurti before he wakes up. Help! Chloe, where are you?

Later

When we were cleaning up Ethan's mess, J. said kids are our reflections. I said I know that intellectually but, on a day-to-day basis, I like to look in the mirror when I want. When we were doing the dishes, he asked me what the first thing is that I think about when I think of my childhood. I said the color black. I said it in jest but now I can't quit thinking about it. J. has this way of asking questions that…I don't know…go in and fester.

HoJo's—Washington, D.C., 1973

Hatia and Heather are here with me and a bunch of other women. We chartered a bus and arrived late last night. This morning I thought I saw Nancy near the Washington Monument but Heather says it was someone else. Right now we are giving each other back rubs and foot massages. What a day! What a rally! Feels like the Supreme Court is on our side. Talk about a high!

Today!

Gerald Ford PARDONS Richard Nixon for any criminal offenses while in office. I am so sick of outrage. This is absolutely, positively my very last, very, very final march!

March, 1974

Couldn't sleep last night. Neither could J. We met in the kitchen over hot milk and honey. He went on about OPEC and the oil shortage and I began to long for him to say something personal. I don't care that I'm not supposed to be having these thoughts…we are drowning in metaphors and I am getting sick of hot milk and honey! He is so goddamned responsible and disciplined. So proud of the way Ethan and I are living our lives that I have grown to resent his faith in me…in my work and in my character. Sometimes I even become bored and, though I often deny it…edgy. Mother's so lucky. If she has these thoughts she doesn't know it. Maybe that's all there is to Unconditional Love.

July, 1974

Heather starts her first job job on Monday. Wall Street. High finance. She told Hatia she thinks equal pay for equal work can only be achieved from within the System. She's probably right but sometimes when she talks about the movement I feel as if she's just repeating all the stuff she picked up at Barnard. I mean, I know she's my sister and I want to be supportive but sometimes I feel it's more important for her to appear hip than to question deeply. I don't know, maybe it isn't her. Maybe it's me.

August 9, 1974

NIXON RESIGNS. I keep thinking about the Color Black. It's like there's a wall starting with Timmy's death and going back as far as I can remember. Look at that ASSHOLE! Getting on Air Force One and making the <u>PEACE</u> sign with both <u>hands</u>! I feel sorry for Pat. I hear he beats her. Look at him! Smiling that fake fucking smile...like he's the fucking victim! FUCK YOU, ASSHOLE! (Good thing the boys are watching TV in Pennsylvania) I mean, Gerald Ford? God, if You are out there, maybe You could show me how to find this funny.

Whenever

Devon retires from the world of books and Hatia takes over as manager making me her assistant. I get to be in charge of religion, philosophy, social studies and children's books. (Read "A Hole is to Dig.") We're going to call a halt to the Talk-a-thons...move the Women's Section into the reading area and expand African Studies.

The Day After <u>D Day</u>! 1975

No one here when I got home from work. Nice. Took a hot bath and listened to Stevie Wonder's new album, "Songs in the Key of Life." Fell asleep reading "Breakfast of Champions." Crashing and banging of utensils came from the kitchen about an hour later. I got up, pretending sleep and surprise at finding Johnson there.

 Oh...hi...I said rubbing my eyes.

 Did I wake you?

 Yes. No. Not really. I was writing.

 I'm not a very good liar (which I know J. appreciates). He lifted the honey out of the jar, twisting it around the spoon.

What were you writing about?

Oh…nothing much…I said. That letter we're going to send to the *Times* about the oil shortage. I got to the paragraph where the U.S. has enough oil in Texas and I started thinking about you.

What about me?

The way you talk.

About what?

Everything but the way you feel.

I hate it when I blush…but he doesn't. He has this theory that people who blush are still innocent and innocence is one of the many things we must keep from extinction in order to save the world.

Guilty…he said.

Except with Ethan…you're very open with Ethan.

He stirred the hot milk into the honey and licked the spoon. I wondered…yes, I did…what it would be like to be…well, either the spoon or the honey. And later, as he drank…the mug…and the hot milk. I wondered what it would be like to be his lips. Soft… sensitive…

Last night…he said…I had a dream. About you.

What kind of dream?

A recurring dream.

Good or bad?

Prolific.

Ethan stirred. Johnson went to him, of course, and I went back to my room, took the piece about the oil crisis out of my typewriter, got into bed and tried to fiddle with it. The next time I looked up Johnson was standing…toes on the threshold of my room. Eyes dark and direct. Mouth soft and…

I dreamt we were making love…he said, casting his eyes to the floor. When I woke up my heart was exploding and my soul was adrift in an electric sea.

There was a silence. Then he looked at me…well, more like into me…and I could feel him, in spite of the distance, pressing up against me. His hips calling out to my hips. His fingers finding me as wet as I have been for all these years.

We could go on waiting…I said, uncertainly.

He wandered to my desk and turned the paper roller knob on the typewriter. He let his hand drift along the wall, then my bathrobe, then he gently closed my closet door. He stood in the doorway, his back to me, looking for answers in the hallway.

You probably think I'm a tease...he said.

I think you're scared...like I'm scared.

Then neither one of us said much of anything. He turned around. Our eyes met...skittishly at first...then dark and tender... and finally gently, gently...we reeled each other in.

February, 1975

Two weeks ago we explained to Ethan that he was getting big enough to sleep on the rollaway by himself which often means he climbs in bed with us.

Chapter Four

Molly flushes the toilet and considers going for the razor. Giving in to the Color Black. Somebody once said somewhere deep in the Self-Help Section that the only way to dissipate Fear was to go toward it. Someone else said it was an Illusion. And the person next to him said it was all Fate anyway so what the fuck? Molly had overheard this conversation while moving the Women's Section into what had been the reading area. She had thought about it for a long time. She'd begun to question her abilities, especially when it came to Unconditional Love. She was having trouble converting her Rage or Frustration or Whateveritwas. Not that she took it out on others, but her poor journal.... It was almost as if she were two different people. Then she and Johnson started sleeping together and her Rage disappeared and she was finally able to blame her shortcomings on lack of sex and return with a clear heart to her original mission. It was for all those reasons, and others that never fully caught up with her, that she eventually came down on the side of Illusion. It was very simple, really. If Fear was an Illusion then it only existed in the mind which meant it was nothing more than a thought form which meant it could be replaced or, if need be, dominated by Love...preferably Unconditional.

Molly was very easy to get along with when her purpose was clear. When it wasn't she paced and fretted and demanded answers to questions that were never meant to have any. She had always done that. Challenged, then pressed, as if knowing could save her.

"Oh, what do you know?" she mutters as she pushes her barefeet

into the cracked tile floor, pulls up her underpants and staggers into the hallway. The person upstairs turns on the TV. Molly pulls her coat around her and as she turns toward the bedroom she hears a cry. Wild, primitive. And deep inside the Color Black her mary janes slam onto flagstone steps.

"I didn't ask to be born!"

Molly sees her mother's eyes grow dark and beady. She hears her willful determination to do as she pleased lock with her mother's willful determination to turn her into a good little girl. Then, as swiftly as they arrive, the phantoms of her childhood disappear.

When she comes to she is chewing the tip of her thumb and the chatter is back in full force.

'You disgust me. The way you blame your bullshit on your mother. She had Conrad and Heather to deal with! And what about Timmy? Have you forgotten about Timmy?'

Molly looks toward the rollaway in the living room. Timmy... small, sickly and off limits. Molly turns back toward her bedroom. Timmy...fragile, exotic looking, actually...with this almost translucent skin...

Molly shines the flashlight on the journal with the flower decals that lies on her closet floor. Hadn't she written something similar about Ethan? Yes! She starts toward the unmarked box. A shadow skuttles, rat-like, into her closet. Molly stops short. The refugee who lives on the grate across the street starts yelling obscenities. Molly wants to yell back. Something...anything. But her heart is bouncing off the walls and suddenly she knows if she is going to get out of her apartment alive she has to rescue the unmarked box; has to walk into the jaws of everything that is against her and, like a pioneer facing a new frontier, penetrate the Color Black.

Molly shuts her eyes.

'God, I know it's been a long time since we've talked. Yeah, like no one's thought of that before. I'm sorry. If we could just—'

A car alarm goes off underneath Molly's window. Molly means to make a dash for her journals. She really does. But the sour whine is tearing her eardrums and stretching her nerves over the edge. She turns sharply. Slams her bedroom door and walks purposefully through the living room briefly taking in the rollaway. She doesn't have to read her journals to remember what happened next. Ethan started *kindergarten and Johnson got a job working for Alice Crenshaw, a widow somewhere in her eighties who wanted to invest her fortune in keeping the wilderness wild.*

Molly liked Mrs. Crenshaw. She was reserved and high strung and slightly scatterbrained, not unlike Molly's mother, but there was understanding in her eyes and a soft-spoken respect for Molly's desire to live a useful life.

Molly marches into the kitchen and grabs hold of the refrigerator. She doesn't have to read her journals to remember Johnson's visit to Matilda or his suggestion that they begin to think about divorce. She doesn't have to read her journals to remember Matilda's refusal followed by a sudden interest in Ethan followed by an equally sudden retreat.

"Fucking refrigerator. Moooooove!"

She doesn't have to read her journals to remember the collage by a Nancy Lurie that was hung in the lobby of Heather's building on Wall Street. Nancy had always been artistic. Always been torn between what was expected of her and what she expected of herself.

"Just fucking move, will you?!"

She doesn't have to read her journals to hear Ethan call her Molly Mom or feel her heart explode when it shortened itself to Momly.

"Stupid thing."

She doesn't have to read her journals to remember her first Christmas on the farm and the letter she'd written knowing full well she had nowhere to send it:

Dear Chloe,

We've been here for three days and this place...this trip...this everything...is totally magical. Right up your alley! And, there is even snow! As soon as we got here, J. put on his work boots and dug up a tiny Christmas tree which we will replant in the spring. Then we strung popcorn and cranberries. Baked bread. Chopped wood. Built fires and threw snowballs. J. is like another person. Wide open. Silly. Free. We roll around like a litter of puppies. I don't know when I've laughed so hard. And Ethan...the dark cloud, the mood swings, the trembling upper lip, the sudden affection...what you said...or, what I imagine you said, about pretending I'm inside a symphony instead of...well, at the dentist. Unconditional Love...some days I think I'm going to make it and this is definitely one of them. Oh, yes…we finally finished the poem thing about the moon. We made it Chinese. I think you would be proud.

December 31, 1975

Dear Chloe,

J. brought me up here (to his meditation room in the attic) about an hour ago. We sat on satin pillows (with tassles) and watched the moonlight come through the dormer window and make its way across the altar. I can see why he misses being here when he's in New York. The vibration is rich with a Higher Power. I don't know how else to explain it but when you take off your shoes and walk across the threshold the air is thick and still and you know you are some place Other. There are pictures and incense and statues everywhere. Muktunanda, Krishnamurti, Buddah, Jesus, Ghandi and Martin Luther King. This vacation…The trust. The care. All three of us. I told J. I thought it was going to be really hard to leave. Then he said, very quietly and very simply: Why do we have to? I said: Well, my job…my apartment…my struggling philodendron. And he said: You could bring your philodendron here. I started to cry. I don't know why. He held me so tenderly…the way he did at Woodstock and I started babbling about the bookstore. Not that I don't love working with Hatia…it's just…ever since the Talk-a-thons went the way of the sixties…I feel so at sea. And I take it out on Ethan. The irritation. The knee-jerk impatience. My big mistake was letting him write in my journals. Now he thinks they're his, too. Three days ago we had a discussion about privacy. Now, whenever I sit down to write he interrupts me. Even if he's in another room. It's uncanny. And, I mean, I know it's important to go toward the things that irritate you. J. thinks Ethan's still reacting to Matilda. They were very close when her ducks were all in a row. If you ask me I think he could use a little therapy (Ethan). I said as much to J. and his eyes began to jitter so I asked him to be patient with me. Told him I'm sorting out my short-comings with you, Chloe. That made him laugh. I thought it might. Then he wiped a strand of hair off my cheek. He said maybe it isn't so much Ethan as the universe trying to tell me it's time to slow down…quit spreading myself so thin. He said one cause is enough. I said: But I don't know what my cause is anymore.

Then why don't you take some time off?...he said...I'm a working man again. Why don't you let me take care of us for a while?

It's funny...you want this time to come but when it does...I don't know...you think angels will sing, I guess. I suppose if they were going to, this is when they would.

Chapter Five

Molly kicks the refrigerator vent with the ball of her foot.

"Fuck you and the horse you rode in on!"

Then she aims the flashlight into the crack between the refrigerator and the kitchen counter. Aims it as a surgeon aims a lasar. And there it is. The razor blade. Rusty but, more than likely, still sharp. Molly looks around the kitchen. She needs something long and skinny. Something like…. She opens the kitchen drawers, frantically searching for a chopstick or a knife.

"Great! Fucking great!" she says slamming the last remaining drawer. "Everything's gone along with everything else!"

The drawer bounces back. Molly rips it off its tracks and throws it into the sink.

"Not even a fucking chopstick!" she mutters as she heads for the refrigerator, wraps her fingers around the doorhandle and remembers Chinese New Years in Oakland with Johnson's mother, Meimei, and a trip deep into Chinatown to eat sparrow's tongues, bat's lips and wizard's gizzards. She can still see the cloud crossing Ethan's face as Meimei dumps a wad of Mystery Mein onto his plate.

"One bite," says Johnson. "I had to eat it, too. It's like admission to the club." Ethan turns his face away.

"You no raise him Chinese way," says Meimei.

"Because he isn't Chinese," says Johnson, "any more than I am."

"Good Chinese boy obey parents," says Meimei as she approaches Ethan's lips with something long and dangly.

Molly gives the refrigerator handle a good yank. The smell that bursts forth is warm and rank. Molly grabs her nose and sees a post-card from Hatia leaning against some moldy take-out. Underneath the postcard is a box wrapped in yellow paper. Molly slams the refrigerator door. Now she is seeing presents inside the fridge! She puts her hands to her ears.

'We have to find something long and thin to fit in the crack. Something stiff, but not too stiff. Something that will help us retrieve the razor.'

Molly picks the flashlight off the floor.

'What about that emery board in her purse. No…too short. Unless it could be attached to something. Something like…the cover of a journal!'

Molly returns to her bedroom and opens the door. The refugee is trying to tame the car alarm with the battered lid of a metal garbage can. Molly turns the flashlight on the unmarked box. It is infinitely more dignified to die than go mad and a lot less trouble for the "family." Molly heads toward the closet. She moves quickly in case she encounters the rat-like shadow. The unmarked box is heavier than anticipated. It tips as she drags it out of the closet. The car alarm stops. The refugee mumbles and returns to his grate. And as steam drifts past her window, Molly feels a hand on the center of her back. She takes a sharp breath, rescues the journal nearest her and runs into the living room. Her upstairs neighbor turns off the TV and, for a moment, there is silence. Molly follows the moonlight as it travels down the airshaft and presses against the window casting a warm light on the eviction notice. She shines the flashlight anywhere but at the floor. Hatia has taken everything except for a stack of books. But, then, everything was all hers to take. Molly looks into the kitchen then scrunches her feet underneath her and, even though she doesn't like it, takes refuge on the rollaway.

January, 1976
Oakland, CA

Toured San Francisco today then celebrated the Chinese New Year with Johnson's mother…a short, solid woman with a gold tooth who lives simply in an old apartment building in Oakland. She sure has a lot of friends. And the phone…you'd think she was an activist.

I don't know…maybe she is. Her eyes absolutely sparkle. She stabs at the English language with such confidence you go right along…getting what you can and imagining the rest. She speaks to Johnson in Chinese and he answers her in English. They have a running joke about his father that seems to grow and flourish with every telling. It has to do with their courtship. How Meimei realized on their first date that he thought she was Japanese. And how she cleverly decided not to deny it and so…walked behind him.

First date. No kiss. Like this goodnight.

And she would bow low…trying not to laugh at the truth about her tactics.

It turned out Meimei was in her thirties when she arrived in America and married. Her husband had left China fifteen years earlier and while she waited for him to send for her she learned acupuncture…became a doctor. Three months after her arrival her husband was killed in a traffic accident and she was left to fend for herself. She moved to Oakland where she had a distant relative and where she met Johnson's mostly Fundamentalist, part Native American father. And where, the story goes, she pretended to be submissive when she had always been her own woman.

Chinese women always…

And she made the peace sign but I think what she meant was 'liberated'…then she threw her head back and laughed, a stocky arm finding Johnson's shoulder.

You fault! You tell me: Now I born. Make self Japanese quick.

Oakland

The last day

Ethan and I gave Meimei a copy of our poem thing about the Chinese moon when we got here…complete with illustrations. She made a big fuss about receiving it then put it, unopened, on the kitchen counter. This morning its condition was unchanged so I asked her if she was ever going to open it and she said: A bad wind from top blows all strength down hill.

Johnson warned me of her "annoying habit of predicting the future." He said you have to be careful not to give her predictions too much power.

February, 1976

Keep thinking about the farm. The peace and quiet. Could have used it today. Ethan had a temper tantrum on the bus. I tried to reason with him. The bus driver told him to listen to his mother. He said: She's NOT my mother! And a bus load of eyes stared at me as if I stole babies for the black market. It was all I could do not to shout: Want to buy him? I can't seem to shake the feeling I'm doing it all wrong. I try but I always go to bed feeling slightly dirty. Except on the farm. It's just…I'm not sure what else I'd do there. J. says I could help him. Alice Crenshaw's driving him crazy. Keeps changing her mind about what property to buy. When J. gets irritated he loses his ability to speak in complete sentences so I finish them for him and, unlike Davis and my mother, he doesn't seem to mind. It's really sort of sweet.

March 8, 1976

Dear Mrs. Crenshaw,

I found the enclosed article in an obscure newspaper that somebody left behind in the bookstore where I work. I am sending a copy on to you at Johnson's request as we both thought you might be interested.

> New Mexico. Mysterious accidents continue to plague the construction of a roadway and tourist center near the remote cascade known as Walking Spirit Falls. The 55 acres were recently purchased from a private owner by S&N Developers. The Laquot Indians who live on the reservation that abuts Walking Spirit Falls, have repeatedly stated that the land surrounding and including the waterfall was illegally obtained and is, in fact, part of a sacred burial ground. Two weeks ago tractors arrived and began to uproot the Laquot's ancestors and place of worship. Flash floods occurred. Lightning struck trees and sent them falling on equipment and yesterday on a portable john. One construction worker was hospitalized with a broken shoulder. Three other workers quit. John Harris, foreman for S&N Developers, is convinced the accidents are the work of a local shaman, Bill Sudden Thunder. S&N Developers was not available for comment.

Later, in the bathroom

Can't sleep. Keep thinking about something else Meimei said even though I know I'm not supposed to. She and I were sitting in her kitchen stuffing dumplings. Turtles were clanging against the metal pot turning into soup and I was telling her how I'd met Johnson when she said: Watch out. Matilda…not finish. Drive mind crazy. Stay 'way from house. You, Johnson, baby…New York City always.

Chapter Six

Molly takes the cover of the journal between her fingers and pretends it's Matilda's neck as she twists it slowly and deliberately away from its spine. Johnson had given her this particular journal for Christmas. The pages are creamy and thick. The spine is covered with hunter green cloth and the back and front are covered with handmade rice paper in its purest form. Molly has never liked it. It doesn't have any lines. But it is beautifully bound. Johnson had pointed that out to her almost immediately.

"Sewn," he'd said, "not glued."

Now she curses his pride in buying her nothing but the best. The cover of the journal refuses to budge. Molly sits on one side and tries to pull the other up. Nothing. Then she stands on one side and pulls on the other. Still nothing. Then she throws the journal on the rollaway, slaps it open and rips out a couple of pages.

March, 1976

Quit my job today. Sublet my apartment to Hatia for six months and bought a secondhand station wagon. J. says we are moving to the farm just in time. All the horseshit about the Centennial. The tall ships might be kind of fun...but pretending we're this great nation...

July, 1976

Mother came with her rototiller shortly after we got here. We spent the whole day in the garden. She threw in the bone meal while I turned the soil and now you should see the results! The garden is positively bursting with tomatoes, basil, zucchini, arugula, corn, eggplant, beans, marigolds, chard and squash. The bird feeders are overflowing with seed. Wild ducks are returning to the pond. Whippoorwills are singing in the swampy patch in the woods. And an owl has discovered the barn. Johnson said he's never seen so much wildlife. For his birthday Ethan and I gave him a pair of binoculars.

September, 1976

Dear Chloe,

Ethan started first grade today. He was wired and shy and kind of sweet. We are doing much better. And J. is really good about pitching in when he's at home. Really aware that I can't DO IT ALL! Plus there are a couple of play groups and, even though I don't relish my turn to have the kids here, I know it's oh, so right that we came. But you know what's weird? Every time I think I've got what it takes to be a good mother...every time I start to appreciate the "calling"... Matilda telephones. Almost as if she can feel me falling in love with her son. I tried talking to her at first. I told her about the poem Ethan and I wrote. Offered to send her an illustrated copy and she hung up. Now I just take messages and sometimes I don't even do that. At least, not right now. Johnson's preoccupied with a piece of property in New Mexico called Walking Spirit Falls. The Laquot Indians are saying it's a sacred burial ground that was lost illegally in a poker game. I've been helping Johnson with research and correspondence. He wants to be familiar with prior claims before he approaches the developers. It's kind of interesting. Complicated. And sometimes he tries to explain it to me in detail and goes on and on and on. I've never been much of one for dates...and history...I never know whose version to believe... Anyway, this morning when we were packing Ethan's lunch box for his first day of school, Johnson put his arms around me, nibbled my ear and called me the Little Woman. I said: Please translate. And he said: I don't know what I'd do without you.

November, 1976
Walking Spirit Falls
New Mexico

For the last six months I've been immersed in the natural beauty of the farm. And now this! It is almost more than my big city bones can bare!! The cliffs are a dusty orange, the pine trees are a vibrant green, the water is a clear blue...almost turquoise...and, only a few miles away, we're surrounded by desert! As I write, Johnson is sitting with his back against a sapling that is growing out of a crack in a mustard yellow boulder. His eyes are closed, his legs are crossed, his palms are up, his thumb and index finger are gently touching. Except for his new, short haircut, he looks like Siddhartha. Anyway, when we got here, we had a couple of hours before our appointment with S&N so J. rented a car and drove us to Walking Spirit Falls. The air is thin and cool and smells like frozen pepper. A delicate column of water is falling free from inside a series of magnificent red and yellow boulders. At first we just stood...our faces moistened by the mist. Then J. asked me if I could feel something quiet and inevitable. I said I didn't know and he sat down to meditate. I wish I could meditate but I get too...well, my mind...I can't shut it off the way he can so I write in my journal. It's probably for the best.

                                                              Later

Remember what I said about J. feeling something quiet and inevitable? Well, get this: When we returned to the car it overheated as soon as we hit the desert. In minutes, and I mean minutes, a pickup truck appeared on the horizon. Johnson stuck out his thumb and this older man got out. Tall with gray braids and a round, weathered face with a battered cowboy hat and eyelids that pointed down. He said his name was Bill Sudden Thunder and that he'd been expecting us. He got right to the point...any outside interest in Walking Spirit Falls would only make the developers hold on tighter. J. asked how he'd known we were even approaching the developers and he said Johnson had come to him in a dream! I don't have to tell you there was this rather long silence. Then we got in the back of his truck (as if it was inevitable) and he drove us to the nearest payphone so I could call S&N and cancel our appointment.

Then we returned to Walking Spirit Falls and climbed the narrow path alongside. At the top Bill Sudden Thunder showed us where S&N has begun to cut the access road. Then he showed us the burial grounds. Then he said his time is running out. He needs Johnson to work with his people. To help them understand their rights and how to fight for them in the white man's world.

Tonight

Met Bill Sudden Thunder's son, Willie, and the tribe's other religious leader, Quanah. We warmed up frozen enchiladas on a pot-bellied stove. Quanah has a very round face. Weathered like Bill Sudden Thunder's but his features sort of fold together. You wouldn't notice him in a crowd. Except for his eyes. They are deeper than Johnson's. They don't hypnotize you the way J.'s do…they behold you. I can't explain it. It's compelling and unnerving and most of the time I looked at the floor. Quanah's house was hardly more than one room but it was sweet with sage and woodsmoke. It was sort of thrown together with whatever was available. Doors, corrugated metal, recycled 2x4s and plastic bags over the holes in the windows. When we were through eating, Willie scraped the leftovers together and put them outside for his dog. Then he asked us if we had seen the moon so we stood outside while his dog licked the dishes and he smoked a couple of cigarettes. Willie is short and compact. His skin is pockmarked and he has a bit of a beer belly. He wears thick glasses. His shoulders are round and apologetic and the whole time I had the feeling he was there against his will. Anyway, when the dog was finished, Willie put out his cigarette, picked up the aluminum dishes and threw them in a sink that was leaning against the house. Then we went inside. Quanah lit some sage and Bill Sudden Thunder said something clipped and guttural that felt like a blessing or a prayer. Then Quanah lifted up a floorboard and got something long and narrow that was wrapped carefully in a piece of cloth. It turned out to be the dried hide of a red fox. Head, tail, everything but the guts. Quanah reached inside its neck and pulled out a pipe. He put something in it and handed it to Bill Sudden Thunder who smoked it in four directions…north, south, east and west. Then Quanah reached under his house once again and pulled out an old cigar box. Ancient treaties and documents were passed around with a certain reverence. Mostly I listened and took notes. After Walking Spirit Falls was lost in a poker game...well, the guy who won it thought it was a useless mountain of rusty rocks in the middle of nowhere and the Laquots weren't about to tell him differently because they didn't want strangers finding out about the falls. It wasn't until the hippies started backpacking that word got out and graves began to be plundered (not necessarily by hippies) for souvenirs, if you can believe it. Enter the National Park Service and a convoluted paper trail that ended up placing Walking Spirit Falls under their jurisdiction which meant it was only a matter of time before the arrival of S&N developers.

Still November

Dear Mrs. Crenshaw,

I just got off the phone with Johnson who said you have decided to withdraw your support. This couldn't be coming at a worse time. Two days ago, Bill Sudden Thunder lay on top of Walking Spirit Falls and died. Yesterday the tractors returned. Willie and Quanah, and several other members of the tribe, were in the middle of a ceremony that involved peyote. They lay down on the ground and refused to let the tractors pass. They were subsequently arrested and jailed for obstruction and use of an illegal substance. That is why Johnson flew to New Mexico instead of the Texas panhandle. He is not trying to defy you or your wishes to invest your money elsewhere. He's become involved with the Laquot people and it goes against his grain to leave them high and dry. Remember our conversation about the still, small voice? Fuck it. I'll just call.

Tuesday

Took me about four phone calls to get Mrs. Crenshaw to come out from behind her cultivated vagueness and talk to me but I did it! Told her it was time for her to have the experience of NOT changing her mind! (Told her gently...pretended she was Ethan, or my mother, on a bad day.) Told her the Laquot believe their souls go to the high country when they die which is why they believe Walking Spirit Falls is sacred. She said the National Park Service has a history of siding with developers. She said it over and over...almost as if she didn't know what else to say. So I suggested she set aside the money she would have invested in the land and invest it in the Fight. Then, when it is used up, she and Johnson can get together to reassess. When she finally caught my drift I wasted no time (but I was smooth about it) in asking her to ante up so we could get Willie and Quanah out of jail. Felt like the old days!

Saturday

Willie was last seen a week ago Friday buying a substantial amount of beer at a 7-11. Quanah says he's gone to dance with the white man's fire.

Sunday
Bad Mother's Day

Heather called. Conrad got a letter from Nancy. I don't know the details. Heather said Mother said Conrad said Nancy is living with a woman in SoHo and wants to see the kids! Then Matilda called after, what?...almost two years! I think she's left the ashram. I never know how much to ask. She grudgingly gave me her new number. Wish J. would get one of those answering machine things then she could talk all she wanted...as if I didn't even live here.

Later

Keep thinking about something Mrs. Crenshaw said about sadness. How everyone comes up against a loss that is so big that there is nothing to do but let go and let life...whatever that means. I mean, I know what it means. But not what it MEANS.

Wednesday

Two days ago Ethan saw a toy machine gun on television and yesterday Matilda went out and bought it. It's waiting for him when he goes to visit her in her new three bedroom condo in June. A year ago this woman was in an ashram. Now she's living in style in the real world and buying her son machine guns...and he's only six years old! J. says we can't ask him not to play with those things...that they're part of growing up. I say Matilda's bribing Ethan to spend the whole summer. Bribing him with violence. Violence and junk food. J. says she's his mother. I say he (J.) is abnormally understanding.

May

Yesterday the Santa Fe lower court decided the public's interest in tourism superseded American Indian religious rights and Mrs. Crenshaw decided once and for all to withdraw her support. Right now J. is on his way to New Mexico for a few days. He asked me to stay behind on account of Ethan. I said: But I'm not the mother...then J. asked me if I'd like to be. I reminded him that we aren't even married. He said: Ah, yes, marriage...and drifted off.

Thursday

When J. got home from New Mexico there was a letter waiting for him from Matilda's lawyer. He was out back splitting wood when I showed it to him. She wants full custody and total child support. As soon as he saw the words he threw the axe at the side of the barn.

I knew when she got pregnant...he cried...I knew as I was pulling it out of her that fucking bitch had me fucking where she wanted me and there was nothing I could do because I had made a promise to my mother and some fucking friend of hers that threw the I Ching when I was fifteen that I was going to live a life that was "honorable." And I try, you know?

You more than try...I said rubbing his back. You succeed.

Then the floodgates opened and we fell to the ground by the woodpile, J.'s heart breaking in dry, awkward sobs on my lap and found ourselves, for the first time I could remember...awash in uncertainty. Johnson's strong sense of purpose shattered by a woman he rarely talks about and I have never met. And as I let my heart find his, a strange excitement began to grow in my body at being needed by him in a whole new way. And in a sudden, steady rush everything about him became extraordinary. His courage. His pain. His confusion. And I wanted to take him into me...as far inside as he needed to go. I wanted to open to the feelings of a child...our child...growing inside us. Was this the Urge? I moved one of his legs between mine and pressed my excitement against his thigh so he could feel my thoughts through his blue jeans. I kissed and drank his tears and took his tongue into my mouth and undid my blouse so he could feel my breasts beating hot and unafraid of everything he was. And when all our clothes were almost off and underneath us, I found myself on top of his groin twisting him deep inside me...his hand on my cheek...a finger in my mouth...and I stretched backwards...breasts in the sunlight...and felt him take me...hold me in his eyes with such affection I was sure I heard him say: I love you.

What?...I asked (just to be sure).

I didn't say anything...he said.

Uh huh.

What did you think I said?...he asked

I thought you said you loved me.

His laugh was shy and gentle.

Words...I said and blushed.

You make them too important.

You know me...I said as he pulled me down on top of him and found his way into my upper back and with his long, inquiring fingers caressed and held my aches and pains with such tenderness I—

Yes...yes...yes, I will marry you. Yes!

And later in the grass full of quiet laughter and the possibility of a child he placed his hand gently between my legs and said: I didn't know I'd asked.

Chapter Seven

Molly wraps her coat a little tighter and sits on the chill in her feet. The moonlight adjusts itself, strokes her shoulders then curls inside her lap. Sometimes she wonders if she was born without a womb. No doctor has ever said as much. Still, she is pretty sure she's never really felt the Urge. Never felt the ticking of the so-called biological clock all her women friends carried on about.

"Momly?"

"What, Eth?"

"Who are those people on the lawn?"

"Uh…birdwatchers. Remember I told you about the Audubon Society. How they will sometimes be taking walks here?"

"Momly?"

"What, Eth?"

"What's so great about birds?"

"What do you think?"

"They poop on the lawn."

"Well, the ducks do…but what did Pop tell you?"

"They tell us about the air by where they fly."

"Yes. Open the oven door, will you? And for some reason they've begun to fly to us. Or anyway, to where we live."

"Why?"

"I don't know. Ask your father. Now open the door so I can put in the bread."

"Why?"

"Why what?"

"Why should I ask my father?"

"Because he remembers what he reads."

"Why?"

"Because he just does."

"Why?"

"Because facts make him feel good...I don't know..."

"Why?"

"I don't know. Ethan, open the oven door!"

"Why?"

"Gimme a break, buddy."

"Why?"

"Because I say so and I am God. Now open the oven door before I make lightning."

Molly takes the pages she has just read between her fingers and very slowly begins to tear. When they are free of the spine of Johnson's journal, she stacks them neatly, folds them in half and tears again. Then she tears them in quarters, into eighths and throws them in the air. And as the moonlight begins its slow retreat from the airshaft torn pages float like ash onto the rollaway.

July 15, 1977

Dear Matilda,

I know we don't really know each other and that Ethan is your son...but Johnson is my mate ~~husband~~ the father of our maybe child...conceived behind the barn. ~~I bet you never gave that to him.~~

July 15, 1977

Dear Matilda,

Johnson is a very fair man and I know for a fact he would never deprive you of being with Ethan...but I would...because you are a selfish and manipulative bitch who probably went crazy for effect...and all I can say is, if I were you I would kill myself out of respect for the human race. (Scribbled over)

July 15, 1977

Dear Matilda,

When I become a mother maybe I will understand your desire to separate your son from his father, one of the most excellent, most patient, most giving fathers I have ever encountered…who is so devastated by your recent decision he is finding it hard to get out of bed in the morning and into it at night which is why I have taken it upon myself to write…even though this has nothing to do with me (Torn in half)

July 15, 1977

Dear Matilda,

My brother recently won sole custody of his three children. Like Johnson, he was left to raise them when his ex-wife, Nancy, left to find herself and then decided her children were a part of the self she was trying to find and wanted them back. I haven't seen Nancy since she left. I always liked her when I knew her but now I think she's evil. ~~In any case, she didn't stand a chance in a court of law. She is gay where you are crazy.~~ I hope you will take a long, quiet look into your heart and ask yourself if it's really necessary to take Ethan away from Johnson entirely when he would never dream of doing that to you. ~~He doesn't know I am writing you…he is too devastated to think straight.~~ If, however, you insist on devastating him…as well as your son…my brother is completely prepared to give Johnson the benefit of his experience and we will beat your ass in court.

P.S. My brother is a ~~dentist~~ lawyer…and he is very bitter and very thirsty.

July 15, 1977

Dear Matilda,

(Here my pen came to rest…on the verge of the sentence that would say it all with wit and wisdom…while I quietly proceeded to draw a major blank.)

July 15, 1977

Dear Matilda
Fuck you.

August, 1977

Shortly after my abortive attempt to write Matilda, Johnson and I drove to Connecticut to pick my brother's brains and eat my mother's tomato aspic shaped like a salmon…something I never understood but once, as a child, I'd complimented her on it…probably because I wanted her to let me go to the movies…and she decided it was my favorite food so for over twenty years I've been holding my breath every time I swallowed it. And then there were the dreaded second helpings. And watching it shake like that. It made me think of the housekeeper who gave my mother the recipe in the first place…and the hair that grew out of the mole on the end of her nose and how Conrad used to tell me I was going to end up like her if I didn't learn how to lose gracefully when we played Scrabble…and that made me think of the Color Black and how no one in my family ever talks about Timmy. His life or death. No one. No one even mentions his name. So, naturally, I thought this visit would be the perfect time to dig him up…or, maybe Resurrect is a better word. So, anyway, I'm sitting on the patio with Johnson and Conrad drinking a Perrier. Conrad has just asked Johnson if he'd like a vodka and tonic and Johnson has just said <u>Yes</u>. I haven't said anything. I am preoccupied. My period is one-going-on-two weeks late. I am convincing myself it is probably stress and trying not to think about it when I hear: Yoo hoo…Molly? Come back, come back wherever you are. It's almost time to pick up Heather at the train station and I forgot heavy cream. Want to go with me?

I look at Johnson. He smiles an absent smile. My brother slaps him on the back and hands him another vodka and tonic. Johnson raises it in my direction.

To you, Babe.

Babe?…I think. What a strange word to come from Johnson.

You got lucky, Johnson…says Conrad toasting me with the dregs of his martini straight up.

They don't make 'em any better…says Johnson.

'They' who?…I ask.

The gods…says Johnson putting his arm around my hips. Do I have to tell you everything?

No…but you should…I say playing with his hair.

Johnson looks at his vodka and tonic and smiles mysteriously.

When did Johnson start drinking like a normal person?…asks Mother as she and I get in the car.

I don't know…I say. Today, I guess. He's probably just letting off steam.

We ride in silence past the country club.

Heather brought a young man home last week…says Mother. Works with her on Wall Street. She wanted to know if we thought he was "a good specimen." I wish you'd have a talk with her…she treats men like sex objects.

Mother…how did Timmy die?

The car swerves onto the shoulder.

What kind of question is that?…she asks.

Nothing…it's just…because when I think about my childhood starting with Timmy's death and going back to…I don't know…my birth, I guess…all I see is the Color Black.

Mother eases us back onto the roadway. We hang motionless in a long, dark space.

I'm sorry…I say when we get to the A&P. I didn't mean to bring up Timmy. I just thought…I was hoping we could talk about motherhood because I think I might be pregnant.

Mother wrestles a listing shopping cart through the automatic doorway.

I want my daughters to have weddings before they get pregnant and so does your father…and that is that.

Mother, Johnson's divorce…the custody thing…it's going to be time consuming and probably nasty. It's important for us to become a family in case we have to go before the judge.

Mother shakes her head and is about to mutter: You children… when I relieve her of the reluctant shopping cart.

We'll start in frozen food…she says tightly.

I thought all we needed was heavy cream.

We might as well get something for tomorrow. Does ham sound good? Oh, no, that's right, Johnson doesn't eat meat. You'd think once a year…one little bite…

Mother, we'll be gone by dinnertime.

Oh. I thought you were staying until Monday.

Johnson starts his new job with the law firm in Philadelphia.

He's leaving Mrs. Crenshaw?…she asks as if it were a medical emergency.

He's going to live at home full time…I say for the millionth time. We both are. That way we have a better chance of getting custody if we...you know, start our own family. Like what happened with Conrad...it meant a lot to the judge that you and Dad...well, that you were there for him and that...you know, your whole life is kids.

I have my bridge club.

That wasn't a criticism...I say rather critically.

On the way to the train station Mother asks if Matilda has a good lawyer. I explain that her father's very wealthy. Then Mother says she and Father will help any way they can.

When we return to the house with Heather, Johnson and Conrad are in a heated debate about rent control and how it will eventually ruin New York City. Conrad sees welfare as the major culprit and Johnson keeps trying to say Military Spending without slurring which launches them into a whole thing about the defense budget and the Viet Nam War. Heather pours herself a double scotch no rocks and suggests they have no business debating about the war since neither one of them had a direct involvement. My brother does not want to be reminded of his cowardice and is, fortunately, rescued by my mother when she asks him to do the one thing he has always done better than anybody...get the coals started in the bar-b-cue pit. Then she says she thinks she should wake my father or he'll keep her up all night. I say Johnson can keep him company...they can cruise through mail order catalogues. Johnson is not amused. Evidently, his nocturnal excursions into military surplus are beyond private...and I'm supposed to know even though we haven't TALKED ABOUT IT. Anyway, he shoots me this really mean look and I pretend to throw what's left of my Perrier in his face and when he laughs and tries to pull me onto his lap I get away and sit on the boulder in the lawn. Then Heather makes some comment about men and how she doesn't get the really good promotions because she's a woman.

You're not a woman...says Conrad. Your sister's a woman.

Why? Because she's sacrificing her life to help Johnson raise his kid?

Conrad squirts on the lighter fluid and hisses: Feminist.

Look, pig...I know you're pissed off because you got stuck...but Nancy had to do what she had to do and so do I.

Do me a favor, Heather…stay away from my kids!

Swoosh! Flames fill the bar-b-cue pit as Johnson's elbows find their way onto his knees and he lowers his head into his hands.

Maybe this isn't the day for this…I say.

Mol…if we don't get through to them…who will?…asks Heather.

But you talk about men like they're the enemy.

You live for him…says Heather pointing an accusatory finger.

Yes…says Johnson into the brick patio…and I live for Molly.

Except you don't sleep with her…am I right?

What are you talking about?…I say ever so curious about her source of information.

His nocturnal excursions into military surplus. The catalogues under his cushion in the shrine room. The pistol…or whatever it is from World War One.

Johnson shakes his head and gets up slowly and moves onto the lawn. He knows Heather and I talk. Now I know why he wishes we didn't.

I love Johnson, Heather, and if you want to turn me into a bowl of Jello because I put him ahead of…I don't know…what you think I should be doing with my life… Men are a part of this universe. They are hurting. They don't have each other to talk to the way we do.

I used to look up to you. You were the one who sprayed Reddi Whip on the walls!

There is nothing wrong with owning a gun if you're trying to understand yourself in relationship to it…I say defiantly.

Stand by your man…sings Heather.

Sacrifice has its place!…I holler.

Yes, Mother.

Alright, I'm Mother. Look at me! I am Mother!!

And I spread my arms, expose my possibly pregnant belly, then run sobbing across the lawn toward the hammock.

What a great discussion we're having about custody…I say as J. approaches.

He snaps a twig in two.

Personal things, Mol…you live with someone…you should be able to figure them out.

I'm sorry...I say wiping my eyes. It's just...guns and meditation ...I was trying to understand...when Heather called...and you were firing it out back. I knew I shouldn't've brought it up just now.... But...sometimes

Shhhh...says Johnson, stroking my hair. It's okay.

Johnse...what if we're trying to get pregnant for all the wrong reasons?

I didn't know there were wrong reasons.

Well, I mean...you know how...what if this is all about getting custody of Ethan and not the baby?

Mol...getting pregnant is something you just do. You start to analyze it—

Have you always been faithful?

He turns away rather suddenly. I look at him startled. He turns back.

Mol, I won't do anything stupid. I'm a lucky guy.

I sit on the edge of the hammock and wonder why the only time he tells me he is lucky is when I'm in pain.

Oh!!!...I moan, banging my fist on my head...I'm so sick of my brain! I wish I was one person!

J. takes my fists in his hands, looks me in the eyes and says: Guess what? I wish I was, too.

Chapter Eight

The corner of a bent and spattered index card slides from the pages of Johnson's unlined journal and pokes the underside of Molly's wrist.

MOTHER'S BASIL JELLY

1½ C boiling water. Pour over:

2 C basil leaves—packed. Let cool. Reheat. Add:

1½ C white wine vinegar (plus)

6½ C sugar. Bring to a rolling boil for 4 minutes. Strain into a pitcher. Immediately add:

1 bottle of Certo

6–8 drops of green food coloring.

Pour into sterilized jars. Seal with paraffin when necessary.

Makes 9 jars.

Good with lamb. M. likes it on tuna sandwiches. C. likes it on cream cheese and crackers.

Molly stares at the word Sterilized. She can still see her mother, lost in the steam of boiling jam and jelly jars, "lovingly filled and sealed to perfection." Molly turns the index card in her fingers. On the other side she has written a phone number: Hatia's MD—Dr. Bozniak—212-867-9346. And alongside that: Botulism.

Under ordinary circumstances, Molly would have returned the index card and the pages of her journal to the unmarked box and gone on with the daily business of forgetting. Now her feet are cold and something cruel and determined wants to see how much she can take before she breaks in two forever.

August

Ethan came home two days ago from Matilda's. He was very angry at us for "ditching him for the summer." Johnson reminded him of their conversation about the holidays and how he had agreed to spend them with Matilda until the custody issue is settled. Today Ethan took one of his toy guns across the field to play war with Thomas only to discover he was not allowed in Thomas's house. This prompted a haphazard conversation about the Amish and nonviolence as Johnson was putting on a tie (I still find it weird) and preparing to face another day in corporate America. As soon as Ethan was through waving goodbye he turned his fingers into guns and aimed them in my direction.

Pow, pow, pow…you're dead.

Funny…I said opening the screen door…I don't feel dead.

You're dead. When I say you're dead you're dead!

I stumbled into the living room, clutching my heart, and fell onto the couch. Ethan climbed on top of me and started hitting me with his fists.

Hey, Ethan…slow down. Slow down. We're just playing.

He pulled the pin out of an imaginary grenade and threw it into the corner of the room accompanied by the sound of an explosion.

At the same time an Audubon tour walked thoughtfully across the front lawn toward the woods.

Duck, quick…the enemy!…said Ethan as he crawled on his belly across the living room floor and out the screen door to spy on the intruders through the porch railings.

Company crossing south toward bird sanctuary…he continued. We suspect their binoculars. Poisoned gas. Read me?

I'll read you as soon as you pick up your clothes in the living room…I said.

Reconnoiter…said Ethan sneaking off the porch.

Ethan…I said firmly…I'm asking you to pick up your mess from last night.

Ethan slid off the porch and picked up a rock.

Ethan…I warned in a low voice.

Kill the women and children!…hollered Ethan throwing the rock like a grenade in my direction.

What has gotten into you?…I yelled as Ethan made a beeline for the barn.

I was just playing…he whined as I grabbed his arm.

You threw a rock at me! What did your father just say about throwing rocks?

You're hurting me.

Does your mother allow it?

You're hurting me!

Does she?

Ow! I don't know!!

Right…I said, letting go of Ethan with a sarcastic push. Well…maybe you'd like to go to your room to figure it out.

No.

Then why did you do it?

I don't know.

Then go to your room.

I was just playing!…said Ethan kicking open the barn door.

I said go to your room. This is not your room.

I didn't mean it to go that far.

What have we told you…over and over…about rocks and guns?

Pop has a gun.

He doesn't point it at people.

I didn't point mine at Thomas! I went over there to play. Just like now. There isn't even any hay. There's supposed to be hay in a stupid barn. I don't like it here anymore! And I don't have to stay!

Then fine…I said…go! GO!!

Ethan rubbed his arm and looked at me as if I'd thrown a knife into his heart. Chloe would have taken a deep breath, realized she was the adult and transformed her frustration or Anger or HA-TRED into understanding eyes and a reassuring smile. And J. would have negotiated a truce. But today my eyes locked with Ethan's and he saw the dark cloud I normally confine to the pages of my journal and in a chilling second we both knew there was no turning back.

Friday
The bathroom

Had the worst nightmare. A woman, sort of like Chloe, sort of not…was coming toward me out of a mist. I was in some sort of boat with a shadowy figure trying to row across a bubbling body of swamp water. The Chloe-woman was all in white. The boat was small and crudely crafted. The shadow kept changing. Shifting. As if it were incapable of keeping still. Then the boat started to sink. "Chloe" was standing above me…but really sort of skimming the surface of the swamp which was turning all acid-y. I knew I was in danger. I called Chloe for help but my voice was muffled as if my cries were stuck inside my throat. The shadow smiled a mischievous smile and started to rock the sinking boat. Chloe planted her feet wide, picked up the hem of her long, misty dress and pulled a sword from between her legs. I tried to grab it but when I reached out my hand my fingers disappeared. Then my arm. Then my shoulder. Then I swallowed my teeth and my face began sucking on itself. When I woke up my heart was pounding so hard I thought I was going to break. The bedroom was still dark but I could feel Chloe like a terrifying angel. J. was still asleep so I put on my bathrobe and decided to come in here. Can't quit thinking about the bruise on Ethan's arm. Told J. about it as soon as he got home. Admitted I behaved immaturely. Told Ethan we all have monsters inside us that we are responsible for and today, when I wasn't looking, mine got out not on a leash. Then I said I was sorry and asked him if we could shake. He said No and, quite honestly I couldn't blame him. When J. and I were getting ready for bed I told him I didn't think it was so much Ethan that caused me to go off so unexpectedly…as me feeling so adrift. J. looked at me almost hurt like: But you're pregnant. And right then and there, I decided to ask him about the chicken coop. About converting it into a workroom or office. He said: For what? I said: So I'll have a place that's my own where I can go and feel…like why you meditate. He said he doesn't want to make any improvements until he and Matilda have discussed the fate of the farm. I said: You haven't discussed the farm? He said: One thing at a time. I hope this lawyer friend of J.'s knows what he's doing. I hope he's a bona fide mother fucker (pun intended).

Still August
Where Else?

Morning sickness! Whoop dee doo! Quanah invited Johnson to New Mexico for a ten-day ritual on top of Walking Spirit Falls. J. says I should stay here with Ethan. I said why don't we take Ethan with us? Of course, he's got school plus the camping trip with the Walters…so for now…J.'s right…it would be best if he went by himself. CALL HATIA! DO IT!!

Later

Ethan's arm isn't quite so purple with the details of my fingers. I've been dressing him in long sleeved t-shirts for school. He continues to keep his distance. Won't let me kiss him goodnight. Won't let me read him his bedtime story. At dinner he informed me that he doesn't like his food touching. I said: It touches in your stomach. His lower lip began to tremble. I could feel another tantrum in the making. I asked him if he was about to let his monster out for a walk not on a leash. Steam began to pour from his ears. I took his plate back and put everything in three separate bowls. I served it to him with as much om, shanti, om as I could muster. Crocodile tears fell onto his cheeks.

On a plate!…he wailed. On a plate!!

I removed the bowls and the food which was now lukewarm to cool, and got another dinner plate out of the cupboard. Om, shanti, om. I stood at the stove as if I were Chloe, planted my feet wide, raised the hem of my diaphanous skirt and pulled a wooden spoon from between my legs. Then I loaded the food with Love on his untouching plate. Om, shanti, om. I turned and served it to him…calmly…as if he were The Little Prince and I his humble stepmother. Baba ganoush.

Dear You,

I am afraid I'm going to bring you into this world then wish I hadn't. Then I'm afraid I'll take it out on you the way I take it out on Ethan even when I don't think I'm going to. Sometimes I think Ethan would be better off with Matilda. I really do. I don't know how to break it to your father. Obviously he wouldn't agree with me and would probably be very upset if he knew I was writing you this letter. But he won't be around the way I will be to clean your diapers and strain your food. I need a job. I need an office and a purpose. I am haunted by this feeling I am standing to one side of my life. I don't know how else to explain it and I am tired of thinking about it! Hatia says I should fold a piece of paper in half and make two lists. Likes and Dislikes. But it's not that I don't like my life. I love my life. I mean, look at my garden. I close the gate behind me and I feel part of a miraculous process. I even understand what Mother means when she says all the chatter comforts her. All the growing and pushing and giving up of self. So it isn't that I don't want you…it's that I need you to wait until I understand…I mean, when a beet is coming into its own it doesn't say: Sorry, you can only have my greens. So what's the difference between giving up of Self and mindless surrender?

Still September
New York City
Waiting for the car to become legal

Hatia went with me this morning. She was right…it was pretty quick and painless…until the sucking started. Then I felt this sharp twinge. Like a deep and fiery ripping. When it was over I sat up and turned as white and clammy as crushed ice. The nurse wanted me to lie down again but I didn't want to keep Hatia waiting. She had fixed up the back of my station wagon. I knew I could lie down there while she drove back to 31st Street. We didn't say much. There wasn't much to say. Last night when Hatia and I were weighing and balancing she said you never feel totally right about it. Well, she's wrong. I do. It wasn't as if that baby or fetus or whatever and I hadn't talked. It wasn't as if I hadn't acknowledged its existence. I mean, let's face it, I'm not ready. Maybe that's why we came together…so I could learn in my gut what I've known in my head: That kids are a lifetime responsibility so if you're going to have them you have to be prepared to put them ahead of everything else otherwise you end up like Matilda and Nancy. If I didn't believe in the depths of my soul that I had acted in that baby's best interest I wouldn't feel so at peace. Well, maybe Peace isn't the right word…but I'm definitely not writhing in sorrow and self loathing. In fact, I don't feel much of anything. I'm just lying here in the back of my station wagon waiting for 2 o'clock when the parking space becomes legal. Thank you, whoever you are or would have been. I hope one day we can meet and you can see how deeply you are woven in the fabric of my being.

Later

The apartment looks good even though Hatia could stand a cleaning lady. She's taken down some of my pictures. She can take them all down for all I care. Anyway, I'm glad I decided to drive instead of taking the train. I'm going to take some more stuff back to the farm. My prints, my good knife, my tool box, my sewing machine and maybe my coatrack if it will fit. Fascinating, huh?

Later 2

I keep wondering how I would have felt if J. had asked me to marry him behind the barn. I mean, even when he found out I was pregnant...not a mention of the word Wife. Not that we could literally marry...but, still, just to know that he was thinking about it.... Maybe it's the Yacht Club rising up in me like a disapproving eyebrow. Maybe it's my mother looking startled when I told her I was pregnant. Or maybe it's all those Milk Duds and Doris Day movies before the Cinema Palace became a mini-mall. But, whatever it is...here on the rollaway...my head 'in the airshaft' where J.'s used to be...I wonder if it would have made a difference.

Tonight
The Farm

J. came home tonight full of the harvest ritual. Said it made him glad to be working with Quanah and Willie post-Crenshaw (who, Mother says, may have to go into the hospital with her liver). Anyway, J. said the Laquots make his days in corporate America more bearable. I said if there was anything he needed me to do.... He said they're in a wait-and-see mode and, besides, he's got a secretary (minor body blow). Then he gave me a ring. Turquoise and silver. An old Hopi design. Willie made it. I said: What's this for? And J. said Quanah has offered to marry us...not literally but heart to heart (major body blow). I looked away. He asked me what was wrong. I said something stupid like: I thought you were through with marriage. He said he'd been planning to ask me ever since I told him I was pregnant but Willie had to make the ring and he wanted it to be a surprise. I held out my hand and burst into tears. The ring fit perfectly. J. said he'd measured my finger when I was asleep. I couldn't tell if he was kidding or being romantic but either way was fine with me. Then he took both our hands and put them on my stomach and I lost it. Started sobbing and sobbing. I was going to tell him the truth, the whole truth and nothing but and started to several times...but his eyes were so full of tenderness and his arms so full of anticipation and trust...

The baby...I said. I was fitting...Hatia was helping...my coatrack in the back of the station wagon when I felt a twinge. I thought it was a muscle. I got in the car. I wanted to beat the traffic. Get home in time to pick up Ethan. From his camping trip. With the Walters. I started...hemorrhaging. On the New Jersey Turnpike!

J.'s face was ashen. I kept saying I'm sorry, I'm sorry, I'm sorry. We just held each other. So full of...I don't know anymore...I really don't!

September

The Supreme Court upheld the Lower Court's ruling and Walking Spirit Falls is on its way to becoming another tourist attraction for the state of New Mexico. Quanah, Willie and J. returned to the farm in various states of defeat. I set the table with Mother's linen and good china. No one said much of anything. It was too depressing. We all thought we had a good chance with the Religious Freedom Act about to go before the Senate. Anyway, halfway through dinner, I decided to lighten things up so I put on the wedding ring Willie made me and gave the boys a fashion show.

It fits perfectly...I said, sounding cheery like Mother.

I make a better jeweler than a lawyer...said Willie opening another can of beer.

Then I showed the ring to Quanah. He turned my hand over, studied my upturned palm and smiled a smile that could have meant just about anything and for a split second I felt totally naked. Then I took orders for dessert.

Pumpkin cheesecake...said Ethan. She makes it better than anybody.

She does...said Johnson.

SHE...I thought looking at my reflection in the window over the kitchen sink. SHE? Last month it was BABE. This month it's SHE. SHE BABE, SHE BABE, SHE BABE WHAT YOU DO TO ME.

Anyway, after dinner Willie showed Ethan how to use his camera and J. took Quanah upstairs to meditate. When I finally got in bed J. was still shuffling about overhead. I closed my eyes and all I could see was Quanah's smile. Then I had a dream. Or I think it was a dream. I was standing at the bedroom window looking out the back toward the clearing in the woods. Quanah was on the lawn thrusting his naked chest into the moonlight like an offering. A skewer moved under his flesh and out the other side. His face was expressionless. I stood transfixed. Then, suddenly, Quanah looked at me standing in the window. Looked at me the way he did at dinner when he took in my wedding ring and studied the secrets of my palm.

The Morning After
The Garden

Came here to pick pumpkins for pies, pull up what has become of the tomatoes and eggplant and get away from Quanah's smile. I am totally spooked. I am positive he is trying to tell me something which if I don't hear I'll turn into a dead soul in a living body. I better tell J. the truth about the baby before Meimei comes for her visit. Today is the perfect day for her arrival what with the heart to heart ceremony. I was thinking maybe we should do it in the bird sanctuary but now I'm not so sure I want to get married in the woods...metaphorically speaking.

Later
Airline Terminal

Ethan and Quanah were in the bird sanctuary when I finally got up the nerve to approach Quanah. I had decided to tell him what I did about the baby then ask him if I should tell J. the whole truth before we had our heart to heart ceremony...or if that would...I don't know...get us off to a bad start. When I got to the clearing Quanah and Ethan were sitting crosslegged on the ground with Quanah's drum between them.

Its round shape represents the whole universe...said Quanah.

And its strong, steady beat is the pulse…the throbbing heart of all things. So when we beat the drum…it is not a casual thing. It is to reconnect with the heart of the Mother.

To reconnect with the heart of the Mother? The words flashed on and off in my brain like a neon sign on the road to salvation when I suddenly remembered: Shit! Meimei! The airport!

I nodded nervously toward the house. Quanah nodded back. I took long, self-conscious steps out of the woods.

Oh, my god. Quanah can see what became of the baby!…I thought as I broke into a run on the lawn, bounded into the house as J. was making his way down the stairs and gasped: Breakfast…whatever's there. Meimei. I'll just make it!

I grabbed my fanny pack and threw a shirt over my overalls and decided to tell J. I'd had an abortion. I ran into the kitchen, took one look at him, stuffed a pumpkin muffin in my mouth and decided to reconnect with the heart of the Mother first. But what Mother? I got in the car and stepped on the gas. I'd tried my biological mother so many times it wasn't funny. I straightened out on Farm to Market Road. Who else was there? Matilda? Nancy? I don't think so. I made my way through the airport just as the arrival of Meimei's flight was being announced.

Meimei!…I thought as her plane taxied to the gate. Of course! I will reconnect with Meimei.

                                        Insomnia in the Bathroom
When Meimei got off the plane she was a lot thinner than I remembered and using a cane. It took us forever to get to the baggage claim, let alone the parking lot. When we were finally on our way I told her about the heart to heart ceremony and how lucky I feel to be in Johnson's life. She smiled and nodded and said: You eyes gray. Here. No good. Look.

I stretched my neck and adjusted the rearview mirror.

Those are my bags. I've always had bags.

Gall bladder…she said. Too much angry.

I shifted into reverse and decided to tell J. the truth as soon as I got home. Tell him before the heart to heart ceremony and fuck the fucking heart of the fucking Mother.

When Meimei was getting settled in Ethan's room I flipped

through the mail. Another letter from Matilda's lawyer. Full custody, no child support and J. can have the house except for the furniture. I slid it under the toaster oven. A drumming sound came from the woods.

Sounds like the men are in the bird sanctuary...I said as Meimei made her way into the kitchen.

We stood on our toes and looked out the window. Had the heart to heart ceremony already started? Was this some sort of purification ritual for the groom? Should I blush like a bride or prostrate myself like a sinner? And what about the frozen baby that had attached itself to the boney plain between my breasts?

I put my hand under Meimei's elbow as we made our way down the porch steps and across the lawn. When we got to the bird sanctuary...Ethan, Willie and Johnson were dancing this way and that while Quanah sat to one side playing his drum. An eagle feather was by the birch tree along with a rock, a leaf and a walking stick J. had found in the woods over the winter. Coming out from what I assume was the altar were four lines of cornmeal. Willie circled the configuration, each circle growing smaller and, as he did so he sang...his voice coming from deep inside to penetrate the sky.

We're not going to stop...all day...said Ethan holding out a rattle. We're blessing the land so the same thing doesn't happen to it that happened to their waterfall.

Blessing the land?...I thought as Johnson unfolded a chair and helped Meimei sit. What about joining our hearts?

Aiiiiwaaaa aiiiiwaaa ay!...chanted Quanah as Meimei took Ethan's rattle and found her way into the spirit of the ceremony as if she'd been expecting it.

I took a deep breath, put my hands over the frozen baby and leapt into the breach and as the sun followed its path across the sky a ceremony grew in a clearing in the woods. We sang. We danced. We jumped and ran. We sat, exhausted, in a circle and spoke in quiet conversation. We lay on our backs...heads touching...and listened to the stillness. And once when we were all breathing in unison Johnson said: Imagine yourselves in a safe place. And I imagined myself in the arms of Chloe and when I opened my eyes the frozen baby was gone. Had I reconnected with the heart of the Mother? I tried to catch Meimei's eye but she was trying not to nod

off and just as she was gaining ground, Johnson asked us to close
our eyes and fill ourselves with light and when we were all Out
There somewhere Quanah said a prayer in Tewa. Then Meimei said
a poem in Chinese. And I said the only thing I know in Italian:
Frutta fresca per me, per piacere. And Johnson said: Borscht. And
Ethan said: Tortilla. And Quanah said: Black-eyed peas. And Willie
said: Atlantis. And sang the *Ave Maria* with a lifetime of feeling as
he led everyone out of the woods to the spot on the lawn where
Quanah had pierced his chest in my dream. It was there we sat in
our final circle. There that Quanah lit his pipe and blew the smoke
in four directions and, as Willie raised the prayer stick, Quanah
dove into Johnson's eyes and told him he and Ethan and I are the
keepers of a Power Spot. Johnson's face became deep and serious. I
looked toward the farmhouse. Johnson put his arm around Ethan.
Meimei felt a chill. And I thought I saw the frozen baby standing in
our bedroom window. I jumped to my feet. Ethan looked at me,
startled, then took refuge in his father's lap.

I'll get you a wrap...I said gently touching Meimei's shoulder.

And as the afternoon sun fell from the sky, Willie followed me
toward the house.

So do you do this a lot?...I asked as he returned to his beer on
the porch. You know...ceremonies.

Not like this. No. I don't know what this is.

I laughed, partly relieved and partly annoyed. I had given myself to the ceremony...taken it seriously and now I was feeling like a
fool. All the mystical smiles and metaphors. Had J. and I gotten
married or hadn't we?

Later when Meimei was fast asleep in Ethan's bed and Willie had
passed out on the couch in the living room and Ethan had been given
permission to sleep next to Quanah under the stars, J. and I lit a fire
in the woodburning stove in our bedroom and I decided to ask. J.
looked at me sideways and shook his head as if I were incorrigible.

You put today into Words you rob it of its Mystery...he said.

I just want to know if we were married...joined. That's all. You
know...in our hearts. Come on. One question a day. It's good for
balance.

Johnson shook his head again and smiled.

I thought we were...he said squirming under my mircroscope.

When Willie sang the *Ave Maria.*

You were moving your mother's chair.

I know...but I heard it and I knew it was doing the same thing to you it was doing to me.

What was it doing to you?

Mol...

Oh, come on. A little clarity won't kill you.

Johnson got out of bed and poked at the fire.

Didn't you hear what Quanah said?...he asked. This land is sacred. There is a convergence of energy that is—

But all I was hearing was Johnson's voice shaking when he said the word Sacred and I didn't know if he believed what he was saying or was saying what he hoped he believed.

Johnson returned to the bed, crossed his legs, took my hand, looked in my eyes and when he was satisfied he had me he said: We are the keepers of a Power Spot.

I know.

There is no greater honor.

Yes, Professor.

Don't...Molly...I'm serious. I am very, very serious. We were married today...we were married to the land.

How romantic...I thought as I looked at the fire in the woodburning stove.

Without the land...Johnson continued...there would be no life. And without life there would be no...

I looked out the window. The face of the frozen baby shimmered in the chill on the darkening pane.

What is it?...asked Johnson.

Nothing.

You can tell me.

I...uh...When you were in New Mexico...I just think if two people...because when they don't know they're getting married... whether it's to a piece of property or to another human being.... Because, what you said about Mystery...I mean, if all we do is experience our own interpretation of life...then are we opening ourselves to deeper truths or perpetuating unspoken lies?

Come here...he said tenderly.

I don't feel like coming there.

What is it, Mol?

Nothing…really. There's a letter…that's all. Under the toaster oven. From Matilda. I opened it by mistake.

Oh.

She wants to talk about the house.

So you read it by mistake, too.

She says you can have the house but she wants all her furniture.

Johnson looked toward the fire. The red glow on his face played with the dark lines of his weary spirit as I scolded myself for pushing him when I was the one who hadn't followed through…partly because I can see how ravaged he is by the game of chess Matilda continues to play with his heart and the thought of adding the frozen baby.… Maybe Johnson is right. Maybe some things are best left unsaid. Especially when there's no turning back. I looked at Johnson's long, sloping back and dug my fingers into his rounded shoulders.

Mmmmmm…he said…that feels good.

And as he ran his hand along my thigh the shadowy figure from my dream about Chloe skuttled across the Color Black. I need to get a job! Something to take my mind off Johnson and Ethan and out of my fucking, pathetic, self-absorbed self.

There's a meeting next week to discuss the dumping of toxic waste into the river…said Johnson after a moment. I thought we should take Ethan.

I rested my cheek against Johnson's upper back. He nestled the back of his hand under the inside of my knee and twisted himself around until his face was a blur to my eyes and his mouth the gateway to my lips.

I keep thinking about the baby…he said as I fell backwards onto the bed.

So do I…I said softly.

They say you shouldn't let too much time go by or you'll start putting it off…said Johnson settling himself on top of me.

I smoothed his hair and kissed him quickly and as he reconnected with the warm spot between my thighs, I heard a baby cry.

Johnse?

What…oh, wife of my life?

Nothing…just, uh…you're the best father.

Sunday
Willie and Quanah left this afternoon and Meimei is still in bed. J.'s
going to have a talk with her about her Chi energy. She (and it) are
all over the place and we both know traditional medicine is out of
the question. I got on the phone just in case. Found a possible homeopath in Philadelphia. Then I cruised the classifieds. I don't
know what I'm qualified for but I'll find a job if it kills me!

Tuesday
Ethan took the picture he drew of our bedroom ceiling to school for
Show and Tell and called it: Pop Meditating for Peace on the River.
On the way home, according to the bus driver, the Hogan boy told
Ethan his father was a slant-eyed sissy so Ethan hit him over the
head with his homework. J. and I did our best to explain, once
again, why violence is not an option. I'm sure it didn't help that J. is
still given to firing his pistol or rifle or whatever-it-is from WWI.
Not a lot…and usually when Ethan's not around. But, still, it's not
like Ethan doesn't know it's there.

Monday after Thanksgiving
J. taught Ethan how to respect and assemble his rifle and Meimei
taught him how to respect and play mah jongg. Whatever she got
from her herbalist friend in San Francisco seemed to do the trick.
This morning we tried to persuade her to stay with us through
Christmas especially now that we've seasoned the wok. But she
misses her friends and hates the cold weather.

When you get Quanah make it summer all time I come back…
she said as we helped her onto the plane.

J. and I drove in silence to his lawyer's office. Matilda continues
to loom. J. continues to disappear and I continue to raid the refrigerator. Only Ethan seems oblivious and only God knows for how
much longer. Anyway, it was interesting meeting J.'s lawyer friend,
Eliot. He certainly doesn't look like his voice on the phone. Small
and disheveled. Books everywhere…lining the walls and piled on
the floor next to moving cartons that looked as if they hadn't been
unpacked for years. File cabinets overflowed. Legal briefs exploded
on his desk. When he wasn't on the verge of looking for something,
he chewed Kleenex and tapped his pencil and listened intently, his

eyes wrestling with the fairest approach versus the smartest.

We can try for split custody...he said twisting what remained of his hair around his finger. She takes the furniture...you get the house.

Alri-i-i-ght...said Johnson slowly.

ALL THE FURNITURE?!! I couldn't believe J. was even considering it! I bit my tongue to the point of injury. Eliot poured me a glass of water and explained if we are lenient with the furniture then we might get Matilda to loosen up about Ethan. Good intent and all that. On the way home about all J. said was that split custody would hurt Ethan's schooling. I couldn't tell if I was meant to respond or be a sounding board so I said: Does Ethan ever have a say in this? Johnson adjusted the static on the radio dial. A blast of hard rock came at us and he started singing along with it. He hates hard rock. He won't even let Ethan listen to it. Babe. She. And now heavy metal.

What's her name?...I joked, sort of.

He laughed and switched to NPR.

Whose?

The chick who taught you the lyrics.

Graciela...he said with flair. Graciela Mish Mash.

And that was pretty much it for the rest of the ride...except for a dead feeling in the pit of my ever-expanding stomach.

January 1978

Ethan returned yesterday from Christmas vacation with Matilda. She gave him a picture of herself in a silver frame. He put it on his bedside table. I've been staring at it all morning...waiting for her to turn a little more this way so I can get a look at her head on. She is very, very skinny. Ethan has her pale coloring all right...and her hair. But while his is straight hers is thick and curly. It twists itself effortlessly into an auburn Gibson Girl...the shorter strands framing her face like a halo. I don't like that part. I also don't like that she looks so fucking happy when she's really a high strung, anorexic pile of...hair on a stick.

Tomorrow

Ethan is at Thomas's even though he hasn't finished his chores for the second day in a row...and Johnson is upstairs meditating with a vengeance. Not only meditating but becoming macrobiotic. Nothing that comes from an animal is to cross his lips for the rest of his life. No eggs, no butter and certainly not hot milk and honey. Feels a lot like penance to this pilgrim. Penance for indulging Ethan, if you ask me. But then, what do I know? I'm only the family "drive slaver." 'Tis best to remain mute and close to the refrigerator. Homemade granola on coffee ice cream. Shake, rattle and roll.

Started working in the local nursery (plants not babies) about three days ago. It's a harmless job. Organizational stuff. Nice people. Plus we need the money. And it gets the Boys used to me being out of the house.

J. put a bullseye on the side of the barn. Ethan fired his sling shot and J. fired his rifle. Then, judging by Ethan's stride into the kitchen for dinner (and the occasional rubbing of his shoulder) I think they traded off.

Tuesday

Went to a fund-raiser (in the green dress that sags, according to Mother) for the citizen's committee that wants Johnson to save the river. J.'s speech went really well. This morning in the shower, J. said they made him an offer. He wants me to help him with his acceptance speech, too. We were getting all sweet and cozy when he muttered something about Eliot. How he feels he (J.) is paying him to do what he could have done on his own. Later, as I wiped the steam off the mirror I realized J. was trying to tell me he wants to handle his divorce himself so he can quit his job and become a local hero by saving the river that runs into our pond that attracts the birds that attract the bird-watchers who snap the snapshots that are developed in the chemicals that end up in the river. AND WHY, FOR ONCE, CAN'T THINGS STAY THE WAY THEY ARE?!? GOD!!! It's like all this jockeying for personal satisfaction. It's exhausting!

Next Week

Eliot called this morning. Matilda is immovable. Eliot thinks we should go to court even though the judge is a woman. I think we should do whatever Eliot wants and I say as much.

Under no circumstances is Ethan going to be put in a position where he has to choose…mutters Johnson putting on his undershirt. That's why I hired Eliot. That's why I'm pushing paper in a fucking highrise.

But it's just a threat.

You don't know Matilda…he insists.

I know Matilda! She's why you can't sleep. Why Ethan throws rocks. Why we tried to get pregnant, for god's sake. Never mind the baby. Just…let's look All-American for the judge…who you don't even want to go before.

My father never spoke to me again!

You're not your father, Johnse. You and Ethan are close.

Eliot was supposed to settle out of court. That was the whole point!

Fire Eliot if you want…I say sitting on the bed next to him…but get another lawyer…a lawyer who's a shit…like hers.

Johnson falls back, his arm over his eyes, a sock dangling off his right foot and mutters: We can't afford to start all over again!

Then what's all this talk about quitting your job?

Because I'm drowning in bullshit! In corporate bullshit!!

Well, I'm drowning in ficus trees and fertilizer…and that may have to be the way it is for a while. It won't kill us.

Johnson stiffens his back and clenches his teeth.

It's okay to fall apart…I say running a strand of his hair between my fingers. No matter what you decide, I'm not going anywhere.

I fall apart…he mumbles sitting up. I fall apart all the time.

In your meditation room.

He stands up and puts on his suitpants. I sit uncertainly then head for the walk-in closet.

Are you having an affair or something?

That's all I need…he says buttoning his shirt.

Then why is it so hard for you to accept my comfort?

You're the one who pulled away in the shower.

I button my jeans and come out of the closet.

Well, I just thought…well, when I got pregnant…well, that there would be…I don't know…time taken. You know, between us. That it wouldn't just be about getting an erection and sticking it in.

He puts on his jacket and mutters: You're never satisfied, are you? Then he leaves to go downstairs. I put on my down vest and try to compose myself. I make it to the count of three.

We're talking about a human life!…I holler. We're talking about bringing a baby into a world with no…no…(No what? Quick!…I think…Money? Love?)…<u>Furniture</u>!

I stand at the top of the stairs and he stands sullenly at the bottom, impatience hunching his back and shaking his head.

Look at me…I say.

And when he doesn't I say: Look at me! And throw a potted plant in his direction. Johnson turns around and glares.

I AM YOUR BEST FRIEND!…I scream as Ethan comes out of the kitchen. I've put my life on hold to help you get yours together. And the only time you touch me is when you're trying to get me pregnant. You make me feel like a goddamned uterus!!

February, 1978

Johnson has fired Eliot, quit his job, rented a grubby office in downtown Philadelphia and gone to work for the Citizen's Committee to save the river. I dive into bottomless bowls of buttered popcorn over the weekend and stay as late as I can after work during the week to earn all the money that is humanly possible. He chooses a time like this to have his gd principles. Unbefuckinglievable.

March

I was waiting for a delivery of steer manure. I was running late. But it wasn't as if Ethan hadn't walked home from the bus before. Only this time when he opened the door the phone was ringing and it was Matilda. When J. found out Ethan had been by himself for about half an hour he had another attack of paranoia about child neglect and the judge's ruling (and the fact that she's a W-O-M-A-N) and insisted I quit working at the nursery until the custody thing is resolved. I was afraid to challenge him. I was afraid he'd say something cutting about my right to find myself then go upstairs to meditate. And I know, I know…Matilda's got him by the short and curlies and he doesn't mean to take it out on me but he does because I'm Here trying to decide how much more of being Here I can take.

Friday

Johnson and Matilda preoccupy themselves with fighting about the furniture because it's easier than fighting about Ethan…who hit the Hogan boy again…this time with a stick. When Matilda found out that I had gone with Johnson to speak to the principal she said:

That does it! And slammed down the receiver. When Ethan was do-ing his homework, J. took his rifle apart then hid it in the basement where it is to remain forever, I hope...or at least until Ethan is a little older and his parents have discovered Forgiveness. Then J. took Ethan upstairs to introduce him to the principles of meditation, non-violence and divorce.

First week of April

Two weeks before we go before the judge!

Ethan and Thomas were splattering flour water on the kitchen table making papier mache rocks. I was in the living room trying to re-work a funding proposal for J. One of the women on the Citizen's Committee to save the river heard I wrote J.'s acceptance speech and decided I was "a writer." (I didn't tell her all I ever think about is food.) Anyway, the boys were getting rowdy and I was beginning to feel the presence of an "adult" might be called for so I decided it was time to clean out the freezer and that was where I ran across some odd bits of mushrooms in a Ziploc bag.

Where do you suppose these came from?...I asked anyone who cared to listen.

Quanah gave them to Pop...said Ethan. You chew them and you see things.

Thomas looked at Ethan in disbelief and ran another strip of newspaper through the pasty water.

Ethan flicked some pasty water at Thomas who hesitated then flicked some back and they both began to giggle.

I'll tell you right now...I said, returning the mushrooms to the freezer...I'm not cleaning up your mess.

You better not...said Thomas as Ethan approached his face with a strip of pasty newspaper.

I'm wa-a-a-rning you...I sang firmly.

But temptation won out. Ethan lunged for Thomas who turned to avoid him and knocked the bowl of pasty water on the floor. I slammed the freezer door as Ethan ran into the living room and Thomas looked at me...panic overwhelming his otherwise placid nature. I marched across the kitchen as Thomas put a roll of paper towels in one of the puddles and began to smear the sticky water all over the linoleum.

Ethan...I said entering the living room...you clean up that mess or it's all over.

Ethan crossed his arms and turned his back and knew, as I did, how badly I wanted to grab him by the throat and throw his coddled little ass out of my narrow, unfocused, petty, fattening, self-absorbed life.

Fine...I said regaining my composure...if you aren't going to clean up after yourself then neither am I.

I returned to the kitchen.

Thomas...leave everything where it is. We're going to live here like pigs...I said loud enough for Ethan to hear. And when Ethan's father objects he can answer to him.

A Week Later

The standoff continues. Doors are routinely slammed. Dishes pile up in the sink. Milk turns sour. Socks are lost. Shoes are tripped over in the middle of the night. Ants march in a steady stream across the kitchen counter. Junk mail buries the phone. Sticky fingers dirty the TV screen. Toothpaste hardens in open tubes. And Johnson begs us to negotiate.

I'm not going first...I inform him. I don't care! This place can become a landfill. I don't care!!

Mol, you're being childish.

He doesn't recycle. He leaves the water running when he brushes his teeth. He doesn't turn off the lights. He interrupts when I write. And he treats me like I'm the maid!

He's in pain.

We're all in pain. Ever stop to think about that? All of us. So fuck you.

Alright...what do you want me to do?...he asks reluctantly.

Stop protecting him! It's like you're so afraid he's going to turn against you. You and Matilda both. So I end up doing the dirty work!

Mol, I grounded him. What more do you want?

He can't clean up his mess if he's confined to his room.

Johnson's body tenses.

Ethan!...he yells up the stairs.

Whaaaaat!

Come into the living room, please.

I can't...I'm grounded.

Well, I'm ungrounding you for five minutes.

Ethan slinks down the stairs, his eyes on the floor.

It's time for us to have a talk.

I didn't spill the sticky water...Thomas did...he says sullenly kicking a sneaker toward the fireplace.

You were going to papier mache his face...I say as Johnson digs his fingers into my arm.

Hold it. Now just hold it. Both of you.

YOU'RE NOT MY MOTHER!

I rip my arm away from J., grab Ethan by the front of his shirt and hiss: WELL, YOU'RE NOT MY SON!!!!!

Ethan glares at me from the mean side of hatred. Chloe trips over the shadowy figure and falls backwards off the brittle edge of Unconditional Love. I grab myself by the hair and yank it...hard. Ethan bolts up the stairs like a startled animal. J. turns sharply in my direction.

Do you honestly think if he has to tell the judge which parent he feels like living with—

Fuck the judge...I say. It's not about the judge and you know it. It's about Matilda...fucking-squeeze-your-balls-until-you-die Matilda.

Johnson's fingers curl into fists. Then he turns on his heels, climbs the stairs two at a time and knocks on Ethan's door.

Ethan! Let me in.

I'm not here.

Then where are you?

Nowhere!

Nowhere's a pretty big place.

Shut up!

I sit heavily at the bottom of the stairs and wonder if I've seen the last of Chloe. Five minutes later, Ethan bolts from his room and into the kitchen. He and J. have struck a deal in record time. If he cleans the kitchen floor he can go hot air ballooning with Thomas and his father tomorrow.

Saturday, late
Six days before the WOMAN judge
Ethan and Johnson got their own breakfast while I lay in bed fantasizing about French toast, melted butter, brown sugar, lemon juice and a double caffeinated cappuccino and tried to finish the funding proposal. After the screen door slammed and Ethan was off I decided to get up but fat and depression beached me like a whale. Then J. came up the stairs with a glass of fresh squeezed orange juice. He handed it to me and sat on the edge of the bed. He was feeling guilty about giving Ethan permission to go ballooning, I could tell. I turned away. I didn't feel like getting into a whole discussion about Ethan's manipulation of his parents because Johnson would only pat me on the head like he had the truth on ice in his meditation room and I was not to be enlightened until he was good and ready.

So what's the deal with the psychedelic mushrooms?...I asked as he bent the toes of one of my feet through the covers.

Quanah left them. For guidance.

You don't suppose we need it, do you?

A short while later I dumped some of the mushrooms in the ashtray that had my wedding ring in it and left the rest on the kitchen counter. Then I climbed the stairs to J.'s meditation room.

Remember...he said as I handed him some mushroom bits...there are no accidents.

I know...I said as we smiled tentatively through the tattered veil of Woodstock.

Then Johnson got on his knees, held the ashtray full of mushrooms in the air, bowed his head, lowered everything onto the altar, put his palms together, said something under his breath and kissed the floor. Then he held a piece of mushroom out to me as if he were a priest and these were high holy days and said: Chew it thoroughly and ask for guidance.

We put the mushroom bits in our mouths. They were earthy and bitter tasting. We closed our eyes and waited. Whatever happened I didn't want to babble. Chloe. I wanted to find Chloe in all her Unconditional splendor. The shadowy figure laughed a loud, hollow laugh and I was a little girl lost in a thousand mirrors. I had a chameleon pinned to my shirt. It opened its mouth and swallowed me so I entered my own shoulder and when I swam toward my heart it began to snow. I was shivering in my nightgown on the edge of the roof when I heard Johnson's voice...maybe for real...maybe not.

Jesus. Mol. What are you doing?

I'm looking for Chloe.

Take my hand, Mol. We can look for her together.

If I move...I said...the world will stop.

Then you lie down and let me look for her, okay?

Where will you look?

In the basement. By the ladder.

Can I go with you?

And I must have...because the next thing I remember is lying on the lawn making angels. And J. was lying a few feet away with his eyes closed...talking to me about the ancient souls that had lived on this land. He was meeting them personally...Native Americans, Pilgrims and...I don't know, maybe even cavemen. And his voice was getting that same little shake as it did when he said Sacred. Uch! I was getting tired of the quivering romance of how things used to be. I wanted to know how they were going to turn out!...so I started crawling on my hands and knees toward the bird sanctuary and when he asked me what I was doing I said I was a horse from ancient times because if I'd told him my heart had congealed into a frozen baby, he would've laughed at the fantastical absurdity and I would have burst into tears and cried for all eternity.

Pegasus...I said. I'm pretending I'm Pegasus.

Then, to J.'s credit, he whinnied, got on all fours and joined me.

Around the same time we were heading for the bird sanctuary on our knees, Thomas was coming down with a violent flu which meant his father brought Ethan home early. No sooner had Ethan curled up on the couch with a comic book than a stranger knocked on the screen door. Said he was a friend of Matilda's. When Ethan told him she no longer lived here he asked if he could look around while he waited for Johnson. Then, Ethan says, the guy killed a few ants, made a remark about how the place looked lived-in, took a camera out of his brief case and took photographs of the clutter on the kitchen counter including the leftover mushroom bits. Around the time he returned to the living room, Johnson and I were rediscovering each other (not as horses) on a pile of leaves in the bird sanctuary.

The first time I saw you...I said dreamily...I thought you were
Jesus.

The first time I saw you...he said...I thought you were Artemis.
Stoned and lost...but Artemis.

Save me...I said throwing my arms open.

Anytime...he said rolling on top of me and easing my nightgown over my hips.

And as I opened my legs to what I prayed was the Urge, a
shadow fell across us and a stranger cleared his throat.

Oh...excuse me.

Johnson looked up...not moving. A man in a brown polyester
suit was standing at the edge of the clearing.

The bird walk was yesterday...I said uncertainly.

I'm looking for Johnson Stillwater...he said loosening his tie.

You're looking at him...said Johnson rolling off.

I'm sorry to intrude.

Then why are you?...I asked and, things being what they were,
found that incredibly funny.

Whoops...said Johnson trying to stand.

Drugs...I said...you can't take him anywhere.

Newtown Development...said the man as he shook Johnson's
hand. Matilda Stillwater has decided to sell this piece of property.

A large paint brush, drew a stripe from the top of his head, over
his face and down his body. When it had crossed his arms it moved
onto the trees, over the sky and into the next day...then into the day
after that...until it had successfully painted the spring of 1978 the
Color Black.

The Week That Was
Johnson hung up the phone and called us over to his desk in the
dining room. Matilda had spoken to the developer, heard we were
living in a pig sty on drugs and was relishing her moment in court.
Johnson threw some stuff on the floor and motioned us to sit. He
seemed tense and professorial. He started by telling us Newtown
Developers had made an offer. Then he turned to Ethan and explained that Matilda loved him so much she wanted him to live
with her full time and if Pop said No to her one more time, she
would sell the farm. So Ethan, quite rightly, suggested we get

Quanah to do another dance. Then Johnson reminded Ethan of what Quanah had said about the farm being a Power Spot and how they had a responsibility toward it...Johnson for now...and Ethan when he was older. Then he asked Ethan to be very brave and think hard about what he wanted to do. The operative word was Consequences. J. had never been able to think in small, day to day ways. Ethan knew this and when his father had finished his little sermon, Ethan picked up the sneakers that normally lived in the middle of the living room, and turned, without expression, toward the stairs. Later J. would join him in his bedroom as I puttered in the living room listening to muffled explosions and tear-stained reasoning. And when J. had taken the consequences of his Understanding with his son into the attic, I walked quietly into Ethan's bedroom to kiss him goodnight.

You know, Eth...you and I have always told each other the truth...and a lot of the time it hasn't been easy. Your father—

I know. He loves me.

Yes.

And you do, too...he said with a shrug.

Yes, Eth. I do, too.

It's only until I'm eighteen...he said throwing a half empty box of crayons into his wastebasket.

It'll go by really fast, you'll see.

It's because I said you're not my mother, isn't it?...he asked, his brave eyes welling with anxiety.

Eth...it's not because of anything you said or did. Whatever you think IT'S NOT. Your mother and father haven't figured out how to get along and you've ended up in the middle.

But I don't want to live with her!...he cried, flinging his arms around my waist. I want to live with you!

Oh, Eth...I said as he buried his face in my belly. I'm so mean to you.

Then...he sobbed...I'll be good, too!

Chapter Nine

The flashlight flickers on the final page of the rice paper journal. Molly rips it, tearstains and all, from its mangled spine and lets her heart fall backwards into silence. Her feet are freezing and a chill is marching up her legs and back. She looks quickly into the hallway. The streetlight is making sure (as it always has) that the bedroom stays nicely illuminated. Little Norway. All that is missing is an aurora borealis. And maybe it isn't…missing. Molly had seen something when she was sucking her thumb. It was brief and colorful and she'd had the feeling she could have melted into it. Merged. Become one with Unconditional Wonder. Then the chatter started and Molly made a conscious decision to stay wherever she was as sucking her thumb was, evidently, more important.

Now Molly stands up, sees the eviction notice and moves with purpose toward the kitchen. It is definitely time to go fishing for the razor. She closes one eye and squats alongside the refrigerator. She can't see anything. She bangs the flashlight on the palm of her hand. It flickers then shudders and dies. Fuck it. She'll use female intuition. It has to be good for something. She opens the cover of her journal and slips it sideways into the uncharted slot. She figures the razor is about halfway back. She won't lower the journal to the floor until she's gotten it as far in as she can then she'll point and drag and see what she comes up with. She focuses what is left of her conscious mind.

'One, two, three…Point. Draaaaaag. Greasy dust balls. One more time. Point. Draaaaaag. A pencil stub. Shit. I need something longer.

What about the emery board? I don't want to go there. Motherfucker.
Go where? It's just a handbag. It's not just a handbag…it's a handbag
that's too close to the eviction notice! Do you mind? Will guns come
out of the walls? They will if the eviction notice doesn't reach out and
grab you first.'

In a desperate attempt to still the chatter, Molly kicks her purse
across the living room and locates the emery board under her wallet.
Then she returns to the kitchen, takes the pencil stub and makes a hole
for the emery board in one end of the journal cover. The contraption is
wobbly but her will is high. She slides it into the crack between the refrigerator and the counter. She points. She drags. Greasy dust, a piece
of dried cheese…and no goddamn emery board!

Molly slumps against the refrigerator and listens to horns honking
and people telling each other to go fuck themselves. Ethan's sad eyes
look at her from the airplane window and she feels nothing. Just as she
felt nothing when Matilda's movers denuded the farmhouse. Or when
President Carter signed the American Indian Religious Freedom Act
into law and Johnson left for a four-day ritual in New Mexico. She
could have gone with him. He had asked her (without much enthusiasm) but she had declined in favor of a trip to New York City to pick
up the rest of her furniture and visit Hatia.

"Read this!" said Hatia throwing a paperback on the trunk that
used to hold Ethan's toys.

"'When God Was a Woman?'"

"Yeah, and guys knew it."

Molly watches herself take the paperback and put it in a box
marked: Books T–Z.

"I better not show it to Johnson," she says. He's not big on women
these days. I went to my gyno for my annual pap smear. I was lying
there with my feet in the stirrups thinking about couple's therapy and
how Johnson doesn't want to go because he's afraid we'll talk about sex
and he doesn't want to remove the Mystery. And there was this virtual
stranger sliding a cold speculum into my vagina and it was like: What
Mystery? Then my gyno said I am built to have babies. And I knew…as
I had never known before…I do not, Not, NOT want to get pregnant
until our relationship has Us in it again. But the thought of communi-
cating this to Johnson…. Forget it! He's already running up the attic
stairs. So, I bit the bullet and asked my gyno to fit me with an IUD."

Molly pulls her knees under her chin, works her sweatshirt over her thighs and tucks part of her overcoat under her feet which have made the move from pink to purple and are merging nicely now with white.

"Pain is the breaking of the shell that encloses understanding."

"What made you think of that?" asks Hatia as she and Molly carry the trunk that used to be the coffee table out the door and down the stairs.

"I don't know. I was thinking how good Johnson is at suffering. It's his drug of choice. Like mine is self-analysis. I've got to lose some weight."

"Girl, are you sure you know what you're doing?"

Molly grabs her white toes with her white fingers. It is time for a hot bath...fuck the razor. She'll boil herself to death. She is so cold she won't feel it anyway.

"I've been thinking about going back to school."

"Going back to school?" asks Johnson as he and Molly put the trunk in front of the fireplace.

"I want to do something with my life! Get a degree. Learn a language. I want to be good at something more than writing grants and growing vegetables."

"You're good at planning benefits."

"Good at planning benefits?!?" says Heather as the waiter pulls out Molly's chair and they sit down for dinner.

"Well, I am. It's just..."

"Not e-e-enough?"

"He's not a bad man."

"I didn't say he was a bad man...says Heather. I said he knows you have this thing about being useful which is fine as long as it's to him."

"I told him about my IUD. I said I'd have it taken out as soon as he agrees to couple's therapy so don't start about how I never stand up for myself."

The waiter lowers two mineral waters with no ice as Heather leans over her salmon-au-something.

"Speaking of IUD's," she whispers, "You'll never guess! I'm pregnant."

"By whom?" says Molly choking on her mineral water.

"They don't give you his name. Just a rundown of his body and brains. He has a lot more going for him than those assholes I've been dating."

"If you have a boy...when he becomes a man...will he be an asshole?"

"Don't you understand?" says Heather moving her broccoli spears to one side. "Men need to fight. It's their rite of passage. Just like ours is giving birth. Except now the price of war is total extinction...so, instead of fighting with each other they fight with us. All this bullshit about Ethan going to live with Matilda...Johnson didn't make the most humane decision...he made the most romantic one."

"What's romantic about giving up?"

"In his mind. I'm talking about in his mind. The Romance of Martyrdom is far more acceptable than The Reality of Weakness."

"I don't mean to hate him," says Molly, bursting into tears. "I really don't."

"You need to have an affair."

Molly jumps to her feet and starts hitting herself to stay warm. Then she tries running in place but the balls of her feet thud on the linoleum like bones on a frozen lake.

"So get this, Hatia," says Molly twisting the phone cord around her fingers. "We are walking through the door of the hotel on our way to some ballroom for another benefit to save the river when I ask Johnson if I can fix up the chicken coop. Turn it into an office. And he says Meimei is coming to live with us and the chicken coop might be just the place for her to stay as she's gotten so frail she can't climb the stairs. And I'm like...speechless. I am. I mean, this is the first I've heard that she's even coming and just as I'm about to bring that to his attention, this Asian woman looks at Johnson knowingly and he points to me nervously and says, 'This is...uh...my...uh...' 'You must be Molly,' she says extending her long, skinny fingers. 'I've heard a lot about you.' 'I hope it's good,' I say treading water. 'Elizabeth Lee,' says Johnson...then adds: 'Elizabeth is our press agent.' Hatia, I knew that. I was on the benefit committee. It's like...am I ever on his mind? Anyway, she went off with some older professor type and Johnson went to the bar to get himself a Perrier and came back with a scotch on the rocks. I've only seen him drink once before and that was a Guy Thing he got into with my brother. So I look at him like: Is there something I

should know (aside from the fact that your mother's coming to live in the chicken coop and we have practically no furniture) and he says he's nervous because he has to give a speech (which he's probably forgotten I helped him write) and I decide to believe him, Hatia, even though I have this creepy feeling that I have just shaken the bony fingers of Graciela Mish Mash."

Molly enters her almost dark living room on tiptoe and runs her hand along the lopsided bookshelves in a last ditch attempt to find something long and thin to retrieve the goddamn razor. Midway through the upper shelf she comes across a letter on top of a large manila envelope stuffed with what feels like books and papers. She carries everything into the hallway and finds herself looking at a post-it from Hatia stuck on the manila envelope:

Found this letter when I was packing. Thought you might want it back. The rest is self-explanatory. Love ya, H. PS My new zip is 91604. Not whatever I told you.

Molly turns the letter in her fingers then lifts the post-it off the manila envelope and sees her name in Nancy's handwriting underneath. A garbage truck rattles down the street. Molly knows what's inside. Knows it as sure as she can barely bend her fingers so she grits her teeth, rests the manila envelope on the palm of her hand and hurls it into Little Norway. But her arm flies wild and the manila envelope goes sideways instead of straight, bouncing off the top of her closet and falling lengthwise onto the composition book which, in turn, falls sharply onto one end of the coat hanger. Molly watches the hanger flip and jangle and come to rest at the foot of her bedside table. She moves, trance-like, toward the bed. She trips over a spiral notebook in the process and it so startles her she kicks it into the hallway. She hears a sucking sound. In a panic, she grabs the coat hanger, bolts for the doorway, grips the doorjamb, bends over, clenches her teeth, catches her breath and begins to work the coat hanger bending it back and forth, smacking it on the spiral notebook, twisting the neck until it springs open. She crosses the living room blinded by purpose and when she reaches the kitchen she falls to her knees and fishes for the razor. She can feel it through the wire. Can feel when she has it and when she doesn't. Can feel with the sensitivity of a healer in spite of her freezing fingers. Meimei has taught her well. It's a good thing she and Johnson made the chicken coop livable. It's a good thing they worked late into the night sheetrocking…plastering.… Point. Draaaag.

"Come on, Baby…come to Mama."

They had had a couple of good laughs that were only partially at-tributable to exhaustion and paint fumes.

'But maybe when he kissed the back of my neck…maybe when I flipped around in his arms covered with joint compound and tasted his salty lips…maybe when he drove his tongue deep into my mouth with a force and passion I could only long for…maybe the whole time he was driving himself deep into Elizabeth.'

Molly closes her eyes and reinserts the coat hanger. She makes contact with the razor and recovers her emery board.

'Mystery,' she stews, 'You can watch men falling for it like flies to rotting fruit.'

Meimei flips on the light. Molly jumps then grabs herself. She has to stay focused or the razor will wedge itself under the refrigerator.

"Big feeling?" asks Meimei.

"Oh," says Molly looking at Meimei disoriented. Meimei takes Molly's hand, folds it in hers and strokes it with quiet understanding.

"Cold. Here. Begin here," says Meimei laying a hand on Molly's heart.

"There are things," stammers Molly. "I thought when Ethan left.… Don't get me wrong…Johnson is a special man."

"No man so special," says Meimei smoothing Molly's hair.

Molly squeezes Meimei's hand. Meimei squeezes back.

"Strong," she says.

"Cold," says Molly.

Meimei points toward her feet then takes off one of her shoes.

"I teacher," she says pointing to the sole of a wide, square foot. "No needles. Fingers. Bottom foot. Everything bottom foot. You do me. I do you. Both get better."

"Point. Draaaag…yes!" says Molly as Meimei clicks her teeth and turns her back on the rusty razor.

April

Dear Hatia,

A week ago, when Johnson was in the shower, I rescued "When God Was a Woman" from the depths of the moving carton that has be-come an end table…and began to read it. I have never been a big reader of things dry and archeological but as I began to familiarize myself with a society that crafted ceramics rather than weapons… that sought to communicate rather than dominate…I began to fall backwards and forwards in time…all in the same moment. So yesterday, unable to contain my excitement and eager to appeal to Johnson's love of history…I decide to show him what I've been reading.

Look…I say opening to the pictures…statues of Goddesses. Amphoras…celebrating the Feminine. A whole period of history has been unearthed and it's like—

Johnson grabs the book and gives it a perfunctory glance.

Read the introduction…I continue. What she says about no longer being able to ignore the existence of a matriarchal society where there was peace and people lived off the land and treated each other as equals.

He cruises through the first paragraph then says: Speculation. And throws the book across the room with flair, casual flair, but he throws it nonetheless.

What's the matter?…I ask in a voice I've never heard before… has she left you for somebody else?

Who?…he asks innocently.

Graciella Mish Mash…I say quietly.

I have my shortcomings…he says…but I'm not faithful.

You mean, not unfaithful.

If you know what I mean why do you correct me?

You correct me.

Because you're wrong!

You know…I say…when we criticize each other all we're really talking about is ourselves. So maybe it would be easier or kinder or something to apply the things we don't like about each other to ourselves…like if I could think of…well, the fact that you didn't fight for Ethan…not that you did or didn't…but that I see it that way…so, if I could think of that as my own fear of my own Weakness and if you could think of my lack of Mystery as your fear of…well, I don't know…exposure or something…well, then maybe we could let go of some of our ideas about how we think we <u>should</u> be because you're a man and I'm a woman. Because, when you think about it…before we're a sex we're human beings.

He grips the banister and taps his foot like: Are you finished? Hatia, it is all I can do not to ask him why he is so frightened of the E word when he sits in his meditation room on a daily basis trying to become one with the universe. Anger coils his back and when the proper amount of time has passed he slithers down the stairs.

Equals...I mutter after him...equals, equals, equals.

After dinner (which we eat separately) I work on Meimei's feet (she is teaching me foot reflexology). Then I do my homework (am truly loving school! Especially Spanish!!) and go to bed. Johnson stays up late reading a book about Pearl Harbor. I am positive it is a gift from Elizabeth which is why I can't sleep so eventually I go downstairs and there he is sitting at his desk in the dining room.

Oh, Mol...he says...I'm such a weak and evil man.

You're a great man...I say sensing an opening. This is just a rough period. We'll get through it. We're good people.

I'm not having an affair with Elizabeth. I'm really not.

Then what are you having?

Nothing.

Well, but the way she flirts with you...

Because she would like to.

Oh...I say relieved and sorry for the information.

I shouldn't've told you...he says.

No...I say...you should. It's like there's a wall. I used to think it was Matilda...and it <u>was</u> Matilda...and, I don't know...maybe it's still Matilda...but is it always going to be...you know...

Matilda?...he says as I sit at his feet.

I mean, don't you ever want to...get on with it?

He twists in his chair and says: I could ask you the same question.

I want to take my IUD out...I say nervously. I really do. It's just...I think we need help. Therapy would give us the tools, that's all.

Therapy would give us the therapist's tools. Just like Quanah gave us his and Buddha gave us his and on and on.

So do we just not do anything?

I know it's been hard...he says placing a hollow kiss on top of my head. You're always the odd man out. And now all this business with my mother.

We're getting along fine...I say, determined to avoid his pity. She's teaching me foot reflexology.

She burned another pot while you were at school. If I hadn't come home for lunch this place would be in ashes.

Maybe we should hire a nurse.

Nothing medical...believe me. Don't even discuss it.

Then a companion. Maybe Thomas's mother knows someone...

Mol, one of us has to quit...he says so softly I almost decide I haven't heard him.

But, Johnson...I feel good about myself for the first time in a long time.

I know...but somebody has to be here.

It's not like I've gone back to school full time.

She has bone cancer! What if she falls when you're running around trying to become...what?

You were going to raise your legal fees.

Not everybody has the money!...he says slapping his desk.

So I'm supposed to not have a life because you've taken a vow of poverty. How romantic. And what a great world into which to bring kids.

Why don't you just admit it...you don't want them and you never have!

I want them! I want them!! I want them!!!

Then stop blackmailing me with your goddamn IUD!

I am not blackmailing you. I just want us to—

You women and your fucking FREEDOM. You're destroying the very fabric of our society.

THERE IS NOTHING WRONG WITH TALKING ABOUT SEX!...I holler.

And then what? And what after that?

I am not Matilda! FOR THE THOUSANDTH TIME...I AM NOT MATILDA!

His body uncoils itself out of the chair and very deliberately he heads for the door.

If children mean so much to you...I say coming up behind him...why did you give up Ethan for an empty house?

Then, Hatia, he raises his hand, whirls around and strikes me across the face. I run into the coat closet. Johnson comes after me. I fumble for the door knob. My fingers find the lock just as Johnson turns the handle. He bangs the door with his fists.

YOU CUNT…he shouts…YOU'RE RUINING MY LIFE!!!

Fuck you!…I holler. Fuck you fuck youfuckyoufuckyou!!!

EVIL!…he screams, kicking the door. YOU ARE FUCKING EVIL! YOU MAKE MATILDA LOOK LIKE MARY POPPINS!!!

Then go back to her! Why don't you fucking go back to her!!!

And you're FAT!…he yells banging the screen door. FAT (bang) FAT (bang) FAT (bang, bang)!!!! When I fuck you it's like fucking a fucking FAT MAN!!! (bang, bang, bang, bang, BANG!)

YOU WISH!…I shout.

The door begins to wobble. He rips it off its hinges and throws it off the porch.

Fat, witch, cuuuuuuuuuunt!!!

I move some shoes aside and sit on the floor. I am not going to cry. I am not going to give him the satisfaction of my Pain so he can indulge in Remorse and we can reconnect through the Drama. I am fine. I feel nothing. I grind my teeth and begin to shiver uncontrollably. I look at my feet. Hiking boots. My feet are in fucking hiking boots! I rip them off along with my plaid shirt, British Army pants and thick socks. Hatia, I am wearing Johnson's clothes! I look at my underpants. They have flowers on them at least…but the elastic is going. I flip on the light and open the closet door. I stand there shivering in the tattered remains of my femininity waiting for Johnson to discover me in all my bizarro splendor. But the moment comes and goes…and so do I…first to the freezer for a pint of butter pecan ice cream…then upstairs to close the bathroom door, turn out all the lights and step into a scalding bubble bath. And as my body turns from a pale purple to brilliant lobster…I eat the ice cream then let the container fall to the floor. My stomach floats up through the bubbles…a lonely red island in the moonlight…and I think about something you said when you first came to work at the bookstore: Why do women clean around the toilet when it's the men who pee on the floor?

Chapter Ten

Molly straightens her letter to Hatia and decides she'll leave it for all to see on the toilet. It is as good a suicide note as any.

She presses her back against the yellowing wall in the hallway and her feet into the stains on the floor. She comes to a standing position and looks toward the bathroom. The tub is still filling with hot water but there doesn't appear to be any steam. She wraps her overcoat around her, tiptoes across the chill in the floor and puts her fingers under the faucet. Ice cold. Fucking landlord. She turns off the water, pulls the rubber plug from the drain and turns nervously toward Little Norway. A shaft of light spills into the hallway. Molly picks up the razor she'd placed in thoughtful ceremony beside the bathtub and turns it in her frozen fingers. Her upstairs neighbor turns on the stereo. Molly can hear the jaunty whine of violins as she presses the razor against her wrist.

'Death to Muzak. They say the last thing that goes is the hearing. I told you she didn't have the guts. Mommy, Mommy! Come on, press. What about the mess? Suicidal Etiquette, that it? Right up there with Unconditional Love.'

Molly slumps against the wall. She will write a note in her composition book with the pencil she rescued from beside the refrigerator…explain her dilemma just in case people think she went down without a thought. She wouldn't want anyone accusing her of being SELFISH! She will have to work this one through. She tucks her letter to Hatia in its envelope along with the rusty razor. Then she picks up the spiral notebook she so unceremoniously kicked out of

Little Norway. It was never intended to become a journal. The first few pages are filled with Spanish declensions and idioms, recommended reading and notes about some of the members of her class. Then comes a page that is folded in half:

LIKES
1. Learning to teach something to someone.

2. Eating a Sara Lee Cheescake in its entirety.
3. Giving Meimei her foot treatments

4. Getting an acupuncture treatment from Meimei.
5. Aprender Español.
6. Writing Funding Proposals (sort of)
7. Living in the daily magnificence of nature.
8. Getting the city council to buy into recycling.
9. Having my own office

DISLIKES
1. J.'s resistance to my interests that don't directly relate to his.
2. Sticking my finger down my throat to bring it up.
3. Brewing her mystery brew with Valerian Root. Smells worse than fish emulsion.
4. Being afraid to tell J. the truth about the frozen baby.
5. Quitting school.
6. Not getting paid for it (at all).

7. Being isolated from the real world.
8. Not having an answering machine.
9. Not being allowed to transform Ethan's bedroom "just in case he comes to visit." PS: Never mind the glaring absence of a bed.

This morning

A delivery truck pulled up in front of the house when I was trying to throw up in the bathroom and two men unloaded a futon onto the front porch. When I signed for it I was handed a note. It read: Let's talk about therapy. Ever, J. Went to the chicken coop to get Meimei's take on the events of the last few days, but she was curled in the fetal position…her pain becoming more frequent and more severe. I had offered her an aspirin yesterday knowing pain killers were out of the question and gotten cursed out in Chinese. Today I took her right foot in my fingers (which only moments before had made their way down my throat in an effort to bring up everything I'd eaten for breakfast). She nodded appreciatively. She is still determined to prove I have the hands of a healer so I do what I can remembering the day she told me that fingers are an extension of the human heart.

About a month later

Talked about Mystery and Openness in therapy today and how we scare each other. Talked about Ethan and the Divorce and how frightened I am that our children will end up in the same predicament if Johnson and I don't get our shit together. I was about to bring up the frozen baby when J. said something about my Anger and how he feels nothing he does for me is ever enough. And that led to how much work I do for him that I never get paid for and how he can see I am chomping at the bit to have a life that is MINE (he sort of growled it out). Then he asked questions like why did he work if not for his family…and if we don't have children because I want to earn a living, too…what is his function… his social, political, economic, historical function in this world? And our therapist asked him to say things like I think and I feel…and J. let her know in no uncertain terms that he was not going to be made over by the two of us into some sort of feminist fantasy of the New Age Man.

Mid-summer

Therapy again today. An effort is being made. A loving, angry, tender effort. And, that being the case, I've decided to have my IUD taken out. I am thinking of it as an Act of Faith. Still haven't mentioned the frozen baby. Probably best to wait until I get pregnant. P.S.: The futon is still in its box on the porch.

Thursday

Meimei had a good day today. Another tightly bound package arrived from her herbalist friend in San Francisco. Roots and herbs in paper bags scribbled with Chinese characters. I made another pot of Mystery Brew. She points I follow. Then, as she sips, she insists she's <u>really</u> improving because I'm getting better and better at working on her feet. She knows where her bread is buttered.

Friday

Have decided not to make an announcement about the removal of my IUD. I am, after all, cultivating Mystery. So, this morning, as soon as J. left for the office I dragged the futon into the house and assembled it in our bedroom. When J. returned I was leaning seductively against the front door in a black, satin slip.

We have a bed to christen, Baby...I said as he came up on the porch.

You put it together all by yourself?...he asked nervously.

No...I said...the other girl did. The one with the hiking boots.

See...he said...I told you she was useful.

I turned my back and headed for the stairs. When I got to the top I looked over my shoulder as if my hair were falling across half my face. He was still standing in the front doorway. His eyes were long and sad. Either he was feeling a perverted loyalty to Elizabeth...who he swears, session after therapy session he never touched...or I was an embarrassment and he didn't know how to tell me.

Fuck it...I thought and disappeared.

When I got to our bedroom, I threw off my slip and put on a rancid flannel nightgown. Thunder rolled in the distance. I lit a candle (in case we had a power failure) and looked at the futon. I could hear J. dragging his body up the stairs.

I'm looking for the woman in the black slip...he said half heartedly.

She's dead...I said.

He laughed shyly and added: So soon?

Not soon enough...I said as he checked out the futon.

You did a good job...he said lying on his back and looking at me.

I didn't know what he wanted so I looked back with a good deal of indifference. That must have turned him on because he spread his legs wide apart. He took himself in his hands and began to get hard. I would play it cool. I would watch. I would watch standing at the end of the bed. I would watch standing on the bed. I would watch standing over him. And I would touch myself...except I was sick of touching myself... Wasn't the whole point for us to be touching each other? He lifted his hips.

Touch me first...I said lowering myself on top of him.

Like that?

Yes...oh, like that. Harder. Higher. Higher.

There?

Yes. Higher. There...yes. No.

I took the curve of his hip bone in my hand, then moved down his thigh and folded my fingers around him. He was shrinking to nothing. I took him in my mouth like a double scoop of banana nut ice cream on a hot summer day.

No...he said pushing me off...I'm trying to give you what you want.

But it's not turning you on.

This is why I hate this...he said. This is exactly why I hate this.

A bolt of lightning split the sky. We sat on opposite sides of the bed and waited in silence for the thunder.

It's because I was the aggressor, isn't it?

No...he said.

Because I told you louder, faster, higher—

No...he said as rain splattered heavy on the roof. I want to quit therapy.

Quit therapy?...I thought. We're finally making progress.

J. fished for his slippers.

I'm going to go on a diet...I said apologetically. Starting tomorrow.

It isn't that...he said walking stiffly toward the window.

You're sleeping with her, aren't you?

No...he said...it isn't that, believe me. It's just...I need some time away.

Do you want to move out, or something?

No...he said...I need to be alone.

But does that mean I can't be in the kitchen when you are? What does that mean?

It means I want to become celibate.

Celibate?

At first I thought he was getting back at me for "blackmailing" him with my IUD...so I told him, with a certain urgency, that I'd had it taken out. Then he turned toward me and took my hand in that too sincere way he has and asked me to understand that what happened to him when he meditated was beyond anything he'd ever experienced in therapy because meditation took him out of his head. Took him into some place Other. He had thought he could separate the two experiences...but the truth was his meditations were a mess. The healing energy he was sending Meimei was filled with too much confusion to do her any good...so until she got better or left her body he couldn't really deal in a deep and significant way with Us.

The Lofty Bottom

I open the door
I don't know why
I am alone in the middle of morning
Going nowhere sideways
Longing has opened its fist
Stretched its intentions wide as a yawn
Somewhere between the chill in our bedroom
And the lofty bottom of the attic stairs
And you are still here
Small vestiges, fractured echoes
Fail to follow you out the door
I know if I sit on your tassled pillow
If I twist my legs into a lotus
And bow my exhausted brain
If I kneel before
The heroes of your inner life
If I raise my hands and offer up
The Best of Us
I will become One with the Wisdom
That doesn't sleep with Words.

I open the door
I don't know why
I am alone in the middle of meditation
Going nowhere sideways

I take off my shoes
I nod my head at the icons of your journey
I fall on bended knee and kiss the floor
I still the Savage
Pulling on
What   Might   Have   Been
I light a candle
To my good intentions
Your pillow has company
A pale yellow letter folded in threes
Words flow like lava
Red hot
They
Curve like snakes across the perfumed page
I feel your voice
Kind, no nonsense
Celibate
You want to become celibate
And I watch your eyes searching mine
For Unconditional Acceptance

I open the door
I don't know why
I am alone in the middle of madness
Going nowhere sideways
Her perfume beats itself into
The secret veins of your two-faced heart
Leaving glistening trails of seduction
Like giant slugs at midnight
Permeating the walls
Challenging the incense
And the whole time you press your lips
Against the drama of her longing
It is my womb you are trying
To salvage with a child

I open the door
I don't know why

I am alone in the middle of mourning
Going nowhere sideways
Longing has opened its fist
Stretched its intentions wide as a yawn
Somewhere between the chill in our bedroom
And the lofty bottom of the attic stairs

Sunday
September
On the train

Heather gave birth to a baby girl last week. I left Meimei with Johnson after breakfast and am now on my way to NYC to meet my niece. Don't know if I should tell Heather about finding The Letter from Elizabeth in J.'s shrine room. She's such a blabber mouth (Heather). But I feel if I don't say something to someone I'll explode. Can barely look at J. I hope he thinks it's because of the celibacy stuff...if he even thinks about it.

Ethan called the other day from a friend's house. He wanted to know if he could come up for a long weekend. All Johnson said was: It's up to your mother. When I asked J. why he continues to give Matilda so much power he said he has no choice...Matilda still owns the bird sanctuary. When Ethan turns twenty-one it will become his...provided Johnson doesn't try anything funny. So I asked J. why Ethan would want to live on the farm as a grown man since the whole place symbolizes the loss of his father. I knew he'd get annoyed with me for asking but I was annoyed that he hadn't told me about Matilda and the bird sanctuary (to say nothing of The Letter) so I asked him anyway.

Missed the deadline for the Wilderness Grant. The article for the Audubon newsletter is due tomorrow. I'm not going to make it and I wish I cared. Am only halfway through the letter to the editor about acid rain.

NYC—Heather's

When Heather opened the door to her high-rise apartment with wraparound windows, she was holding her as-yet-unnamed-test-tube-baby in one arm and a bottle of wine in the other. The first thing she said was: You look like shit. So, naturally, I told her about

The Letter and how Elizabeth met Johnson in New Mexico for the Corn Ceremony and, for all I know, has been meeting him there for years. Heather says I should wait to say anything...that it will all blow over...like the frozen baby, I guess (which only Hatia knows about). But the thought of living with another lie.... And this one isn't even mine.... Anyway, after chitchat about Heather's delivery we made our way into the living room and sank into her beige modular units that overlook the city.

Did you see where the evil Nancy is having an exhibit of her photographs in Soho?...asked Heather as she took the baby to her breast.

No.

Yes. She's becoming a big deal. And not just as a photographer...but as...I don't know if you call it art...but she distresses layouts and makes them into collages. My boss bought one for his office. They're all the rage.

We spent the next hour on our family and how Conrad is thinking of marrying a woman everyone actually likes except for his oldest child, Annie...who says the only thing she wants for her birthday is Nancy.

What does Conrad expect?...said Heather. She's a teenager. All teenagers want to live with the other parent. I tried to explain that to him but he's all hung up on the court having the final say...so...and don't tell anybody...I told Annie she should come here to see the baby...then I got in touch with Nancy—

They're meeting here?...I asked, my voice rising sharply. In your apartment?

Why not?

You sentimental FOOL!!!...I yelled, startling the baby.

Relax, will you?

She's a mother!

Well, so am I.

Heather...you have to think of Conrad. He's your brother. She'll destroy him. Use your head. Mothers will stop at nothing when it comes to their children. I know what I'm talking about. Look at what Matilda did to Johnson.

I don't think it's a good idea for us to talk while I'm nursing.

I shook my head, got up and looked at the sun moving a cold, flat light across the sky.

Nancy made her decision when she abandoned her children…I said. She has no right to reopen their agreement. Period!

Molly, people change, in case you're interested.

So we should all forgive and forget because suddenly she's SORRY?

You're the one who's always yammering about Unconditional Love.

I can love her…I said, thoroughly repelled by the thought…but her actions had consequences and it's time she shut up and lived with them instead of ferreting around after her ex-husband.

God, you act like Conrad is…I don't know…like Nancy wears black lipstick and has snakes coming out of her head.

Well, in case you care to remember…she was pregnant when they got married.

Conrad's rubber burst.

And that's my point. Nancy didn't want her kids any more than Matilda wanted Ethan. She wanted a husband who would take care of her. Matilda knew she was nuts. Ethan wasn't human, he was insurance.

Heather put the baby on her shoulder and rubbed her back.

Well, I don't know how to break it to you but you and Johnson have been getting it on for a few years now and you aren't exactly married.

No…but we will be.

When you get pregnant.

No!

Molly, some men need to be trapped. That's how they make decisions.

Later

Heather swears she'll be back in time for me to catch the 4:13 out of Penn Station so I can get home in time to relieve J. from taking care of Meimei. The baby is asleep in her bassinette and I have just made myself an enormous chicken sandwich and turned on the radio. WQXR. Shades of Davis. Good Old Davis. How is Good Old Davis? Where is Good Old Davis? I try to imagine who we would have become if we had stayed together…now that I am evidently into gays and celibates. I probably would have written perfectly punctuated novels about loneliness and read isolated chapters in dusty bookstores...and when I didn't know what to do with myself I would've walked through misty rain and watched foreign films in movie theaters with broken seats. Eventually I would have taken a lover. Drunk cappuccino in SoHo and been interviewed about life, love, death...and classical sentence structure.

Keep seeing J. putting his arm around Elizabeth in New Mexico as Quanah studies her palm and nods his approval. Oh god, how I want to fly out the window free of the deadly expectations of a long-term relationship! To soar far beyond the familiar into something I don't know I am capable of doing, needing, feeling. To hurt somebody...yes!...hurt somebody and not feel sorry.

Still Later

The baby started to fuss. I lay down on the couch and put her on top of me...belly to belly. The way Mother did when Timmy had a stomach ache. Then I closed my eyes, curled my hands around her feet and imagined her in white light while I swam in white wine. Whatever I'm picking up from Meimei must be working. The baby went out like a light. I reached for a *New York Magazine* on the coffee table and located the gallery that is showing Nancy's collages. And, armed with a flicker of determination from my youth, I decided to set Nancy straight before Heather brings her face to face with Annie.

When Heather finally returned she was forty minutes late. The baby was in an uncontrollable rage and I wasn't doing much better.

Johnson has to meet a client for dinner, Heather! I told you I had to be back in time to spell him. I missed the deadline for the Wilderness Grant. What's he going to think if I make him late for an important dinner?

Jesus, Molly...just because he meditates doesn't mean he's God. TAXI!!!

The cab driver was from another world and had yet to learn where the West Side was...let alone Penn Station. I arrived at the track as the 4:13 was pulling out. I stood in the fumes and cursed out Heather, Matilda, Nancy, Elizabeth and everyone who had ever lived without giving a single thought to others.

As I climbed the stairs to the waiting area, a man with swollen legs and broken shoes asked me if I could spare some change. I dug in my purse for a dollar. Heather would have ignored him completely. Matilda would have spit in his face. And Nancy would have taken his picture. Somewhere in my bag was a lousy dollar. Another man joined us...he was tall and skinny. His hair was matted and his pants were wet with waste. Outstretched hands and wounded eyes pleaded with me for Understanding. A woman with a dummy or a child in a stroller moved into position at a discreet distance. What was this? The express lane?

Take!...I yelled throwing the contents of my bag on the floor...Take! Take everything!

A cop rounded the corner as damaged lives poured over an expired credit card, an emery board, my driver's license, lip balm, an address book, *New York Magazine*, receipts, a checkbook and ancient scraps of notes for Spanish lessons that were all but buried. When I saw the cop I grabbed my wallet and ran. I ran and ran and ran. When I hit Sixth Avenue no one was following me so I headed south. I was going to find a restaurant or a coffee shop. I was going to order something really fattening like blintzes with sour cream and caviar and regroup. Not with only a dollar in my wallet I wasn't. Well, at least I hadn't parted with my spiral notebook.

Reasons I Should Cross the Street
1. The gallery showing Nancy's collages is on the corner.
2. My family needs my help more than J.'s (family).
3. I need to borrow twenty bucks.
4. It's time to quit stewing and start DOING!

Reasons I Shouldn't
1. I don't know what to say which means I'll babble.
2. I might get run over.
3. Nancy might not even be there.
4. What Annie and Heather do is none of my business.

Later

I wish I could say when I saw her face that her eyes glistened with evil. That she grew fangs and spit fire. And that her face fused with

Matilda's...because it did, moments later...but first there was a disturbing moment of recognition when I was struck by her warmth and casual beauty.

It was almost closing time when I finally got up the courage to walk into the gallery. I didn't see Nancy anywhere so I asked for the ladies' room and was directed down a dingy hall to an unmarked door. I would call Hatia when I was through. Ask her to lend me train fare. I turned the door knob and there was a woman standing at the mirror. Her black hair had been stripped and cut so short it stood up in blonde/white spikes exposing a long, graceful neck.

Oh, sorry...I said.

It's my fault...she said. I never lock it.

Nancy?

She squinted her eyes.

I'm sorry...she said...I don't have on my contacts.

It's Molly.

Molly?

Molly...your sister-in-law. Ex.

Molly...what are you doing here?

I...I was in the neighborhood...I'd read about your show...

God...wow...look at you...she said putting in her contacts. You don't look any different.

I'm fatter.

You're married, right?

Well...living with someone. I don't know for how much longer.

She laughed and touched my shoulder. Her fingers felt warm and strong and a little rough.

Tell me about it...she said rolling her eyes.

Then there was this awkward moment where I wanted to hug her and I was pretty sure she wanted to hug me...but things being what they were with Conrad and the kids...

You know what I think?...she said taking me by the shoulders...life is too short.

And she took me in her arms and I hung there feeling taller than she was and remembering the first time I'd seen her...how we'd both known that there was...I don't know...more to us...and once, in a heart to heart about Conrad and Davis...had said so outloud in the woods behind my parents' house...and I had blushed and laughed nervously and she had put a hand on her pregnant belly and become sad and serious.

I have thought about you so much...she said as my arms found their way around her back. And the day we peeled birch bark off the trees and wrote why we thought we'd been born on the inside of the bark...remember?

Yes...I said. Wrote it with a rock.

Cast the truth in stone...she said with a certain irony.

And you wrote: To become whole.

I didn't write that...you wrote that...said Nancy. And my life has been in chaos ever since!

She laughed and put on a pair of long, dangly, triangular earrings. I wouldn't talk to her about Annie just yet.

I'll be out of here in two secs...she said filling the palm of her hand with something that looked like shaving cream. Mousse...she said aware of my fascination. Mousse and bleach...it has come to that.

You look more hip than your kids.

That's what I'm afraid of...she said searching my face for permission to ask all about them.

My spine straightened itself (not unlike my mother's) and Conrad hissed: Manipulative bitch.

Finished...said Nancy heading for the pay phone in the hallway.

I closed the bathroom door, sat on the toilet and counted to ten very slowly. I had to say something right away. If I didn't it would be too late. I took a deep breath. I didn't want the same thing to happen here that had happened with the frozen baby.

Shit...said Nancy as I emerged. My assistant has the grippe and I've got to be in Chicago in three hours. Shit, shit, shit.

What's in Chicago?

What are you doing tonight?...she said her eyes sharp with purpose.

Well, I...

Come with me...she said unzipping a camera bag. Be my assistant.

Me?

All expenses paid.

I shrugged uncertainly as she put on her jacket.

I don't even know what you do…I stammered. Except for col-lages.

Photography. Models. Famous people. Shit like that. Tonight I've got two hours with…shit, I can't even remember his name. Alzheimer's. Major head of a major corporation. Come on…she said picking up her camera bag…it's easy. I'll show you everything on the plane. What else were you going to do? Go home?

I should probably call…I said buttoning my coat.

Call from the airport.

I was supposed to be home before dinner…I said as she handed me a tripod.

He'll get over it…she said as we headed for the street.

In the cab she put two twenties in my hand. If anyone had told me I'd be flying to Chicago with the dreaded Nancy…not only en-joying her company…but putting her money in my pocket…well, I don't know what I would've done…maybe laughed…or thrown up…but I never would've believed it.

Heather says your collages are catching on in a big way.

I've had a good year.

You're doing what you really love, aren't you?…I said as we fas-tened our seatbelts.

Not this shit…she said pointing in the direction of Chicago. This is bread and butter. I get to meet lots of interesting people… don't get me wrong…see the world. Okay…see this? How much do you know about photography?

Well, it pollutes the rivers. Never mind. My…the man I live with is an environmental lawyer. It's sort of a…. So we only use the camera on special occasions. I know how to load film if that's what you mean.

Good. This is the ASA. With 400 you don't need a flash…unless…but, okay…you don't need to know that. You need to know…what do you need to know? I don't know…that's why I have an assistant.

She threw her head back and laughed a lusty laugh, reminding me of Ethan's picture of Matilda.

Whatever happened to Davis?…she asked as we lifted into the air.

I don't know...I said. He sent me that purple letter of apology...or I assume it was apology. I never read it.

So this guy you're with...what's his name?

And in between forays into her lens bag to further acquaint me with equipment and a distant memory of her assistant's routine...I told her how I'd fallen in love and what a good man Johnson was until Matilda drove a stake through his heart in the shape of Ethan...and how I'd lost him to low self-esteem and nothing I did...including trying to get pregnant for all the wrong reasons...would pull him back. And before she could get a word in edgewise, I added that fathers make excellent mothers and it was time the courts recognized that and ruled in their favor.

Whoa!...she said wrestling her bag off the carousel. Take a handle.

And as we lugged her equipment to the taxi stand she said: I know your whole family thinks I'm an irresponsible bitch...but just so you know...I left my kids because I loved them. Because I wanted to give them all of me...not an act. And Conrad and I...let's face it...were an act.

She put her fingers in her mouth and whistled.

Did you ever love him?...I asked with an edge.

I wanted to.

I mean, did you ever think of what leaving him like that would do to him? Not just the kids—

I thought about it all the time...but, well...obviously there were other things.

Like what?

Like what staying would have done to me.

People shouldn't be allowed to have kids until they've gotten to know themselves...I said launching into my speech.

Well, not all of us have the luxury of a trial run—

I knew what I was in for...I said stiffly. Even before Ethan. I talked to my friends. I talked to you! Everyone who's ever had kids spends half the time wishing they hadn't.

Nancy looked out the window.

One day I'll show you the shots I took of you in the woods...she said...the day we wrote on birch bark.

You still have them?

Somewhere…in a shoe box. I've been saving them for…I don't know…something about eyes.

Eyes?

Your eyes, Babycakes…she said lowering her voice and raising an eyebrow.

What about my eyes?

Right here!…she said to the cab driver.

What about my eyes…I wondered as we struggled her bags into the building.

She pressed the button for the elevator, looked at me and smiled a very private smile. Moments later we were standing in a rather large waiting room confronted with chrome, leather and plastic plants. Nancy gave her name to the night guard and we were instantly ushered into an office where we could set up the equipment.

That's not a good place for the desk…she said pointing to the opposite side of the room and I knew instantly I was to move it in front of the picture window. This guy is from Leisure Suit City. They want me to make him look like he has class since, you know, he probably owns the world. So we'll put him with his back to the twinkling lights of beautiful downtown Chicago.

I appropriated real plants from the office of a vice president and arranged the room so neatly that Nancy messed it up. Then she wanted a different phone and a bowl of M&Ms or chocolate kisses…and so I found myself wandering the halls of a Chicago high-rise after hours looking for something cordless and something edible. Eyes. I had beautiful eyes. Maybe I even had Mystery.

Home again, Home again
Jiggety jig

When J. saw me he was pissed off and relieved at finding me…I don't know…ALIVE so he didn't have to inconvenience himself with a trip to the morgue. I told him I got ripped off in Penn Station, went into shock and wandered. Nancy and I had had this really interesting discussion coming back on the plane about the difference between withholding information (which I think is manipulative and disrespectful) and keeping something for yourself. I had gotten onto a Johnson tangent about Mystery and how he doesn't think I'm a Woman because I don't have any. And she said: You don't have anywhere to go. Secrets build places...places to go.

Dear Nancy,
I really enjoyed seeing you again. I was prepared to hate you because of all the grief you've caused Conrad, the kids and, for that matter, my entire family. So being with you was a bit perplexing...mainly because we still seem to be able to talk about EVERYTHING! I particularly appreciated what you said about Secrecy. And why it's important to have a place inside (like a meditation room) that is yours and yours alone. I have been keeping a secret from Johnson for some time now. And have begun to seriously question my integrity. You helped me see that I have a right to choose what I live with and what I don't. I guess one of the secrets I don't want to live with, though, is how I feel about the meeting you and Heather are arranging with Annie. I probably should have come right out with it when I was with you. But I never could find the right moment. Heather is sentimental and impulsive when it comes to motherhood and Annie is navigating the shoals of adolescent rebellion.

Memo To: Molly
From: Molly
LEAVE WELL ENOUGH ALONE!

                                                    Ten Days Later
J. got in really late last night. Spent the night, yet again, in his sleeping bag on the floor of Ethan's room. For breakfast we were careful not to end up in the kitchen at the same time. Apparently we have nothing to say to each other for the rest of our lives.

    Instead of researching possible funders at the library this afternoon, I rewrote my letter to Nancy. It still sounds desperate and didactic. Driving home, I imagined we met in Central Park by the Alice in Wonderland sculpture...and as soon as I opened my mouth to speak, Nancy saw the light and agreed not to meet with Annie until she's eighteen. Then Quanah smiled and Chloe blew me a kiss. And as I boarded the train, all of New York City cheered and there was peace, once again, in the world.

Meimei burned another pot when I was gone. I got home just as the rice was starting to smoulder and instead of turning the stove off I waited for the rice to burst into flame and burn down the entire house.

Today

J.—The woman I told you about named Charlotte will be coming today to look after Meimei as I have family business in New York. Not sure when I'll return. M. PS: Don't panic! It's just for the day.

Later

Oh, god! What a day!! As soon as I got into the city I called Nancy. Invited her for coffee. I was going to give her a piece of my mind about Annie over cappuccino but she was on her way to a theater in the East Village. Well, sort of a theater. People performed...I still don't know what...but it definitely was NOT boring. Anyway, Nancy has a friend who is a performance artist and needs production shots of a rehearsal blown up, glued to foam core and hung like a mobile from the lighting grid. And in exchange for her efforts N. will get an apartment in Italy for part of November.

Florence...she said as we hit Avenue A. Have you ever been to Italy?

I've never been anywhere. I mean, I have...but when you're a kid with your parents a cathedral's just a great big thing you have to look at.

Oh, history...she said...history! When you think of what people did...with no power tools.

A couple pushed a shopping cart filled with god-knows-what and a TV across Avenue A. Nancy readied her camera and we were off on a journey through the Alphabets. By the end of the afternoon we'd made friends with a teenage panhandler who lives in the park, a Ukrainian waitress who wears black stockings and high tops and a woman from the Bronx who claims she's a witch.

Everyone knows something you don't...said Nancy, unlocking the many locks to her loft. And that's about as metaphysical as I get...because, let's face it...the sickest looking people in the world are in health-food stores.

I had to laugh. And when she opened the door I had to gasp.

Whitewashed brick. Tall windows. Tin ceilings. A loft bed. A bathtub in the kitchen. Pillows on the floor. And no walls.

Almost no walls...she said taking my jacket and hanging it on a
moveable clothing rack.

Wow. Woooow! This is so...wow...like you could...I don't
know...take off. Just take off! Run around. Move.

I spread out my arms and twirled until I was dizzy. When I got
my bearings I was looking at an enlarged photograph of a woman's
mouth on another woman's breast.

Want to see what sort of luck we had this afternoon?...Nancy
asked nodding toward her darkroom.

What was it like the first time you went to bed with a
woman?...I asked as she closed the door.

Well, for starters, I was pregnant. Don't get me wrong...we con-
sulted the baby.

Annie?

No. The baby baby. Conrad had always been afraid to get it on
when I was pregnant. He said all that poking and pushing...the
baby would come out brain damaged. It was just as well...all I
thought about when we did it was women. Well, one woman.

Who?

Remember our conversation about secrets?

I laughed a little too hard and my hand touched the center of
her back. It was always touching the center of her back...then making its way self-consciously into my pants pocket. She held up a
strip of yesterday's negatives and cruised through them.

So this crush...how long did it last?...I asked, restless for the
dirt.

The whole time I was married. I kept thinking it would go away.
And it did...sort of...when I met Gillian.

Did you ever tell her? Not Gillian...the—

Almost...she said turning out the lights.

We stood in darkness. She flipped another switch, looked at me,
put her fingers in a square and made like she was framing my face.

Amber light becomes you...she said in a silky voice.

Would you tell her now?...I asked looking away.

Are you kidding? Straight women are nothing but
trouble...and bisexuals are why therapy was invented. Give me a

dyke any day.

She unscrewed a large plastic bottle marked Danger and said: Whatever you do don't open that door. The light.

Are you and Gillian still seeing each other?...I asked as she wiped her hands on her pants.

We're friends...she said exposing a piece of white, shiny paper to a negative. Lesbians do everything backwards.

It was beautiful watching Nancy at work. She lost herself in a reckless intensity. I stood to one side, overcome with admiration. Then I imagined I was Gillian kissing the hairs on the back of her neck.

Riiiing.

You want me to answer it?...I asked eagerly.

Uh...no. Shit. Press the conference button. Hello?

Hello, Nancy? This is Heather!...squawked the speaker phone.

Heather?...asked Nancy.

Heather?!...I thought. Heather promised she'd wait!

I looked at the floor as Nancy poked at a photograph in the developer.

Guess who's standing right beside me?...said Heather.

Hi, Mom.

Annie.... Honey...Annie.... Is that really you?

I don't know...said Annie...is that you?

There hasn't been a day...I hope you know that...not a day when I haven't wondered how you are. Where you are. Who you are. I can't believe it. You sound so...I won't say grown up...you're supposed to be grown up. But you sound so grown up.

I'll be in the next room...said Heather as I closed my eyes and stuck my fingers in my ears.

Honey, look...I've got my hands in developer...said Nancy. When do you have to go home?

I'm meeting Dad at eight at The Numbers.

Then I'll meet you in an hour at Heather's. At least we can say 'hello'. Annie? I know you must feel.... And I want you to tell me. You have a right to be very...oh, god I'm going to cry. Honey, we'll talk...and talk and talk and talk.

Okay...said Annie faintly.

When Nancy finally punched the off button with her elbow I

pressed myself into the farthest corner of the darkroom...if a farthest corner is possible in a darkroom.

I sounded like I was giving a speech...said Nancy grabbing the
end of the counter. Did I sound like I was giving a speech?

I better go...I said reaching for the door knob.

No...she said...the light.

And for a brief moment I considered opening the door and ruining everything. I mean, if it was so important why didn't she have
a lock? Seconds later, embarrassed by my inner life...I moved in the
direction of the developer and watched in silence as two rock stars
with crosses in their ears and haircuts not unlike Nancy's...came to
life in black and white.

I just want to see her...said Nancy when the air was thick with
thought.

And then what?...I asked carefully.

And then what what?...she asked, poking at the rock stars.

After you see her are you going to keep on seeing her?

Molly...she's my child.

She wasn't your child ten years ago...I blurted out...she was
your jailer.

Maybe if Ethan had been your son...she said hanging the rock
stars up to dry.

He was my son!...I said, panic introducing my voice to another
octave. He was! Until Matilda came back. He was fine. He was
healthy. He was happy. HE WAS <u>NORMAL</u>!

And Annie is going to become a dyke if I breathe on her, is that
it?

I didn't say that. Did I say that?

You sound like the fucking Judge...she said pouring fix down
the drain.

I'm just saying—

I should've pretended Gillian was my roommate...she said with
some bitterness...but, no...I was going to lead an out-there kind of
life.

It wasn't Gillian...I said. It was that you disappeared...for several years. And now you think just because you're sorry you can
waltz back into their lives like you're doing them the big favor when
all you're really doing is fucking things up again. I saw it happen

with Matilda. In two more years Annie'll be eighteen. What's two more lousy years?

A long time when you've waited ten.

But it isn't about you. It's about Annie and the boys. They have grades to get. A new mother to adjust to. A sense of themselves to—

Molly...she said approaching me...you don't have to yell. I know it hurts.

It doesn't hurt...I said with complete conviction. Not if you make the right decision in the first place. Then you feel proud. Proud...because you thought things through. And you and your kids, who probably wouldn't've even been born...would at least be in the moment.

The timer rang...fortunately for me because I had no idea what I'd just said. Nancy opened the door. I fell into the largeness of her loft. Located my jacket in a shaft of light on the clothes rack. Nancy watched me from a distance. I waited for her to retreat into her darkroom as Johnson closed the attic door and crossed his legs in meditation.

My children weren't my jailer...said Nancy coming toward me. I was. And, no, I didn't think things through. I won't pretend there weren't consequences, but finally—

I know, I know...it's none of my business...I said trying to undo about twenty locks in the right combination.

Is that what he says to you about Ethan?

It doesn't matter what he says...I said yanking on the door. Shit!

Nancy moved me to one side and studied the chaos that had become her security system.

You piss me off...she said turning this and that...but you still have a right to your feelings.

Words...I said. Words, words, words.

I don't think so.

Well, I do.

Well, I don't!

Well, why not?!

Because you're the woman I had a crush on the whole time I was married. Shhh...she said opening the door...that's a secret.

1979—Fall
God Help Me!

She's a photographer...I said to Johnson...no one you know. She's doing a coffee table book on Tuscany. Wants me to write the text...isn't that great?

A month is a long time.

I turned on the vacuum. We lived together like roommates. Why, as Nancy said, did I still need to ask his fucking permission? He turned off the vacuum with his foot and looked at me...his eyes full of Don't Leave Me. And since that was more feeling than I'd had from him in ages, my heart rose up one more time.

I'm not leaving you...I said cautiously. I'm just going to Italy. Or I would like to go to Italy. Or I think I would like to go to Italy. Or maybe I don't want to go to Italy. Maybe I just want you to ask me to stay.

His laugh had an edge.

What?...I asked with some annoyance.

I don't know...he said.

Yes, you do...I insisted.

Molly, stop! You'll only do what you want to anyway.

I threw my bag in the seat beside Nancy.

So I said to him...I said: I know why you say I Don't Know all the time...because if you did know then you'd have no one to blame for being Aggressive and Uncompromising and all those things you're not supposed to be because you meditate!

The stewardess yanked the door shut and twisted the handle.

I'll do anything you want...I continued. Drink espresso, go on long walks down dark alleys, speak bad Italian...but I don't want to know from Suffering, Meditation or the inside of a Church!

Seven hours and one sleeping pill later we found ourselves in the chaos of the Rome airport and later that afternoon on the train to Florence. That evening we opened the wooden shutters to our small, slightly worn apartment and looked out onto the Piazza Santa Croce at a pink, green and white marble structure that bore a striking resemblance to...oh, why not?...a Church.

We won't think of it as a Church...said Nancy...we'll think of it as the place where Michelangelo is buried. Assuming his bones survived the flood.

A soccer ball bounced into the center of the square followed by three boys. We watched in silence as the piazza filled with lovers, dog walkers and the occasional tourist free until morning from the rigors of sightseeing. Nancy said something about not being much of a one for groups.

Hmm hmm...I nodded, jet lag overwhelming my determination to make the most of every second.

Try and stay awake...she said massaging my shoulders...and tomorrow you'll be on Italian time...no problem.

Maybe we should get something to eat...I said sitting on the edge of the bed and staring at my shoes.

This one goes on this foot and this one goes on that foot...she said as I fell backwards onto the bed.

I won't be very good company...I said as the fog descended.

She sat beside me and moved a strand of hair from my eyes.

Mmmmm...I muttered.

I'll make us some espresso.

I could smell her coming toward me, brushing the side of my cheek with her...huh!...and half asleep I turned my mouth in her direction and let myself know for one careless second...the softness of her lips.

Sometime later I felt her fingers on my forehead and smelled the smell of something fresh and hot and deeply caffeinated.

Molly...she said...you gotta get up.

She let her hand fall onto my stomach. A rush of laughter bubbled out from underneath the weight of sleep...and without opening my eyes I said: Make me. And slowly, tenderly she undid every button on my blouse as if each one held a secret more intimate than the one before...and when my blouse had fallen open she looked at my breasts and without touching them described them to me in a deep whisper that put life in places dark and undiscovered. Then she sighed and took a sip of espresso and when she turned around again I was still lying there...half awake and half excited that I wasn't. She put a hand over one breast.

Ooooo...she said...they fit. I always knew they'd fit.

I opened up my eyes with a start and we looked at each other for a moment so raw with uncertainty that anything could have happened. She took her hand away.

Once...I said...when you and Conrad were still married I watched you dressing.

I know...she said...in the bathroom mirror.

You knew I was there?...I asked.

Why do you think I took so long with the baby oil?

I bit my lower lip.

What, Baby...what is it? You want to stop?

Baby. She called me Baby. Like I was small and fragile and sexy and worth protecting.

I used to want to be your laugh...I said. To be that deep inside you.

The anxiety that comes with confession sent a sharp pain through my heart and tears sprang to my eyes.

Am I a pervert?...I asked.

I don't know...am I?

Johnson does that...I said wistfully...answers questions with questions.

No...she said...you're not a pervert and I've known perverts. Trust me...straight...gay...you're no pervert.

Then what am I?

Well, one thing you are...she said after some thought...is awake.

No...I said looking right at her...not awake enough.

And she put her arms on either side of me and kissed me on the lips. Hard this time and I could feel the walls of waiting melting, melting...as her hands, rough from years of playing in developer, stroked my body as if it were made of smooth, slithery silk.

I'll stop...she said...if you're feeling—

Yes...I said...I'm feeling. I'm feeling. I'm feeling. I'm feeling!

And before I knew it I was on top of her...opening her blouse with far less ceremony than she had opened mine.

You wear a bra!...I said. I thought all you girls burned them in the '60s.

I don't want to dress like a man, Babycakes...I just want the same privileges...she said as she moved her fingers in slow circles over the black lace. It opens in front.

Good...I said then got up and lit a couple of candles.

I watched her from across the room waiting for my mouth. A

mouth she'd only dreamt of knowing. I licked my lips slowly, sensuously.

You're bad...she said. You're so baaaaad.

She snapped her bra open, put her hands under her breasts and offered them to me...her nipples hard and erect. I slipped one knee between her candle-lit thighs and took her breasts in my hands, lowered my head and brought my mouth to within a whisper.

Where to begin...oh, where to begin.

Oh, god...she said...just get it oooover with!

I blew on one breast and tickled the other with my nose. She laughed that laugh that went right through me and sent my hand on a mission all its own between her legs. She pushed herself against my fingers.

Is there anything I'm not supposed to do?

No...she said with a certain urgency...nothing.

I worked my way under the elastic of her underpants and felt the line between the softness of her belly and the coarseness of her hair. I lowered my mouth onto her left breast and twirled my tongue around her nipple.

Oh, god...you have no idea.

She arched her back. I pressed my fingers farther down into her underpants and like a rebel with a machete cut a clear path through the jungle to the waterfall where I dove off the cliff without looking and swam in dark caves that hung wet with wisdom. And slowly, gently, I made my way up the mountain and turned and twisted on the moss that clung to the rock that opened like a flower. Moments later, I watched her yield to the ecstasy as if for the first time. A candle hissed and flickered. A pillow fell to the floor as Nancy dissolved in delicious surrender. I moved quietly to one side and looked at my hand. What had I just done? Where had we just been? And how would I ever explain this to my mother? Nancy threw her forearm over her eyes. God, she was beautiful! Or Conrad? Or, for that matter...jesus...how would I ever tell—

You've been with women before...she moaned.

No, I haven't...honest.

Then you've thought about it.

No. Really. I just pretended you were me...I stammered.

And who were you?

Johnson.

Johnson?

Or who he could be...if only—

Come here, Johnson.

She pulled me to her and unzipped my jeans the rest of the
way...and before she took me in her mouth she said: It takes a real
man to turn a good man into a real woman.

The next morning, buried under a down pillow, I heard the ur-
gent double ring of an Italian telephone and felt Nancy's breasts
against my back as she reached over me to answer it. I heard what
sounded like Italian and felt Nancy's fingers examining a mole on
my shoulder as the sun strained to find its way into the room
through wooden shutters.

What time is it?...I asked as she hung up the phone.

Italian time...she said and looked at me, her face flushed with
hope and fearing the worst.

I'm not sorry...if that's what you're wondering...I said. Are you?

Oh, Baby...how could you even ask?

I thought maybe...you know.... It's so hard for me to relax.

Last night was about a lot more than coming.

Because maybe I've forgotten how.

Yeah...and maybe I'll remember how to remind you. Who
knows?

You know.

I do know.

Oh, yeah...what?

That there is this tall (kiss), graceful (kiss), sexy (kiss, kiss) crea-
ture in my bed with her heart in her eyes and—

—fat on her hips.

Mmmmm, yes...fat (kiss, kiss, kiss)...and I have nothing to offer her but cold (kiss) espresso.

She took a sip.

I wish I was that cup...I said...then I'd be inside your overbite.

Kiss, kiss, kiss.

I wish I was your long, straight spine then I'd always hold you
up.

Sometimes the things she said.... And it got so all she had to do
was look at me and...

Who called?...I asked sliding down her body.

A friend of the woman who lives here. Wanted to be sure we knew where everything was.

Everything?...I asked kissing the gentle round that was her stomach.

And in this way everything we thought, saw, said or did became a part of the passion, lust, love or whateveritwas that drove us...transported us for three full days everywhere but outside the apartment. And when we finally opened the front door, our legs weak, our hearts great, our stomachs empty...and faced the afternoon sun; the tourists who couldn't hope to experience the true meaning of exhaustion...and the never-ending parade of stuttering motor scooters...we burst out laughing. Everything was closed.

Not everything...said Nancy grabbing my hand and leading me down an alley past blue dumpsters, souvenir shops and a house where someone famous had died or been born or spent the night.

The Duomo...she said as we rounded a corner.

An orange bus spewed its waste into our lungs as we stood in awe of centuries of hard labor that had miraculously organized themselves into a single vision. We walked absentmindedly through taxis, our eyes fixed on the cathedral...Nancy filling me full of stories about popes and corruption and the competition to build the dome. She had an appreciation of history that had the wonder of discovery in it...where, with Johnson...there was always the threat of a test. Not that he didn't know what he was talking about. He did. Often in greater detail than Nancy...but to her—

Quick!...she said grabbing my hand again and before I could say: Gold doors...look!...we were winding our way through the hillsides above Florence on a crowded No.7 bus heading for the hill town of Fiesole.

This will orient you...she said as we got off the bus and trudged up what felt like the side of a cliff.

I'm oriented, I'm oriented...I said as she took the lead. I'm so oriented I'm disoriented.

Not that...she said disappearing around a corner...the book.

The book...I thought holding my sides and catching my breath...I'd forgotten all about the book. Or I'd tried to forget all about the book.

I pushed on up the hill. When I finally caught up with Nancy she stood like a defiant goddess...her arms wide.

Everything I have is yours...she said stepping aside to reveal the entire city of Florence...the Duomo rising like a beating heart over terra cotta, sandstone, marble, cypress, leather and steaming espresso.

Imagine being the first person to come over those hills...said Nancy...and because you decide to stop here...because you decide to call it home...it turns into all that.

Home...I thought as Nancy leaned her body into mine.

How's my Honey?...she asked.

I keep waiting for it to feel strange.

I know...she said, laughing in gentle recognition...and it doesn't, does it?

I got up and wandered among olive trees as Nancy busied herself with her camera. I ran my finger along a stone wall and made my way up stone steps to the courtyard of a monastery where I wondered if Johnson had told Elizabeth he was celibate or if he was just saying that to me so they could carry on IN SECRET. I saw Nancy go into a church and made my way down a dark, cool path behind it. I smelled the murkiness of the woods and saw my hand on Nancy's thigh. I tried to imagine Johnson's face when I told him. If I told him. My heart began to race. I turned a corner and found myself walking through a large cast-iron gate. I had never cheated on anybody. I broke out in a sweat and looked at my feet. I was standing in a graveyard. Plastic flowers. White crosses. Real flowers. Marble monuments. Polished placards. And photographs in ornate frames keeping memory from merging with forgetting.

There you are...said Nancy minutes later...I just saw the most unusual fresco depicting...not the life of Jesus, not the life of a saint...but the life of, hold your breath—Ah, yes...she said suddenly aware of her surroundings...Italian graveyards. They always feel like they're—

ALIVE...I said in disbelief.

I know...she said putting more film in her camera and continuing on about the fresco which traced the life of the Virgin Mary from her birth to her—Death!...said Nancy with some excitement. And haven't you always wondered like...what happened to her after

Jesus rolled back the rock? So this artist comes along and paints his version of her story. And, at the risk of sounding like a Feminist…it remains curiously unrestored.

I want to do a really good job on the book…I said with urgency. I have a good mind but I don't know much about art and the only writing I've done is funding proposals. So if you want to hire somebody else—

And to what do I owe this sudden surge of self-doubt?

I don't know…I said as two men approached us with a bouquet of flowers.

This book is my project…said Nancy watching me look at them. We can turn it into anything we want.

The two men nodded politely. I smiled. They looked like a foreign country. They were a foreign country. They smiled back. Nancy returned her camera to its bag with an abrupt efficiency. They circled us. I blushed. One of them held out a rose. I took the rose and looked at Nancy. Her eyes were dark and darting. Was she jealous? She moved toward the gate. I looked back at the men as they placed the remaining flowers in a routine manner on somebody's grave. I smelled the rose and tried to imagine their reactions when I told them it had been a long time since I'd had an orgasm and I was through with faking it.

Week Four
The Last Night
A few days ago, a crunched gelato cup fell from my fingers and landed on the sidewalk. I looked at it as if it belonged to somebody else…and when Johnson crossed my mind I couldn't see his face. Nancy and I were in Siena at the time looking at pottery in the window of a gift shop wondering if Johnson and Gillian expected us to buy them presents. Then Nancy said: Whatever happens when we get home we must never doubt the depth of our feelings for each other. I wasn't sure why she felt it was necessary to say that. I knew as soon as I saw Johnson I was going to tell him I was leaving. I had rehearsed the conversation over and over. I wasn't about to return to the farm in the arms of another lie.

I walked up steep stone steps and stood face to face with a giant Cathedral. Nancy and I had agreed to spend a portion of the day apart so, in her words: We could work up a Miss…or in mine: We'd have something to talk about at dinner. I put my hand on a massive, wooden door and pushed it open. I couldn't believe my eyes. Black and white striped marble pillars. Intricate drawings carved in the marble floor. Frescos, statues and stained glass. A chaos of art and style blending into something so full of celebration I instantly understood why people dragged whining children through crowded airports…humiliating themselves in foreign languages and currencies. The sense of wonder was awesome. I sat, dumbfounded in a pew. I watched a small Mass that was in progress and tried to imagine the Cathedral when it teemed with people who had come to worship instead of gape. I thought about the two men in the graveyard…and about the flash of white hot feeling that had had its way with Nancy. I couldn't shake the feeling she was going to come to her senses when we got back to the States. I worked my way onto my knees…and so no one would think I was actually in the act of Meditation…left part of my rear end on the bench.

Oh, god…I thought the first time I kissed Nancy…I thought that that would turn me off. But every day I feel more and more like a Woman. So, if this is nothing more than an affair to her.… On the other hand…if it isn't…I've been wondering how to tell Johnson and my family. I've been thinking about telling them all at once. Lining them up in front of the fireplace on New Year's Day. Saying: You all know how I've never thought I was particularly beautiful. Or, for that matter…Mysterious. And if Mother makes some excuse about having to see to dinner and if Conrad needs more rum in his eggnog…I'll pick up Father's bullhorn and say: This is the last time I will ever ask you to listen to me…so if for no other reason than Auld Lang Syne I would appreciate it if you would sit down. Sit down!

And they would slink back to their seats and when I had their undivided attention…I'd say: When I'm with Johnson I have learned that if I ask for what I need we either start to fight or he goes upstairs to meditate.

And he would look shamefully at the floor.

But when I'm with Nancy…I feel celebrated. Heard. And I know that for me love isn't about coming…it's about connecting.

Ethan slammed his bedroom door.

You're not my mother!...he hollered as a stranger inserted a gloved hand between my legs. Johnson's eyes filled with tears. I jumped off the operating table and ran and ran until it was the day after my baby brother died and I was running to my father.

You're too old to sit on my lap...he said.

Too old? I was only nine. I was still wearing sun dresses and mary janes. I wasn't too old...I was too big. God...I hated my body! Its size, its longings, its deadness to feeling something...anything! It takes a fucking cordless vibrator to make me come alive! I banged on the door of Johnson's meditation room.

I'm not trying to destroy you!...I screamed. I'm trying to talk to you about my body!

My entire family took their places in a jury box. I stood before them in a suit and tie.

And finally I ask you to look deep into your hearts...I said...and consider the defendant's question: Is putting the quality of her relationship to Johnson ahead of having his children ...selfish...or is it the ultimate compliment?

YOU HAVE A DUTY!...said my mother straightening her spine and putting earplugs in her ears.

I HAVE A DESTINY!...I screamed leaping into the jury box.

Order, order!

I wheeled on Johnson. He took my face in his hands and kissed my cheeks.

Let us pray.

I fell to my knees and looked through the bars of the crib at my baby brother. He was still breathing. I put my head close to his and told him about my day...how I got a tummy ache at recess that wouldn't go away. I pressed the palms of my hands into my stomach. My mother was coming! I slid under the crib. She would kill me if she found me there...especially if I wasn't feeling well.

Sweet baby...she said...sweet, sweet baby.

I held my breath and focused on the toes of her shoes darting under the dust ruffle. My stomach ache was getting worse. I bit my lip. My father stuck his head in the door.

Come to bed...he said as my mother kissed my baby brother goodnight. We'll leave the door open.

I listened to them leave. I wouldn't move until they had turned out all the lights. I wouldn't breathe until their voices faded in the hall. Until my stomach stopped aching and my eyes became heavy with sleep. Around four in the morning I heard a sharp intake of breath. Then Mother ran from the room. I rolled out from underneath the crib.

Wake up...I heard her say to my father. Quickly, quickly!

I ran down the hall into the bathroom. Germs. I had given my baby brother the germs from my stomach ache!

Oh, my god...cried my mother returning to Timmy's crib...oh, my god...oh, my god.

I sat on the toilet.

Shhhh...said my father doing his best to give her comfort. Shhh, shhh, shhh.

I put my head in my hands.

Oh, no...oh, no...oh, no! There was blood between my legs.

That morning at breakfast my parents gave us their little speech about my baby brother and how he would have wanted us to be as brave as he was...so I choked down my cornflakes and decided not to tell them I was bleeding to death because I'd killed him. The next day...sad and confused and loathing every frightening minute in the clutches of my secret...I climbed onto my father's lap to tell him the awful truth and was reprimanded for being too big. Days later my mother would set me straight. My body was changing. In a couple of years I would feel like having babies of my own.

Never...I shouted in the quiet silence of my soul...never, never, never, never, never!

I sat back in the pew. My period had become a monthly exercise in the mastery of feeling. The only thing worse than cramps was sentiment. I looked at gold stars in a brilliant blue vaulted ceiling. At the age of nine I had made the trip from my belly to my head and had spent my adult life trying my utmost to stay there. And as tears ran down the black marble wall of recognition...Chloe put her hand on my belly and I watched it swell with Laughter and give birth to Acceptance.

Fall, 1980

J. met me at the train station. He looked awfully ragged. I didn't know if he wanted that brought to his attention so I rattled on about an Annunciation I'd seen in the monastery of San Marco...and how it led to other Annunciations that opened my mind to art history in a very visceral way. I used the word Visceral several times before adding Luscious, Breathtaking, Ecstatic...but stopped short of: An Orgasm of Color...remembering my promise to Nancy to keep our relationship secret. We had had a good talk in Siena after my whatever in the cathedral. She said she had a history of falling for married women and she'd needed time alone to ask herself if she could wade through another onslaught of Ambivalence.

First of all...I said...I'm not married...and secondly...and most important I am not nor have I ever been Ambivalent. I think it's Manipulative and Rude...not only Rude...but Disrespectful.

Honey...she said...if we make a life together there will be a certain amount of secrecy.

I know...I said...and you're worried it'll build up inside me and I'll blabber in frustration to my family and wreck it for you with Annie and the boys.

It's crossed my mind.

Well, just so you know, I've stopped thinking of Secrecy as duplicitous and started thinking of it as a Human Right. And if I EVER begin to feel I'm going to explode with the truth and you aren't around...I'll write and write and write it out in my beautiful, new journal. I mean, what's the alternative? Not to see each other?

Don't be silly...said Nancy. Besides, there's the book.

Johnson turned the key in the ignition and I decided not to talk about the book. Nancy's faith that something concrete will rise out of lots of photos spread on the floor of her loft would sound like a fool's mission to him.

How's Meimei?...I asked hoping we still had her to talk about.

Not good...he said pulling onto the turnpike. I finally took her to the homeopath.

I'm sorry...I said. Did it do any good?

It's too soon to tell...he said and fell silent.

How about you?...I asked carefully.

Fine, fine...he said tooting too long and hard at a car that cut in front of him. I put an air mattress on the floor of her room. We sleep. We talk.

He tooted again, stepped on the gas and flipped the bird then looked at the speedometer and said: And she tries to teach me how to do her feet.

I watched familiar countryside roll across the passenger window and struggled with the strangeness of being back among the dying...barely able to contain my excitement. Johnson cleared his throat.

Molly...he said as if he were about to give me a lecture...I had no idea how much you did for my mother until I had to do it.

Johnson opened his hand so I could put mine in it. I patted it like a puppy. He got hold of my index finger and held it until he had to shift gears and I remembered the first treatment I'd ever given Meimei...how I tried so hard to get my heart energy into my fingers so that one day when Johnson least expected it...I would touch him with the power of Unconditional Love and he would realize what he really wanted was what he already had.

Home again...said Johnson pulling into the driveway.

The house looked exactly the same. Empty. Neglected. Inside the grief was palpable. You could peel it off the walls. When I finally saw Meimei...her wide bones pushing at her pale yellow skin...I rattled on about my trip choosing my words so carefully she lost interest. Eventually I muttered something about jet lag, went upstairs, unpacked my journal and wrote Nancy's name over and over and over (see back inside cover). I must've been smiling to myself when Johnson came up to say Goodnight.

Writing going well?...he asked changing into his pajamas.

Just notes...I said putting my journal under my pillow.

Good trip?

Yes...I said...and no.

Oh...he said...a Woman of Mystery.

Maybe...I said...maybe not.

That sent a shudder of fascination through him... I could see it for a brief second before he returned to his air mattress and his mother...and I realized that if I have to go this far away from him in order to get his attention...well, it's nice to know I have the Power but I'm not so sure I have the Interest.

Saturday

Nancy still hasn't called. I just know she's changed her mind. Told Gillian all about me; Gillian had a fit; Nancy came to her senses and decided they should get back together. Because, let's face it, the last thing she needs is a practically honest, sort of married woman with no Mystery.

Later

J. says the price of gas will never again be under a dollar and I start 'Sophie's Choice'…or try to. But all I really do is throb with Nancy. Today the telephone became the largest object in the house.

Monday Morning
In the Kitchen

Made banana nut muffins for breakfast. As I was taking them out of the oven J. said: Maybe when all this is over with my mother we should go some place.

Where?…I asked struggling to appear enthusiastic.

Some place warm and beach-y…he said slabbing on the butter.

Hmmm…I thought…the Tropics with a celibate.

The tea kettle whistled.

I have to write the book…I muttered. Or, anyway, the text.

I understand…said Johnson, throwing some herbal tea bags into his thermos.

And I haven't even finished unpacking.

Just a thought…he said washing the dishes.

He'd washed the dishes all weekend. He'd also filled the birdfeeders, raked the leaves and gone with me to the dump! Turned to me as we were hurling black plastic bags into space and said: I know you don't respect me.

I stood dumbfounded on somebody else's grapefruit.

I know you think I run from problem solving, too…he continued.

Well…

And for a long time I have worried you were right.

I…I…I just wish we talked more…I said as a caterpillar tractor pushed a mound of trash in our direction.

I don't know how to talk…said Johnson…until I know what

I think.

The tractor shoved broken toys, eggshells, two-by-fours and coffee grounds over the edge of the embankment.

You're not supposed to know...I said. That's why you talk...to sort it out.

That's why you talk!

I had an experience in Siena...I continued...about fear and the Urge and how I've cut myself off from—

What?

Destiny!...I shouted enthusiastically as a station wagon pulled up in a cloud of dust.

You're the lawyer who saved the river!...said the woman driver looking at Johnson as if he were a god.

And as the tractor pushed part of a stove in the direction of scrap metal I watched Johnson take in a total stranger's concerns as if they were the most important concerns in the world and was reminded once again of the size of his dedication and the growing number of people who depend upon him. Elizabeth is doing her job well. In my absence J. bought an answering machine and appeared on local television.

I should be back about 7-7:30...he said stashing some muffins in a bag beside his thermos. Do you need anything from the health food store?

I shook my head No and watched him zip up his battered briefcase to go do battle with the city as it threatens to halt the construction of our new recycling center. And as the screen door flapped shut I filled with a spasm of hope. He was making a concerted effort. And I was holding out for someone who couldn't even find the time to pick up the goddamn—

Flour!...I shouted bounding onto the front porch...cracked wheat. And some of that avocado honey.

Mol...he said rolling down the car window...are you okay?

Me? Sure. Well...you know...it's weird...you, me...life, death... air mattresses.

He fastened his seatbelt and said: I won't be celibate forever.

You can be celibate...it's okay...really.

No, it's not...he said adjusting the rearview mirror.

I mean, maybe if you were still getting it on with Elizabeth...

I laughed nervously.

You can forget about Elizabeth…he said, turning the key in the ignition…I never loved Elizabeth.

Why was I bringing up Elizabeth? The last thing I wanted was a passionate and painful reconciliation. I was positive I'd either cry or cry out for Nancy, Nancy, Nancy!

Alright…I yelled as he started backing down the driveway…you never loved her! But how do I know all this being nice to me isn't some sort of cover up?

You don't…he said putting on the brakes. Okay? You don't.

Thanks…I said hitting the side of the car.

Listen to me…said Johnson…I was becoming somebody I didn't know.

You lied about her in therapy.

Yes!…he said with some impatience. Why do you think I pulled back? It drives me crazy you need everything so unbearably spelled out!

I looked at the pebbles in the driveway and heard his voice say Yes. Yes…he had slept with her. Yes. He had smelled her hair and told her he loved her. Yes, Yes, Yes. He had longed and obsessed…. Oh, God please…Yes!

I'm sorry…he said.

Hey, look…I said…it's not as if I didn't suspect.

He put his long fingers on top of mine. I saw them making their way down Elizabeth's skinny thighs as Nancy's mouth found my breast.

Maybe instead of a trip…he said…we should buy the farm some furniture.

I love you, Johnson…I said somewhat surprised that I'd said it. I love you so much.

Ditto…he said returning his hand to the steering wheel. Ditto.

When he got to the end of the driveway he tooted three times and waved.

Riiiiing.

I waved back and the faint flame flickered as we struggled to shine ourselves in the same direction.

Riiiiing.

I walked into the house and picked up the phone.

Jesus...said Nancy...I thought I'd never get out of there!!

I laughed once before I burst into tears.

Oh, Angel...don't...don't, Baby, don't. I couldn't call. I'm sorry. Oh, Honey...I've thought about you every single, awful, lonely, ex-cruciating, why was I born? kind of moment.

I've thought about you, too...I stammered as my heart leapt into my throat.

Angel, she knew...said Nancy...she knew the minute she saw me.

So did you sleep with her or something?

Oh, Sweetheart...she was sick. Her gall bladder. She almost had to have it taken out. I spent the whole weekend in the hospital.

You still love her. Just say it. You still love her, don't you?

No, Baby. She still loves me. I want to let her down gently, that's all. Talk to me.

I don't know what to say.

That you love me...she said...just please god, say you love me.

I love you...I said uncertainly. Then added: Johnson wants me to buy the farm some furniture.

A few days later

Nancy and I met today ostensibly to work on the book...but really to reaffirm our passion for each other on the floor of her loft. She is determined to keep Gillian as a friend...something I'm coming to understand as endemic to the lesbian landscape. Unconditional Love and all that. Gillian is out of the hospital. Her gall bladder is back to normal. Nancy thinks we should wait until after Christmas to tell Them, though. She says the way we leave who we are with is a sure sign of how we'll treat the person we are going toward. Some-times it all sounds like bullshit and sometimes I think she's the wis-est woman in the world.

Tuesday

Nancy and I celebrated Christmas early. She gave me a pair of ear-rings she bought in Italy. Took me to the Village to get my ears pierced by a survivor of the Vietnam War. Then we took a walk through Washington Square Park. It was a beautiful day. Clear and cold. The kind of day that feels so fresh you think you are capable of anything...including loving two people simultaneously. And talking about it...at least to one of them. I'm so glad N. and I talk. I'm so glad when something comes into my mind I can just say it and she can just hear it. How does she do that? I want to know how she does that. I want to know how she does EVERYTHING! We sat on the edge of the water fountain and I told her so. Then we were silent...taking in the sun, the electric blue of the sky and lovers out for a stroll through a sacred moment in time.

We should tell Them on the same day...said Nancy dreamily.

How about New Year's?...I suggested wryly.

Let's change our minds...she said suddenly. Let's tell them to-night.

She swatted me affectionately on the behind.

You're blu-shing...she teased.

I am not.

You're beet red and you're scared.

I'm not scared...I said...I just don't like hurting people's feelings.

You mean, you don't like hurting men's feelings. And unfaithful men at that.

Alright...I said...tonight. Alright? We'll tell them tonight.

Later

I was in the kitchen making Meimei some soup when I heard Johnson's car pull up. I made my way into the living room. Someone was getting out into the night air. Someone in addition to Johnson. Someone short and Asian with long hair. Elizabeth. He was getting her luggage out of the trunk. Kind of weird...but, okay...maybe he thought as long as their affair was out in the open.... I'd shake her hand. I'd be dignified. Then I'd give my little speech. They approached the porch. Thank God for Nancy. I opened the screen door. Breaking up was going to be a lot easier than I thought. I turned on the porch light.

Ethan?

Hi.

Ethan!

Yeah.

Jesus. Ethan...I don't believe this. What are you doing here?

I put my arms around him with forced enthusiasm. He stood

inert. Johnson hoisted a bag onto the porch. I patted Ethan's back and pulled away.

The place hasn't changed...he said relieved we hadn't replaced his memory with a lot of unfamiliar furniture.

You'll have to sleep on an air mattress tonight...said Johnson.

Ethan shrugged his approval as Johnson slipped his arm around my waist.

Where will you sleep?...I asked as Ethan took his bags up the stairs.

With you...said Johnson with an uncharacteristic wink.

Wow...I said...what a concept.

Johnson laughed and slapped me playfully. I felt Nancy's hand sliding down my backside only hours earlier in the park. I slapped Johnson back as Ethan reappeared at the top of the stairs. When we took him to see Meimei she grabbed his ear as he bent down to kiss her and gave it a yank. He pulled away...somewhat startled by her strength.

In China...said Johnson...when somebody's had a bad fright the ear is tweaked like that to bring back the soul.

Ethan sat tentatively on the edge of the bed. Meimei took his hand.

Chinese way...uh...she said then rattled the rest in Chinese.

The Chinese way is to want nothing...said Johnson. To swallow the misery of other people and eat your own bitterness.

Sounds pretty WASP to me...I said as Johnson carried the air mattress upstairs.

When we were fitting it with clean sheets he brought me up to date. It seems Matilda decided she was cured and quit taking her Lithium. After a certain amount of verbal and physical abuse...Ethan began spending the night with a classmate whose father was a doctor. Matilda was on a downward spiral. There was no telling how long it would last. The doctor finally took it upon himself to call Johnson. He even spoke to Matilda's father about having her committed. A long time ago, in trying to explain his strategy to me for the fiftieth time, Johnson had said: If you give Matilda her way she'll hang herself because there's nothing she hates more than winning.

Still Later

Watched Johnson settle uncertainly into our bed and thought about his extraordinary patience with human nature and how restless people like me come along and interpret it as Weakness.

Is Ethan here...you know...to stay?...I asked as he smoothed the pages of his book.

Well, I don't know about on the farm...he said after a moment... but with us.

He rubbed his eyes, looked at me and smiled a sad, shy smile.

Tell him. Tell him now. Tell him, tell him, tell him!...I shouted to myself as he turned on his reading light.

I don't mean to carry on about Elizabeth...I said studying the shadows on the ceiling. I mean, I'm sure you had your reasons.... Because I know I scare you. I mean, shit...I scare myself.

I stood poised on the brink of the Truth then watched myself segue into Siena, my baby brother and the Urge. How I cut myself off when I was nine. Ran screaming into my head. Which is now why it's important for me to open to life below my waist...but that requires a certain amount of Trust on Johnson's part...or maybe Understanding is a better word.... Just the way he needs me to Understand his thing about being celibate.

Next Day

J. and I woke up this morning in each other's arms. I think we were both a little surprised. He stroked my hair and brought me up to date on the recycling center then I edited his letter to the editor at Mother Jones.

January 1980

We seem to be sliding into the comfort of a routine that has taken us through Christmas, New Year's and various stores that sell furniture. Johnson never questions the days I spend in the city working on the book...or the hushed phone calls from Nancy at odd hours...and I've quit asking him about his involvement with Elizabeth who is turning him into a local celebrity. In fact, two days ago Nancy and I watched J. on the evening news in New York. I thought it would be good for her to see him in action. That way she won't have to live with a ghost as I've had to live with Matilda.

You're still in love with him, aren't you?...she mumbled when they cut for the commercial.

I'm trying to do what you said...I said...leave him in a way I can live with.

I was wrong...she said pulling on her face.

After we get Ethan settled in a school—

After this...after that... You come here...we get close...we work on the book and you take off like I'm expendable...she said getting up.

You can call me.

You can't always talk.

Well, I'm sorry...I didn't know Ethan was coming home.

I thought you didn't care about kids.

Nance...you don't exactly cancel your appointments with Annie so we can work on the book.

I do!...she said tearing up a photograph. I don't always tell you. What are we in here...grade school?

Let's just be friends...I said totally terrified of the notion...let's just be friends until we finish.

And then what?

Then what what?

When the book is over?

I'm not going to leave you!...I hollered taking refuge behind the kitchen counter...YOU'RE THE ONLY PERSON I CAN TALK TO ABOUT EVERYTHING!

We steamed for a good ten minutes in separate corners of the loft pretending to look at photographs. We are still in search of a theme. I think it should be The Doors of Tuscany...and she thinks it should be something about light. Light...doors...whatever it is I'm getting tired of her constant need for reassurance. It's like...she doubts my word! My word. I never go back on my word. That's like accusing me of being Ambivalent!

Winter, 1980

Nancy has thrown herself into her work with a vengeance, trying not to hate herself too much for her incurable attraction to married women. And I reassure her that, even though we sleep on the same futon, Johnson is still celibate and I am still gay. I don't have the slightest idea how I've arrived at that conclusion...but I promise her anyway and we dive into each other's eyes where she still finds me beautiful and I still find her bountiful and we make long, slow love then return to our work with a concentration that is so intense hours pass in seconds and by the end of our time together we've been some place so deep and true and delicate it only belongs to us.

Chapter Eleven

Molly closes the spiral notebook, puts it on the floor beside her and feels a nasty rustling under her skin. She is embarrassed by the long hours she spent taut as a wishbone between Johnson and Nancy. She had hoped her journals would have enlightened her. Revealed something she'd never given herself credit for. Instead, she comes face to face with her Ambivalence and, with the overview of a bald eagle, traces it back to the tired history of the frozen baby.

She looks at Nancy's handwriting on the manila envelope. The bed in the apartment overhead begins to creak slowly and rhythmically. Molly's feet grip the hallway floor. She knows the journal Nancy bought her in Florence is in the manila envelope. She can feel the lush greens and splashes of hot pink bleeding in waves across the handmade cover. Can see the pages, thick and creamy, not unlike the rice paper journal Johnson had given her. And unlined, too. But, at the time, Molly didn't care because every time she opened it she fell heart first into Nancy. Molly's upstairs neighbor grunts. The creaking noise becomes louder, faster. A sharp crack loosens the ice flow in Molly's belly. She knows the Italian journal will not be easy. But she is still seeing rats in the shadows in Little Norway and the Italian journal is her last remaining link to sanity. Molly opens the manila envelope and hears a muffled scream. She no longer knows if it's coming from inside or out, upstairs or down.

'Wherever it's coming from, it's coming for us! Please, God… Chicken. Mommy!! I told you, she doesn't have the— Shut up, shut up,

shutup, shutupshutUP!'

And as a rat-like shadow skuttles into the unmarked box, a warm wind blows and Molly's ice-bound body cracks and falls into the safety of her well-lit bed. And as she pulls the covers over her head, words splatter like wet paint on the remainder of her mind, the manila envelope ripping and swirling through the chatter. And somewhere inside the chaos, Molly falls with a thud on the broken remains of the frozen baby and picks up the pieces with her terrible longing. Tucks them in the bruised spot along with Ethan and Timmy and merges with the irrational passion of the Italian journal.

Early April

On the train returning to the farm

The evolution of the book has been thrilling. Starting with Nancy's absolutely blind faith that I could do it. Your voice…she would say. I want to hear Your Voice. After several failed attempts, I read her one of my letters to Chloe. Then she said: That's it! Postcards. The book will be a series of postcards…and the text will be what each person writes on the back.

God! I have been having…I can't tell you. What a turn on! I've invented ten people…all types and ages, on a tour of Tuscany. The one who writes home the most, though, is Chloe because she's got at least five kids.

Later

On the way to Penn Station, N. wanted to know if I'd like to use my real name or a pseudonym. I said I'd think about it. I mean, I know if I say pseudonym she'll go into one of her moods…but, the truth is, I don't have the faintest idea how to explain our "collaboration" to my family. Heather already knows something's up. Keeps teasing me about the weight I've lost and the glow in my cheeks. I cover with how much better things have gotten between J. and me since Ethan's return. And she says: You always were a lousy liar. I just laugh. I've gotten pretty good at just laughing. At cultivating my secret place. Even Nancy has made me swear I won't get too good at it. I just laughed then, too. Conrad, though…will be scary. He'll demand an explanation in that "teasing" way he has and as soon he realizes Nancy and I are not only coworkers but "friends".… And when he finds out about Annie.... Oh, christ...it's too big and too complicated. I'll tell Nancy I'll use a pseudonym. We can work it out. We can work out anything.

Tuesday

I mean, it's not like the people who'll buy the book are going to buy it to read it...I said as Nancy and I descended into the subway. They'll buy it to look at your pictures.

Photographs...she said slamming her subway token in the slot.

Sometimes you sound just like Johnson...I said as a long line of graffiti pulled into the 72nd Street Station.

Look...she said as the doors opened (or, anyway, as one did)...every woman I've ever fallen for except Gillian has been afraid of coming out.

I know...I said all too familiar with the scenario.

And you said you weren't...so please understand this is not an accusation...I decided to believe you. I have done this to myself. Eyes wide open. I should've seen it coming...because right now I feel like a total asshole as fucking usual.

I'm not afraid of coming out...I said, knowing full well I was...I'm afraid if Conrad finds out about you and Annie he'll—

There are ways around Conrad...she said as the subway pulled into Sheridan Square.

Alright, I'm afraid...I said as we climbed the stairs. When Johnson lost Ethan he took it out on me. I'm just afraid you'll lose Annie and do the same.

I'm not Johnson, Baby. Just like you're not Gillian.

A doorbell tinkled. Two shoppers emerged from a rather funky boutique. Nancy caught the door before it closed and ushered me inside. She tapped a salesgirl on the back.

Look who I ran into...she said as the girl turned around. Your Aunt Molly.

Hi...said Annie with adolescent indifference.

Hi...I said...my god...so this is where you work. What a coincidence!

I smiled politely but underneath I couldn't believe Nancy had brought me there! She has this way of putting me on the spot in public. Annie could definitely tell something was up. I said Nancy

and I had run into each other on the subway. I pretended to be de-
lighted Annie and Nancy were back in each other's lives. Then
Nancy made me swear I wouldn't say anything to Conrad...so I
swore...then said I had an appointment with an antique dealer and
just about ran the whole way to Penn Station.

Heeeeelllllppppp!!!
N. and I met at the public library to do some last minute research
for the book.

It's one thing to withhold information from my family...I said
as she ran up the steps ahead of me...and another to lie to
them...especially to Annie.

It won't hurt her...she said as we swung open the doors. She's a
big girl.

She's conservative like her father...I whispered.

You can say that again...she said pulling out a file.

I will not hurt my family so a lot of strangers can look at my
name on the front of a coffee table book.

Oh, that's right...said Nancy handing me a couple of books on
Tuscany. Family. I must make a point to remember how central
FAMILY is to your existence.

Shhhh!...said a man with a pock-marked face and bulging eyes.

Homophobe...said Nancy under her breath.

Look...I said knowing full well she'd intended the remark for
me...maybe we should be friends until I know what I'm doing.

We looked up the information we needed in silence. Then
found our way to Fifth Avenue. Nancy thrust a handful of notes at
me as we waited stiffly for the bus.

I just wanted to be in the same room with my child and my
lover...she said as the bus arrived. I wanted to know what that felt
like. Forgive my gross indulgence.

I'll see you on Friday...I said getting on.

No...she said...you won't. Gillian is having her gall bladder
taken out. I said I'd be there for her.

Gillian?

Gillian...she said as the doors closed.

I opened the window.

So what are you saying?...I yelled.

FUCK THE BOOK!

I slammed the window...or tried to...and as the bus started to move she banged the side of it with her fist.

AND FUCK YOU!

I looked for solace in my lap as my heart pounded against the confines of my chest and thirty strangers watched me try not to turn every imaginable shade of red.

A Week Later

Still waiting for Nancy to apologize. This morning, while I was working on Meimei's feet...I thought about the remark Nancy made about me and Family and decided not to call her, either. It's so fucking typical...I trust her with the details of the frozen baby and she uses them against me when it suits her. Reminds me of my mother.

May

Parents Day

Went to Ethan's school with Johnson. Ethan did a good job in a bad play about the food chain that included a journey through the human body. Ethan played a corpuscle. During the reception I went to the ladies' room. I was sitting in the stall, to be graphic about it...aching with Nancy and trying not to vomit the contents of my secret fucking place into the toilet...when Peggy Allen came in with that new boy's mother who had said she would carpool on Thursday.

Call Molly...said Peggy. She'll cover for you. She lives with Ethan's father...you know, the lawyer who is trying to save the recycling center. They brush their teeth with baking soda and leave their thermostat at 50.

Then they freshened their lipstick and made jokes about the conservation of energy and thanked God they didn't have that kind of image to live up to.

After they left, I flushed the toilet. Not that I'd actually been able to throw up or go to the bathroom. I just wanted to remember what it was like to waste water.

Tuesday

Got the Italian thing out from under the futon. Turned over a pile of notes and looked at Nancy's handwriting. Am sinking deeper and deeper into the ratty grime of self-loathing. Spend a lot of time fantasizing about the most efficient way to do myself in. Today I concluded a good cry would be the most noble. Just open the flood-gates and let her rip until my heart breaks whatever's left of me and I turn inside out.

Jesus, I am boring! So tangled in the sea of self-involvement it is a miracle I can keep the car on the road! And what is all this bullshit about getting my heart energy into my fingers? Touching Johnson with the power of Unconditional Love? The next thing I'll be de-manding of myself is a stigmata!

Nancy, Nancy, Nancy

Have forgotten how to read. The garden is a riot of weeds. I could care less about food. And now Johnson, ever mindful of my Pain, has taken to putting his hand on my heart and the angrier I get at him for thinking because he meditates he can make It All Go Away…the more I begin to find a kind of sanctuary in the chicken coop holding onto Meimei's feet. Not that I think I am doing her the slightest bit of good…it isn't that. It's that I can just be there with her and she doesn't try to fix the way I am.

Summer, 1980

Had a good "talk" with Meimei today about the Chinese way. About swallowing another person's misery and eating your own bitterness. I asked her how you know when you're really doing it…or when it's all some sort of ego trip and maybe it would be better to go on to something you can actually accomplish? She sighed a deep sigh, put her hand on her stomach and jiggled it ever so slightly…then mo-tioned me to do the same. She has begun to lose her battle with the English language. At first the silences were long and nervous-mak-ing and had I had anything else to do I would've made my excuses and gone about my business…but now I am coming to understand the true meaning of courage. Her pain is unrelenting. Yet every day she sends her breath into the black hole that is sapping her energy and sucking her soul into another world. And every day I take hold of her feet and go with her.

October

Meimei's oldest friend, The Herb and Root Connection, took a fall
and his family closed his shop and put him in an old age home outside San Francisco. As Meimei's supplies have dwindled her pain has
intensified and, now, it seems, wandered beyond the limits of brav-
ery. Last week I went into NYC and bought anything I could find at
Aphrodesia that looked mysterious and plant-like...the whole time
praying I wouldn't run into Nancy. Yesterday I took hold of
Meimei's feet and she howled like a wounded animal. This morning
she refused to eat. Now she can't stand to be touched so I sit uncertainly at the foot of her bed saying inconsequential things like:
Johnson says he's heard of a doctor who has had some luck with a
Vitamin C drip. And she motions me to leave the room so I hang
my head like an overgrown cowboy and climb down slowly, still too
big to sit in my father's lap.

Wednesday

Meimei's still not eating. Not even organic baby food.

Friday

Meimei couldn't get out of bed again to go to the bathroom. The
bedpan has become an instrument of torture and why (in trying to
get her to use it) have I "turned against her"? I try to stay centered. I
take a deep breath, put my hands on my stomach, as she taught me,
and relax into her suffering as if it were my own. I thought I was
doing pretty well until she wet the bed. It wasn't so much that she
wet it...but when I tried to change the sheets she spat at my stomach. At first I thought it was an accident. Then she spat again. J. says
she's cutting us loose. Ethan says we should tweak her ear. After dinner, I contacted the local hospice and arranged to have her put on a
catheter. No sooner had I hung up the phone than Heather called.
Conrad has found out that Annie has been seeing Nancy and isn't
going to let her be Maid of Honor at his wedding. Mother is up in
arms. Heather is morbidly fascinated. And I could care less and I say
as much. Then Heather lets it drop that Nancy has a show up in
SoHo. Something about eyes. I am very cool but inside I feel like a

handball in an echo chamber and over and over I hear Nancy saying: If you take an object from your past and turn it into art you free yourself from the clutter of a former life. Now, alone in early morning, I know I am the clutter and my family is the former life.

Yesterday

Meimei refused her breakfast so I sat on the edge of her bed and ate it for her. Then the hospice nurse came to put in the catheter. It was a painful process. Meimei squeezed my hand so hard I thought she was going to break my fingers. Then she fell back exhausted. Ethan tried to bring her back with talk of the sweat lodge he and J. are planning to build, but she remained clammy and unresponsive. When I went to check on her after dinner, she pointed to a Chinese box. I remembered it coming in the last package from the Herb and Root Connection. I thought it might be a painkiller of some sort so I gave it to her. An hour later she was in a coma. A year ago I might've thought it was all my fault but now I think I helped her.

Tomorrow

Meimei died last night. J. was holding her hand and I was holding her feet. We didn't know what to do with her body so we left her until morning…hoping when we came downstairs she would be all better. It's funny how you wait for this moment to come in all its inevitable inevitability…and when it does you pretend it hasn't. You do strange things like clean the fireplace, eat ice cream and agree to give each other backrubs. And before you know it your boyfriend's fingers are digging into your rigid muscles and you're thinking how strong they are compared to Nancy's. How soft. And he's moving down your spine caressing your long waist as if you are a piece of glass. Then he's putting lotion on his hands and working his way under your T-shirt. And you're closing your eyes and burying your nose in the pillow and wondering if he's through being celibate. I mean, he's curving his hand around the inside of your thighs; Quanah's drum is beating and Nancy is undoing the locks to her loft.

Turn over…says your boyfriend softly.

You smile shyly. He works his hands along your rib cage as Nancy undoes the buttons on your blouse and you hear yourself

say: You wear a bra! And you try to tell your boyfriend that he's got
to stop. That his mother isn't even cold in the chicken coop. Then,
as he takes your breasts in his mouth, he tells you she is at peace and
you hear Nancy say: Ooooo...they fit...I always knew they'd fit. You
slam the darkroom door.

Be careful...she says...the light.

You like that?...asks your boyfriend.

Mmmmm...you mumble as he kisses the base of your throat...
your chin, your nose...making every effort to appreciate foreplay
which you know he learned from Elizabeth. Elizabeth...jesus! How
are you going to get through this without—His hand is traveling
down your thigh.

Oh, God...you say. Not yet. I'm still so—

But he spreads you wide and lowers himself between your legs
as Nancy comes toward you with a cordless vibrator.

Get that thing out of here!...you cry pushing him to one side.

He looks at you...bewildered. Your heart rumbles like an earthquake rolling toward its destiny. You start to apologize.

Fuck you!...says Nancy...AND FUCK THE BOOK!!

You slam the bus window and let go of your breath. Tears
spring from your eyes. Your boyfriend looks at you with a mixture
of compassion and pity.

Oh, god...you sob...oh, god I miss her so much!!

He kisses your tears. Your hand travels down his backside. You
feel your confusion getting him excited.

I miss her, too...he stammers. I miss her, too.

You slip off his underwear. There have always been ghosts in
bed with you. Now there are so many neither one of you really
knows who you are talking about...so you push forward...kissing
eyes and noses and with a fierce intensity rediscovering neglected
lips. You are suddenly certain you can pull it off...then, he enters
you and something rises up...something in such a rage at having
been relegated to obscurity in the name of Mystery that it explodes
the confines of your secret place...and hissing and spitting shapes
poison into righteous indignation and with the cold precision of a
surgeon pushes itself contemptuously through your tear-stained
lips.

Your penis isn't going to take away my pain any more than my hands are going to fill you full of Unconditional Love!

Your boyfriend turns away.

I'm sorry…you say after a moment…I don't know what came over me. I was just…Meimei.… And all the.… I mean, the whole time you were celibate…was I just supposed to wait?

No…he says…of course not.

So, does this mean we're starting over or is this…you know…because your mother is lying lifeless in the chicken coop?

What do you want?…he cries, slamming his hand into his pillow. What DO YOU WANT?

You burst into tears and wail: I want to do something USEFUL with my LIFE!

He turns away. He is sick of your complaining and you want to tell him he is right…but you are all over the place so you babble about how he makes you feel like a fool when you try to focus on something other than his career. His needs. His life.

For the longest time he doesn't respond. Then, very quietly, he turns his back and pulls the covers over his head and from some place deep and sad and exhausted he says: Just go to her. Just get out of bed…and GO TO HER!

On the train to Greenwich

When all the necessary papers had been signed and Meimei's body had been taken to the crematorium, J. and I decided I should go alone to Conrad's wedding. When I got to Penn Station I hailed a cab to take me to Grand Central and as I got inside I heard myself say: SoHo. Moments later I opened the door that stood between me and Nancy's effort to banish me from the rest of her life.

When I entered the gallery, I nodded politely to an officious looking young man in a '50s jacket and string tie. The man nodded back and introduced himself as Arthur. He appeared to be alone so I made my way to the art work.

That collage is my personal favorite…he said as I moved to one side of a support column.

I smiled politely, even though my back was to him, and took in not only my eyes…but pieces of birch bark…and handwriting.… To Become…oh, my god…Whole. Nancy was right…I <u>had</u> written it. And underneath…an old label from a bottle of Johnson's Baby

Oil. But the Oil part was torn so it read: Johnson's Baby. And right next to it was a splash of red paint. Blood I guess. For what I'd done to Nancy...or, for that matter, the frozen baby. I reached up to touch the birch bark. The young man cleared his throat. I smiled weakly and looked on the wall for the title.

There isn't one...he said as if he knew Nancy intimately...but you never know.

I smiled vaguely.

And the red dots...what are the—

Sold...he said adamantly.

Sold...

Yesterday.

Uh huh.

She always sells.

I took a deep breath. I'd been framed and sold. Framed and sold and my secret was out in the open.

She'll be in later if you're interested...said the young man pulling up his socks. We've got a new show coming in tomorrow. If you get her when she's taking things off the walls...you can sometimes talk her down in price.

I'll keep that in mind...I said casually and headed for the door.

She's in town!...I thought loudly. She's in town!

The string tie buzzed me out. My heart began to race. I waved frantically at a cab and just barely caught a later train to Connecticut. I fell into a seat beside a hard-core commuter. I closed my eyes, relaxed my stomach and took hold of Meimei's feet. Or maybe Nancy's. Or maybe the frozen baby's. Well, anyway...they were feet.

Let the Games Begin

When I got to the Country Club my mother wanted to know why I hadn't called to say I'd be late.

I thought you'd joined Heather's boycott...she said as she arranged and rearranged the place cards.

No...I said...Johnson's mother died last night.

No!...she said as if it were totally unexpected.

Yes...I said with deliberate impatience.

I'm sorry.

It was time.

But still...you were fond of her.

Mother, I learned something.

She smiled a distracted smile and exchanged two more place cards putting Annie between her two brothers.

I cut myself off...I said...like when someone leaves...or dies...our whole family...we go dead.

She fluffed up an arrangement of flowers.

So the other two aren't joining you?...she asked from the nervous comfort of self-control.

That's right...I said with an edge...there'll be two empty places at dinner.

I wish you'd told me. I could've asked the Guilfoyles.

You can still ask them.

It's too late. They'd feel insulted.

Mother...I think it's wrong we never talk about Timmy.

Really, Molly...

Never even say his name.

You pick the oddest times to start conversations.

Because people don't die. They move inside you. Don't you see? The relationship continues.

She pointed me in the direction of the ladies' room the way she did when I was five. I put on a pale green something she'd rented so the whole family...or anyway, those who showed up...would look like we went together. The dress was strapless which meant I was always hiking it up or hunching over into it. Heather was not in attendance but we were all sure she would make a surprise entrance because she loves a good party. To say nothing of showing off her baby. Annie, on the other hand, was...thanks in large part to Conrad's new wife who had made Annie promise to quit her job in the Village for one in a Talbot's that was closer to home.

I heard that you and Nancy...well, that it didn't work out...I said as Annie and I circled the punch bowl at the reception.

Want some punch?...she asked with an indifferent shrug.

I held out my glass. She waved at someone who might've been a friend and let go of the ladle. I poked at the melting ice sculpture and wondered if Meimei could see us trying so hard to be a family. I filled my glass with what had to be forty different kinds of liquor. I ignored a nod of recognition from an old classmate and wandered outside. The sun was starting to set. I sat on a stone bench under a tree and listened to the boat riggings clinking in the harbor. I watched a cloud take its own sweet time moving in front of the sun. Maybe Meimei was a part of that cloud…floating free.… Like—

Timmy…I said quietly…Timmy, Timmy, Timmy, Timmy.

I promised your mother I'd wear this confounded thing…said my father as he fiddled with his hearing aid…but I'm about to retract my word.

He sat down beside me and added: Too much clatter.

For a while we watched the bobbing boats…then, for reasons only known to him…he patted my hand.

You're a good egg…he said mustering himself into the moment.

Father…I've been thinking a lot about when Timmy died.

His hearing aid made a sharp, whining noise. He took it out of his ear and threw it into the sound.

Yes…he said…please extend Johnson my apologies.

NO…TIMMY. WHEN HE DIED. REMEMBER WHEN I CLIMBED INTO YOUR LAP?

I took it…when I always take it.

YOUR LAP…I said pointing to mine…LAP…NOT NAP.

Yes…he said vaguely.

WHY DID YOU TELL ME I WAS TOO BIG?

Your mother said I should tell you to come in for the wedding dinner…he said using my arm to pull himself up.

What if we don't? What if we just STAY HERE AND TALK?

And she's mad enough about Heather.

I THOUGHT SHE'D WEAKEN…I said leading him across the lawn. HEATHER. I THOUGHT SHE'D—

TOO MUCH SEX…he hollered. THAT'S THE WHOLE TROUBLE WITH YOU KIDS. NOBODY THINKS ABOUT ANYTHING BUT THEMSELVES. GODDAMN TIMOTHY LEARY. DESTROYED AN ENTIRE GENERATION!

Conversation with my father has a way of becoming one-sided…especially when he's removed his hearing aid…and always when he's been drinking. By the time we got to the dining room all the guests were seated and my mother was desperate for an extra person so there would be fourteen instead of thirteen at the table.

She had that pinched look on her face that provokes my father which may have been why he proceeded to carry on in a rather loud voice about promiscuity and the rapid rise of homosexuality.

And if that isn't enough...he continued...the goddamn poofters have their own parade!

Father...gay men and women have a right to be treated like everybody else...I said. They fight the same wars and pay the same taxes.

They are systematically undermining the human family.

They're creating extended families. Why does it always have to be about bloodlines?

Alright...said my mother trying to regain control of the conversation.

I mean, didn't you teach us Love is what's important?

You women are the real culprits...said my father pulling himself into focus.

Oh, that's great...lose one round...blame somebody else...I said trying not to turn purple.

It's no use talking to him when he gets like this...warned my mother.

You mean when he's been DRINKING?...I said loudly.

Don't use that word...whispered my mother sharply.

Mother...we're hurting. Our whole family—

Because...slurred my Father...you women refuse to KNOW YOUR PLACE.

I threw my napkin on the table, stood up and unzipped my strapless evening dress.

I know my place, Father...and it's not in this!

My mother held her napkin in front of me. Conrad put his hand on his steak knife and ordered me to ACT LIKE A LADY.

Whose version?...I asked threatening to drop the bodice. Yours or mine?

He turned to his brand new in-laws and apologized for my outspoken ways. My...quote mother-in-law unquote...had just died...I was exhausted and it wasn't my custom to drink. They nodded nervously. Conrad's new and naturally submissive wife put her hand on top of his.

Nancy was the best thing that ever happened to us...I

hollered…only we were so caught up in doing what we were supposed to we couldn't appreciate the gift.

That's it!…said Conrad kicking back his chair. That's it!

You can't pretend she doesn't exist!…I said as my toes gripped the floor.

You have no right bringing that woman up at my wedding!

She's the mother of your children!

Get out of here…get out!

You're depriving them of—

How would you know what I'm "depriving them of"?…he asked with contempt.

Annie snickered.

Do you like being a bitch? Does it give you a thrill?…I asked as I fumbled for my zipper.

I don't know…she said…do you like being a dyke?

What's going on here?…demanded Conrad as the Andersons excused themselves.

They've been getting it on…said Annie with cold delight.

Oh, please…oh, please…I said resecuring the pale green bodice.

Who's been getting it on?…asked Conrad as I turned on Annie.

You dirty, narrow-minded little—

Who do you think?…said Annie relishing every moment on center stage. Molly and Mom.

A killing frost gripped the Clubhouse.

Is Annie telling the truth?…asked Conrad, his hands turning into fists.

I stood alone on the red hot rim of the volcano.

Well, I was about to put it a little differently…I said as the volcano began to rumble…but…yes…Annie is telling the truth.

My father ordered himself another drink. My mother covered her ears and muttered something about the number thirteen and how it never failed to ruin dinner conversation. I looked at her in disbelief as Conrad pointed a banishing finger in the direction of the door. I gritted my teeth, lifted my chin, went to the desk, called a cab and made the next train. An hour later I found myself in Soho. I stood in my strapless evening gown before the door of the gallery. Chloe wrapped herself around my shoulders. I put my hand on the knob. I could hear Nancy's voice. I opened the door slowly. When Nancy saw me she took a sharp breath.

It's you...she said squinting slightly.

I know.

It's you!

We stood for a self-conscious second in our last moment on 5th Avenue.

I need to talk to you about the book...I said. I want to use my name. I've already told my family.

Nancy smiled as Chloe fell in slow, ecstatic motion into the roiling mouth of the volcano.

Dear Molly,

Once, a long time ago, shortly after you lost the baby, we got into a discussion about the big sadness. You said everyone comes up against something at least once that is so devastating and incomprehensible that there is nothing left to do but let go and let life. You were trying to comfort me (yet again) about Matilda. You reminded me of what I'd said to you in the car coming back from Woodstock about pain being the breaking of the shell that encloses understanding. I remember feeling irritated when you said it was time for me to get into the second half of the sentence. I believe I changed the subject. Turned to the comfort of self-pity and chastised myself for coming to you with the burden of another life. For expecting you to fit in when it was appropriate and to disappear when it wasn't. But all along, much of what you said to me in your "fits of clarity" has been sinking in. And still I find myself in petty rebellion, loathing every minute inside my skin; dreading every hour in our empty bed. And raging at your perplexing reluctance to have a child. Our child. I thought when we met I could help you find your place in the world as well as in our life together, as you have, so selflessly, helped me find mine. I am sorry that our perceptions collided. That you felt "cut off at the pass." I have blamed myself far more than I have blamed you. And, yes, I have refrained from saying what I deeply believe. That something happened to you around the time of the miscarriage. Around the time you were wisely advising me about sadness...you were, I believe, becoming the victim of your own. I remember saying that we should try again right away. Not let ourselves get spooked. Yet somehow we did. You did. It wasn't that I didn't want to marry you. It was that I didn't think I made you happy. Anymore than I did Matilda. Now I try to imagine what you must be feeling alone in the confines of a strange and unexpected world. Some days I see you flying free of the dictates of a stupid male who would rather "meditate than communicate." Other days I imagine the excruciating pain of having to embrace a deep and disturbing truth. I have never been good at putting my feelings into words. I have depended on you for clarity and feared you for it at the same time. Now I lie awake wishing I weren't so traditional. So rooted in my ideas of how we should be because I'm a man and you're a woman. I look at my relationship to Elizabeth. She KNOWS men. She knows how to charm and listen and stroke our pathetic egos. And still I ache for the sound of your voice booming up the stairs. For your open laugh and challenging mind. I ache and chastise and remember. And I am powerless to change. Yours at large in the second half of the sentence,

J.

Dear Johnson,

~~Where do you come off calling my new life a "deep and disturbing truth"? It's just another example of your need to focus on pain and guilt and all the things you need to indulge yourself in so you feel ALIVE~~

Dear Johnson,

~~As I have said and said and said,~~ there are lots of ways to have children. We have to consider who we are. How we live. What about kids who have nothing? Why does it always have to be about bloodlines?

Dear Johnson,

You're right. I did get spooked...shortly before the incident with the baby...when I bruised Ethan's arm. Suddenly my rage was out in the open painfully displayed on the body of a child. Suddenly I had physical evidence of my fear at being relegated to the confines of motherhood before I had discovered my place in the world. So I latched onto your reluctance to discuss marriage while expecting me to find contentment in having babies as you came and went. I latched onto Matilda's manipulation of you, of Ethan and therefore of Us. I latched onto your fear of the Judge's ruling. I took comfort in making you the one with the problem so I could turn my face from the mirror and lose myself in lofty thoughts of Unconditional Love. Call me a victim of the New Age. Call me a victim of Women's Lib. Whatever I am I have not been honest with you and that, more than anything, is probably what you felt. I ~~never suffered a miscarriage. I bought myself some time in an abortion clinic on the Upper East Side.~~

Dear Johnson,
Thanks for your letter. I left the following items in the trunk at the foot of the futon under Meimei's ashes: The flannel nightgown ~~you gave me last Christmas~~; my overalls, hiking boots, gardening books, some seeds and Willie's ring, ~~whatever that was about~~. I'll come for them when the dust has settled.
    M.

YOU ARE CORDIALLY INVITED
TO
THE LAZY EYE GALLERY
TO CELEBRATE THE PUBLICATION
OF
POSTCARDS FROM TUSCANY
PHOTOS BY
NANCY HARRISON
TEXT BY
MOLLY WILLIAMS
JULY 21, 1981   RSVP

NOW
New York City

Is that you?
    Nancy's honeyed tones floated effortlessly on the steamy air of a summer day.
    It's me…I said opening the door to the loft…is it you?
    It's me, Baby.

Baby?...I said pointing to our names on the invitations.

Baby? At a time like this you call me Baby?

She took an invitation in her hand.

There you are...she said stroking my name...in print.

I blushed and turned away.

I'm not a writer, Nance. I did this for you.

Take a deep breath and take the fucking compliment...she said snapping my picture.

I don't know...I said. What if people think the book stinks?

Nancy rolled a chair in my direction and motioned me to sit.

You smile sweetly and say: Fuck you for sharing.

I laughed as Nancy draped my legs over the arms of the chair, pulled my blouse out of my jeans and opened the top three buttons.

I don't know about those apple fasts...she said zooming in on my ribcage. You're as bony as Hatia.

Do you think I should send them an invitation?

Click, click, click.

Who? The Eastern Bloc?

Yes...I laughed...do you think it's been long enough since Conrad's wedding?

I think one day your whole family will be walking down Fifth Avenue and there we'll be. The book. The photo. The two of us...in Scribner's...all blown up in the fucking window.

Are you ever sorry you told Annie you were gay?...I asked.

Not that I told her...no...just that I assumed that underneath that conservative little exterior...not that she ever was a ragingly curious child...but around the time I met Gillian there was hope. Say Cheese.

I am going to send an invitation to Johnson...I said instead ...just so he knows.

Knows what?

That there's life after...I don't know...denial, disappointment...death.

Mol...said Nancy standing over me...you're never going to get his approval.

I don't need his approval...I said as she refocused her camera.

Well, whatever you want you're not going to get it. He doesn't have it to give. That's why you left, remember?

I can put Johnson down...I said putting my hand in front of the lens. You have to be nice.

                                                              Later
Nancy, who used to say she didn't want to dress like a man she just wanted the same privileges...is going to wear a tux to the book party. Wants me to wear one, too. She thinks we should give the event some class. She's even hired a limo. I called Hatia. All this dressing up in men's clothing...I don't know...I mean, I like being with Nancy because she makes me feel like a woman. Hatia says she has something long and slinky and cut on the bias and now that I'm so beautifully bony...

                                                          Thursday
Nancy just called. We got another good review...this time in the Voice. I still feel I'm reading about somebody else. Nancy says I should get over it. She is getting more and more pumped up. Comes home with flowers...champagne. We are always in the middle of celebrating something. It's almost exhausting. I told Hatia I wish she'd back off (Nancy). I mean, all the attention. I'm used to a guy who locks himself in the attic! Hatia says I should just say Cool It! But I know Nancy. She'll sulk and tweedle and call me her little Control Freak. Come hell or high water, she's going to loosen me up and, come hell or high water, I'm going to let her! It's just... well...she's so driven.

                                                  The Morning After
What a party! Nancy couldn't believe my gorgeousity! I had Hatia make me up in the darkroom then I threw open the door looking tall and slinky in Hatia's dress. My hair fell casually across part of my face and fire engine red glistened on my lips. N. about fell over. I was even wearing heels (not my idea of a good time!). Anyway, after the appropriate amount of fussing, all three of us got in the limo and went to the reception. All the artists had congregated by the hors d'oeuvres and all the suits were by the bar. Then the music started. Very funky. Very hip. Slightly weird. But good to dance to. Gradually, the hors d'oeuvres and the bar came together to twist and gyrate and say next to nothing. It's so odd...we're shy about

sharing our minds but not our bodies. I think it should be the other way around…but then, that's why I terrify the average man. But not the average woman! Oh, no. Anyway, Arthur (who has grown a goatee to go with his '50s jacket and string tie) said Nancy and I looked like Clark Gable and Carole Lombard. Of course, he was whacked. But Nancy liked the idea so she took me in her arms, swept me onto the dance floor and asked me to marry her. I thought she was kidding. I was about to say something flippant when she was called on to speak. She was very funny. At home in front of all those people. Of course, they were all her friends, or if they weren't, they wanted to be. Anyway, she talked about her dream of catching Tuscan light and weathered faces in her camera and how we decided to write the text as postcards. Then she introduced me as her friend, coworker and WIFE! and motioned me to come up beside her. I couldn't believe what she was doing. I smiled, as I was trained to do by Emily Post, and took away her glass of wine. But underneath I had this creepy feeling that she was putting me in a box. Anyway, after what seemed like the longest second in recorded history, somebody asked a question I didn't understand about metaphors and literary conceits and I told him I write the way I speak and if I did whatever he was talking about then I got a lot more out of my Liberal Arts education than I realized. Then a cork popped and next thing I knew we were drinking champagne and signing copies of the book and the whole time I was trying not to feel weird about Nancy. Toward the end of the evening a Pakistani woman asked if I'd like to come to her apartment next Tuesday and read from whatever I'm working on. She has a salon in her living room on East Third somewhere in the Alphabets. Nancy doesn't like it when I tell people I'm not really a writer so I told her (the Pakistani woman) I'd think about it but that my first priority was going back to school.

Nancy's eyes are still bothering her. Probably all the smoke.

Two Days Later

Had a long talk with Hatia about Nancy's marriage proposal or whatever you call it. Hatia was great. Really helped me sort out my panic. I'm glad I didn't respond right away (the way I usually do) because when Nancy and I talked I was calm and clear and she was thoughtful and sorry. I said I didn't think I was ready. That I need to get a job, go to night school and focus on my life in the world! N. said I could skip getting a job. That she would put me through school if I'd marry her. I said I wouldn't marry her until I got my degree…preferably in Social Work. So she said alright, she'd wait… but as long as she was going to foot the bill, she wanted me to take Creative Writing, as well. I said okay. I mean, it's not like she's asking me to become fluent in Sanskrit, now, is it?

Fall, 1981

First day of Spanish. Of course, I am the oldest person here except for the teacher, Mr. Something-Yugoslavian-that-I'll-never-be-able-to-spell. He's good, though. Makes learning fun. Experiential. He also teaches how to teach English as a Second Language. I'm thinking maybe next semester. I like his style. He says language sings in the whole body. And he's right. He's right! He's right!!

Saturday, 1982

Last week Nancy began turning out collages of men superimposed on women; women on men; men on men; women on women…blending through, blotting out. When I was through studying, we began kicking around titles for each collage. Pretty soon we were discussing a possible theme. And before long we were no longer hanging the collages in a gallery but working on another book…or maybe not…we weren't exactly sure so we took a break and went shopping for a king-sized bed with a motor in it.

It's awfully expensive…I said showing Nancy the price tag.

Nancy squinted, shrugged and pulled me down beside her.

If we get cable TV…she whispered…we won't have to go anywhere forever.

The salesman looked at us lying there raising the foot on one side of the bed and the head on the other. Then he cleared his throat and pursed his lips.

Will that be all?

For now…said Nancy…unless you sell dildoes.

We held our sides and fell onto the street but underneath I was beyond embarrassed and I think she could tell.

Get pasta…she said backing in the direction of an art supply store. The kind that's curly! We'll have pesto!

Then she turned around and walked into a trash can. Kicked it as if it had planted itself in front of her on purpose. I waved goodbye and walked to Balducci's, bought the pasta and some fresh fruit. On the way home I pretended I'd gotten my Masters and practised saying: Yes…I will marry you. Yes.

By the time I opened the door to the loft we'd been married and divorced about five times and my stomach was rumbling like acid in an earthquake. I put the groceries on the counter, turned in a circle and opened the mail. I knew Nancy was in the mood to light candles, put on Holly Near and fantasize about our future. It's her way of making sure she's making good on her "investment." It's not like I'm going to go back on my word. I mean, if I knew I was going to do that—

Dear Molly,
Pop gave me your book for my birthday. I've been learning about Italy in school. I got an A on my paper. It was really good. Next week I learn about The Forbidden City.
    Love, Ethan.

Mol,
Am proud and happy for you. Ever, J.

I stared at the word Ever, folded the letter quickly and put it in my purse. It's been almost a year since I tried to write J. the truth about the frozen baby. I thought since I never actually sent him any letter whatsoever that he'd pushed all thoughts of me from his mind. I was definitely not prepared for the elusive breeze of admiration.

                                    Martina Wins Wimbledon!
Have been reading in Mirya's salon once a month now that I have all this material from Creative Writing. My teacher says it's good to have a place to workout. I guess he's right because that's the only reason I do it.

Arthur has an idea for a performance piece. Wants to do it at PS122 when Nancy's collages are finished. Wants me to write something abstract about body parts. The operative word is Androgynous. I said I didn't know. I have a test coming up. He got all fluttery. I told him I'd do it but it all feels so irrelevant.

Whenever

Big lecture in the little auditorium at school about acid rain. How it works. What we can do about it. Stopped by on a whim…in case J. was one of the speakers. He wasn't. Still fantasize about answering Ethan's note and putting something cryptic in it to J. Can't quite bring myself to sit down and do it, though. Maybe it's just as well.

P.S.: Arthur's roommate, Louis, got pneumonia and died…just like that. Nobody quite knows why. He was only thirty-six.

Second Semester

Cut my courses in half this semester so it will take me three years instead of two. Of course, I had to run my new time frame by Nancy now that I'm BEHOLDEN. But I figured out how to put it. Said reading in Mirya's salon, working on the performance piece with Arthur and being a part of the new book, or whateveritis, was too much if I was going to carry a full load. Underneath I was hoping to avoid a scene. And underneath that I was swimming in my own disgust. I worry I'm taking advantage of Nancy. I worry I'm becoming as manipulative as Matilda and as elusive as Johnson. Today I bought myself another year and, while she felt distanced from the possibility of our marriage, I felt uplifted.

March, 1983

President Reagan proposes building a nuclear shield that will protect the U.S. from Soviet missiles and I finally catch up with 'E.T.' No wonder E.T. wants to go home! I think we'd all like to join him. Jesus, god…how can Reagan stand in front of a million people and keep a straight face?

June, 1983
Sally Ride Becomes the
First Woman in Space!

Dear Johnson,

Got on the crosstown bus. Was reading the headline of somebody else's newspaper which is generally how I get my news, these days. Anyway, the page was turned and folded back and back again...and there was an article about the EPA scandal and another salient blunder by James Watt...and underneath it all, an interview with you. I craned my neck. Read most of it...until the guy whose shoulder I was reading over got annoyed. I wanted to explain...but didn't. You know, the New York public transportation thing... nobody is really here except for me. Anyway, it made me think of you even more than I still do. Glad to hear you're still making a difference. I'm very proud of you, too.

I am finally getting my MA in Social Work. Nancy made a deal with me. Said she'd put me through graduate school if I'd take Creative Writing. It's fun and it's certainly helpful to have verbal skills but the course that's the most interesting is ESL (English as a Second Language). The teacher believes learning is the most effective when it's experiential. He is teaching us Spanish the way he would teach English to a foreigner. Plus he's teaching us how to teach. It's like getting two classes for the price of one. Anyway, I just thought I'd write. I think about you a lot. I was worried I'd lost you when I didn't answer your letter. I hope you know I have taken and continue to take all my actions to heart.

Please tell Ethan I loved getting his note. I kept it in my purse for a long time, but today I tucked it safely into my journal.

My love to you both...and to the farm, the garden, the birds....
Molly.

Sept., 1983

Nancy and I performed at PS122 tonight. N. moved and I read a piece I'd written in class about a woman's struggle to become friends with her ex-husband. I wrote it from her body's point of view. I thought it was relevant. Went with the collages of blurring arms and torsos. But when we were taking our bows N. gave me The Look.

You've been meeting secretly!...she said, throwing the contents of her dressing table into a shopping bag.

Right...I said...I'm like this totally out there dyke and he's this highly respected public figure. Why don't we get back together so he can run for public office?

A steam pipe hissed.

You're not a dyke…said Nancy, banging the steampipe with a hammer. You don't have the guts to be a dyke!

If I can't write about what's on my mind—

You can write about whatever you want to write about. I don't want to dance interpretively to it, that's all.

I was taking a risk. You always say I never risk!

I don't care what I say! Why do you always have to do what I say? Whatever happened to original thought?

What do you WANT? What the fuck do you WANT???

No! What do you want?

I opened my bag and located a jar of face cream.

Johnson is a part of me…I said deliberately. I wouldn't be who I am if it weren't for what he gave me. Maybe it wasn't right or what I needed, but, at the time it was my life. I'm not ashamed of that life. I'm pissed and hurt. But I'm not ashamed.

Be careful, Sweetheart…said Nancy. I'm a woman. I know where you live.

A chill went through me. I undid Nancy's jar of face cream.

I'm not seeing Johnson…I said lathering it on. I wrote him a lousy letter. If you're going to make it a federal offense—

I don't know who you are anymore. I really don't.

I grabbed the Kleenex and wiped my face.

Let's…you know…because maybe this isn't just about me. Or Johnson. Maybe it's also about the stuff with your eyes. I mean, when you took the red chiffon and started running into walls…I wasn't sure if it was for real or—

I made an appointment with the eye doctor…she said grabbing the face cream.

Thanks…I said turning on the water in the sink.

I'm going blind…she said digging her hand into the jar. We might as well admit it.

I put my fingers under the spigot and watched them waiting for the water to become warm. I watched them take hold of Meimei's feet and change Ethan's diaper. Then I watched them hand Nancy a white cane and patiently lead her across the street. Quanah smiled his know-it-all smile. I soaped up my washcloth. My inner life was a dusty mantra of stale, predictable images. I straightened up slowly. I caught Nancy's eyes in the mirror. They pleaded for forgiveness.

Don't worry...I said washing my face...whatever the doctor says about your eyes, I'm not going anywhere.

Promise?...asked Nancy as I took a towel off the back of my chair.

Promise...I mumbled into the terrycloth.

Knock, knock, knock.

God...said one of Nancy's admirers bursting into the room. You guys...too much! Wow. Wow! Really out there.

I stood alone in the dressing room as Nancy and her friends headed down the dusty, lopsided staircase.

So, shall we go for margaritas?...asked Nancy's admirer loud enough for me to hear.

I hooked my fannypack around my hips and rearranged my sweatshirt.

A door slammed in the distance. I stood on the landing and stared down the stairs. The frozen baby opened its arms and shattered into a blinding stillness.

Oh, great...I muttered and ran down the staircase.

A taxi honked as I crossed in front of it.

I'm sorry I'm late...I said pulling out my chair at the table. I thought I'd forgotten something.

You want a margarita or a seltzer? You never know with her...said Nancy wrapping her foot around mine under the table.

Margarita! I said with the appropriate amount of gaiety.

Nancy's hand found my knee. I slipped my hand underneath her fingers and sipped my margarita as a gray wind blew my heart into a distant Nothing.

Tuesday

Nancy left this morning for a few days to shoot someone in the Bahamas. Can't get my fight with her out of my mind. No matter what I say about J. she's convinced we're seeing each other. I would like to know when since all I do is study and worry about not upsetting her.

Friday

Met J. at the Souen in SoHo for brown rice and sake. We were both pretty nervous. Lots of looking out the window and twisting the paper from the chopsticks into little balls.

You look good…I said flushing with the prospect of reconnecting.

Same old same old.

Maybe this was a mistake.

No…he said reaching for my hand. I…I don't know what you want, that's all.

Why do I have to want something?

Women usually do.

I shouldn't've written…I said getting up. I thought maybe we could—

I'm new at this…he said reaching for my hand and ending up with my fannypack.

At what?…I asked as he took his hand away.

Talk…he said motioning me to return to my seat.

I pulled out my chair and sat sideways. I would tell him about the frozen baby. I would blast it out and watch his face turn red and fall. He cleared his throat and looked at his menu.

So how's Elizabeth?…I asked straightening myself around.

She arranged the interview with the Times…he said. When James Watt dismissed The Audubon Society as a "chanting mob"—

I mean, is she living on the farm?

He ordered something with burdock and I stuck to the black bean soup.

No…he said…but she comes over.

So are you going to get married?

He shrugged.

Or are you still trying to figure out if you love her, too?

Like Pavlov's Dog…he said…right to the point.

Congratulate me…I said…I have finally left being a lady to my mother.

He let his palm fall upward in the center of the table.

I'm sorry about your family.

I'm not…I said with a cultivated shrug. It woke me up. I mean, I used to think I could put whatever I wanted behind me.

Time...you know...the Family Therapist. But some things need to be—

Mol...he said...I don't know how to give you what you need. I never have.

But what do I need that's so frightening?

Approval. Closure. I don't know. Love!

You know how to love. You love all the time. It's just the way I ask for it...like I'm afraid you'll throw me off your lap.

A couple sat down at the table beside us.

All my stuff with Matilda...I said lowering my voice...mind you, she can still go fuck herself...but just so you know I know she was everything I was afraid of becoming. Sometimes I think that's why I went toward Nancy...to make Matilda human. But everything's reversing itself. Now I'm the one who's making excuses and being elusive and noncommittal and Nancy's the one who needs constant reassurance.

Johnson cleared his throat and squeezed the lemon that was already in his water glass. Then he sighed and looked at me his eyes soft with confusion.

Johnse, I didn't call you because I had hopes we'd get back together. I called because I wanted you to know...to know...I mean, even if we never see each other again...well, that I am who I am because.... I spent an important part of my life with you and I just want you to know that when I think about you.... I just want you to know...I don't hate your guts. I feel sad and sorry...but mostly, I feel lucky. I will always feel lucky. Very, very lucky.

The waiter lowered our food.

Well...he said...ditto. Ditto, ditto, ditto.

It's okay...you can say it...I won't hold you to it.

He laughed a laugh from our early days. Open. Shy. Full of promise.

Things got fucked up because.... I mean, people change but why does that mean we can't be friends? Something drew us together to begin with. Even in our worst moments we've always cared about each other. I know it isn't Mysterious or Romantic... but it's the glue. It makes the long haul...possible. Am I talking too much?

No...he said, looking in his lap...you're just being yourself.

Friday Night—late

Told Nancy I had lunch with Johnson. She thinks we should go into couple's therapy (she and I). I told her the reason I met with J. was to begin to understand myself in relationship to intimacy. I said I'd been drawn to him originally because he was infinitely more frightened of marriage than I was which meant I got to turn him into the one with all the problems while ignoring my own. And I got to do it all in the name of Unconditional Love. But recently, I said, the scales have been falling from my eyes. Especially when I feel myself treating Nancy the way J. used to treat me. Acting out his ambivalence on her. I said I want to stop doing that and I thought returning to the source might be the most effective (and responsible) way to resolve all the stuff J. and I left hanging. I told Nancy I don't want to be ambivalent or elusive anymore. That it's disrespectful and she's going to have to trust me with J. the way I trust her with Gillian. Finally I said I was doing it for US…so when I'm through with school I can go toward our marriage with a willing heart. And I meant it when I said it…every single word. That's the scary part.

Monday

Nancy's paranoia about how I spend my time when I'm away from her has been aggravated by her cataracts and my anxiety that I will get stuck taking care of her before I've even had a chance to finish school. Today her doctor said he didn't want to operate until her cataracts have ripened sufficiently which could mean another six months to a year.

Arthur hasn't been returning our phone calls. N. is worried his HIV test came back positive.

Refuge

As Nancy's eyesight dwindles and my studies increase, the work that has become our bond comes to a fragmented halt. When I try to help N. pushes me away. When I don't, she calls me insensitive. Plus she's always home. And there are no walls! Nowhere to go to get away except the darkroom which is rapidly becoming the symbol of a former life. Today I crammed an armchair through the door, turned on the light and took refuge in the Laws of Immigration. Or, tried to, anyway. But I kept hearing N. last night in the dark lying on that awful, motorized bed…awake…saying, apropos of yet another conversation about J. that I am using her sexually to liberate myself so I can go back to J. a full-blooded woman. Jesus, it's not like J. and I are sleeping together…alright…maybe we've talked about it but it's not like we're actually DOING it. It's more like the early years in my apartment. God! Lesbian love…there is no fucking SPAAAAAACE!

1984

Walked Johnson to Penn Station and watched his long fingers reach into his battered wallet for a hard-earned twenty. Earlier in the park we'd discussed letting go. Johnson said it was hard for him as it involved forgiving himself for the way he'd treated me and he didn't know if he'd ever be able to do that. More and more I'm getting ready to tell him about the frozen baby. I am convinced it's the only thing standing between us and a new, deeper friendship. It's only a question of finding the right time. I've decided to wait until…. Because right now we are so newly present with each other…. Anyway, we wandered slowly to Penn Station. When we got to the track he turned around to say goodbye and I kissed him on the lips…not so much for what might have been but for who we are becoming. For the time and care we are taking. For the time, care and respect.

April, 1984
Columbia Presbyterian

Am waiting in Nancy's room for her right eye to be relieved of its cataract. It is a plain room. Soothing mint green walls and all the furniture is on wheels. N.'s been gone for at least an hour and her roommate for about 15 minutes. Keep thinking about J. and how brave he is being. How honest and articulate. I wish N. would die on the operating table. Isn't that terrible?

Winter

Hatia's been offered a job in Los Angeles buying and selling rare books. I don't think of rare books in Los Angeles…of books being rare, maybe…. Anyway (bad joke), as H. said, she could have overseen the opening of yet another Barnes & Noble, but this job spoke to her and, besides, she's had enough of winter.

Nancy's good eye is still good. She is restless for the surgery that will restore her right so when she looks into her portrait camera…well, she'll be able to focus the lens, for starters.

School is school. I read, I remember, I get tested. Y hablo español cada dia con el gente en la cocina. ESL is still a possibility. One more semester and I'm there.

Saturday

Hatia leaves in a week. Nancy's as sad as I am about her departure. Thinks we should throw her a big party. Invite that woman she had her eye on when we went to see 'Victor/Victoria' except no one can remember her name…including Hatia.

Monday

Don't know what I'll do without Hatia to talk to. Especially if Nancy starts ragging me about bisexuality and how it's not a sexual orientation but an excuse to remain undecided. At least Hatia is compassionate and open-minded. When I first told her about Nancy, she said I should take my time. That when the excitement was over I'd know if I was straight or gay or something in between. Plus I can talk to Hatia about the frozen baby and, for that matter, J….and even though she thinks I'm nuts, she doesn't look at me like I'm crazy.

Oh, God Help Me!

Went shopping for groceries. Nancy was putting the loft in order for Hatia's farewell party. She (Nancy) claimed she was wrestling the arm chair out of the darkroom when my journal fell from under the cushion and opened to the following (see folded down page):

J. and I had an unnerving conversation at lunch today about abortion. I decided to bring up the subject to see if he still stood where I thought he stood. He's not quite as adamant or sentimental or whateveritis…at least not when it comes to women who are raped or fetuses that have health problems…but I said: What if a woman is still trying to find out who she is? He said, under those circumstances, abortion is the ultimate act of selfishness and that he has no patience with women who waste unborn lives while trying to find their own. I said I didn't think it was up to us to place a value on the journey of a soul by determining that its birth is more valuable than its…well, nonbirth. I reminded J. of what he'd said years ago…that children are our teachers and that maybe the lessons they teach are as profound when they don't come into the world as when they do. Then we walked in silence to the train station…each one considering the other's point of view. Neither one pushing the other to back down or change. When we got to the ticket window J. opened his wallet and got out his trainfare.

I miss you…he said after a moment. I miss you a lot.

Johnson…I said…there's something I have to—

Last call for Philadelphia…squawked the loudspeaker.

Whoops…said Johnson…I had no idea it was so late.

And as he came toward me…his arms open…I took his face in my hands and kissed him. Not hard or anything…but we both sort of didn't know what to do for a moment. Then he turned to go. I lowered my eyes. And just as suddenly as he'd turned away he turned back. Grabbed me around the waist and planted his heart and soul on my lips. Needless to say, he missed his train. And the train after that and the frozen baby took a backseat to the most unexpected display of passion in a nearby hotel.

When I got home I jumped in the shower. I was singing away when N. walked in and asked me what I thought of having our wedding at PS122 on a dark night instead of in the gallery. That way we could invite more people.

What?…I said sticking my head out…and there she stood holding the big towel clearly intending to dry me off.

I couldn't exactly say No. Tomorrow she goes into the hospital to have her "other eye taken out" (her words). So there I was only hours later making love to Nancy. She couldn't tell about Johnson. I don't think she could tell. I mean, she couldn't see my face. Or if she could it was mostly blurry.

Later…in the darkroom

Can't quit thinking about J. Hope he can't quit thinking about me. Have finally succeeded in becoming the manipulative, selfish, heartless, aggressive, evil, two-faced woman-bitch-person I always knew I was. Yes, finally…YES!!!

Dog Meat

When I returned with the groceries, the darkroom door was open, the armchair had been returned to its spot by the footstool, my journal was prominently placed on the end table and Nancy's mood was noticeably altered. During Hatia's party I decided it was best not to look at her (Nancy)...choosing instead to dig my heels into the safety net of cheerfulness and raise my champagne glass toward Hatia.

To the rarest book I've ever opened!...I said in a booming voice. Whoops...that doesn't sound right!

A couple of people laughed. Nancy grunted and returned to the kitchen. As soon as I could get away I came up behind her at the sink.

Keep your hands to yourself...she muttered.

What did I do?

Nancy gripped the edge of the sink.

Just get out. Just get the fuck out.

Nance...

You put me through a whole diatribe about Jealousy and how I shouldn't be. I should just trust you, right?

Nance, Johnson and I are trying to understand what we did to each other so we don't—

Don't you dare give me that SHIT about Unfinished Business!

But he's not in love with me. He's in love with Elizabeth.

Need any help?...asked one of our guests.

I grabbed a plate of stuffed mushrooms and handed it to her with considerable force. She backed away as Nancy's eyes formed into nasty slits.

On the day before my fucking surgery!...she hissed.

We are in the middle of a party...I whispered rather urgently. If you are going to involve our private life in a public moment as if it is nothing more than a piece of Performance Art...then I will leave. I will leave right now and NEVER come back.

Do it, Baby...DO IT!!!

And one more thing...I am not your Baby. I never was your Baby and I don't want you to call me Baby until you can treat me like your equal. Got it?

Nancy grabbed a garbage bag and headed for the rack that held our clothes. I started after her.

What's going on?...asked Hatia putting a gentle hand on my shoulder.

She read my journal!

I READ YOUR JOURNAL?!!! I READ YOUR JOURNAL????? Is that what you think this is about? I read your FUCKING JOUR-NAL??????!

The room got suddenly quiet.

I said I would go if you did this...I warned putting on my fannypack...and I will.

Nancy picked up my journal.

Pick a page...she challenged wagging my innermost thoughts in the air.

I grabbed her camera, aimed and clicked.

Oh, you two...grow up!...muttered one of our guests as Nancy closed her eyes and pointed to a paragraph.

'I used to think men were assholes'...she read in a mocking tone. 'It was a convenient thought form that allowed me to remain helpless and enraged and that, in turn, automatically excused me from taking any responsibility for my own thoughts and feelings. But yesterday when Johnson...'

The way she said his name.... She sunk her teeth into it as if he were a piece of shit. I threw her camera to the floor. Nancy looked at it, concerned. I raised my foot as if I were going to step on the lens. Nancy grabbed a handful of pages and ripped them from my journal. I lunged at her, knocked her to the ground and stepped on her glasses. At first by accident...then on purpose. I sat on top of her and reached for my journal knocking over a bowl of guacamole. Nancy pulled my hair. I slapped her face. Shortly after I bit her arm, Gillian had me upright. I wiped what I could of the guacamole off my clothes, grabbed my fannypack and headed for the door.

Coward...Nancy taunted.

Let her go...said Gillian...let her go.

Hatia followed me into the hall.

Fuck her!...I said, throwing on my overcoat.

She's losing you, Molly.

She's not losing me...I'm changing. Why don't I ever have the right to change?

She's afraid. She can't see.

So what do I do? Give up my life one more time? For what? I don't love her. But every time I try to tell her she says I'm homophobic.

Hatia gave me a long, slow hug.

I'd offer you your place...she said pulling up my lapel...but there's nowhere to sleep until the movers come.

I'm okay...I said pushing the elevator button and tying a red cashmere scarf around my throat.

The elevator rattled to a stop. I slid the battered door to one side and stepped in.

Let me know how you like Los Angeles...I said. Maybe when I'm through with school I'll come for a visit. Maybe I'll come to stay.

Mi casa es tu casa...said Hatia.

I put my hand on the lever and started to close the elevator door.

Tell her I'm sorry...I said through my teeth.

No, Girl...said Hatia...you tell her.

I just mean...about her glasses.

Hatia shook her head No as I closed the door and rattled to street level.

Fuck her glasses...I muttered as I put on my mittens and hit the cold night air. And fuck her camera.

Instinctively, I headed north...taking the darkest streets...praying someone would mug me and that I would die instantly. Occasionally I wondered who I could call. All my friends were Nancy's and, for the most part, were at the party undoubtedly reassuring her it was time she got rid of me. I would call home. Tell Mother and Father their worst fears were finally over. They would ask me to get on the train, come for the night, sleep in my old bed...and my mother would brush the day from my forehead and call me Darling...

At 38th Street my hands were shaking uncontrollably. I stopped in a deli, bought a cup of coffee, this composition book and pen. I had to find some place to write or the cacophony that was making mincemeat of my brain would drive me to irreversible acts. I remembered there was an all-night diner at the corner of.... Yes, and there was also an all-night diner not far from the farm. I would go there. I would miss my psych final.... Fuck it! I didn't want Nancy's greasy money sliding down my future. I was through being

beholden. I would stand tall and call Johnson around seven...
maybe he'd meet me for breakfast.

Philadelphia scrapple and applesauce...I thought as I got on
the train. Would go nicely with dried guacamole and a frozen baby.

Don't know where
I took a seat by the window, handed the conductor my ticket and
wrote until the train lulled me into a deep and disjointed sleep.
When I came to I had missed my stop. I'm not sure I'm even in
Pennsylvania.

The Next Day
Arrived at the diner around 11 A.M. and headed straight for the pay
phone. J. wasn't home and I felt weird about calling him at work. I
decided to wait. Got in a cab and told the driver to take me to the
farm. Knocked on the front door, just in case. Turned the handle.
Locked. We always used to leave it open. Looked through the window. Saw a rather large pair of high tops in the middle of the floor.
Ethan has to be about fifteen (argh)! Sat on the porch swing.
Wrapped my coat tighter and rehearsed my speech about the frozen
baby. Took off my mittens. Put my fingers in my mouth. It was a
mistake to have come. Got up quickly and headed for the chicken
coop. Locked, too. Looked through the window. Either Ethan is living there or Johnson has taken in a very messy boarder. Wandered
into the barn. The cinderblock shelves from our bedroom had been
reconfigured and one corner of the barn was being used for storage.
Ethan's school books. A broken bowl. A kitchen chair. The trunk
that I had left at the end of the futon. Opened it slowly. On the very
top was my bathrobe. Put it on over my coat and dug deeper.
Meimei's ashes. Johnson's gun. Ethan's toys. A copy of our poem
about the Chinese moon. The watercolor of the red elephant that
used to be on the refrigerator. Legos. Fingerpaintings. A
blanket...yes! I unfolded it quickly. Something fell out. Two picture
frames held, face to face, by rubber bands. Pulled them apart as far
as the rubber bands would allow. Ethan's picture of Matilda.
Johnson's picture of me. Considered separating us then bravely decided to leave us as we were, face to face in a moth-eaten steamer.
Put the blanket over my bathrobe and headed for the clearing in the

woods. Ran, actually…tripped over a root and fell in front of a big pit with lots of rocks in it. Or not rocks…more like lava. Looked up. On the other side of the pit was a sweat lodge. Sat up. It was exactly as Ethan had described it to Meimei all those years ago. A sudden rush of warm blood rose to my cheeks. I crawled inside. Found myself in the dark on something soft. Pulled part of it over me, revised my frozen baby speech and fell into a heavy sleep. When I woke up, a flashlight was flashing near the opening. Johnson lifted the flap and stuck his head in the sweat lodge.

Molly?…he said softly.

I'm sorry…I said. I shouldn't have come.

Don't be silly…he said putting the flashlight on the ground and crawling toward me. Are you alright?

I was kicked out.

Whoops.

At least I could trust you with my journals.

Ouch.

Johnson, what I'm about to say…I want you to promise you won't hate me. I'm sorry…it's just…I mean…

What is it?

Uh…is there a whole group coming over to sweat or what?

No…just family.

Elizabeth?

Pop!…phoooooone!…called a rather low voice from somewhere near the house.

Johnson repositioned the flashlight and stuck his head outside. Coming!

I better be going…I said crawling toward the entry.

No, wait…said Johnson…tell me.

I just…because I should have told you years ago…but…. And this whole time we've been seeing each other…. Because I was young. I wanted to live a useful life…so when I got pregnant behind the barn…. And bruised Ethan's arm…I was afraid I wasn't ready. Afraid I'd take my dissatisfaction out on…our…uh, child…so…what I said, you know, about a miscarriage…

Pop…said the low voice as a portable phone was thrust through the opening…I need to use it. Could you be quick?

Yes, Sir Captain Sir…said Johnson turning his attention toward the phone.

Hello? Hi. Yes. Alright.... No, that's fine, fine. A man's night in the lodge. I'm fine. Are you fine? That's fine. I'm sitting down...I'm in the sweat lodge...I don't have much of a choice. Uh huh. Uh huh...I see. Is that right. What do you want me to say? Can we talk later?...Ethan needs the phone. Then after the Prayer Round. The morning's fine, too. I'll be here all day.

He pushed the off button, returned the phone to Ethan's impatient hand and we waited quietly as Ethan disappeared in the direction of the house.

Boy...said Johnson...some days you wish you'd never been born.

I'm sorry...I said softly. I was going to tell you the truth...then you asked me to marry you and I...I was afraid if you knew what I'd done...Johnse...if I had to do it over...I wouldn't act alone.

Thud. Thud. Thud.

How many rocks, Dad?

Ethan...said Johnson sticking his head out. Come here for a minute. There's someone here who loves you very much...

Oh, god, Johnson...not today!

Ethan got down on his knees and stuck his head in the sweat lodge. His features...what I could see of them were nicely chiseled and there was even evidence of hair on his upper lip.

It's Molly...I said...on a very bad day.

Oh, yeah? What are you doing here?

Or maybe the real question is...why did I ever leave?

I'll light the fire...said Johnson clearing the path between us.

Is Elizabeth coming or is it just us?...asked Ethan.

Just us.

When the rocks were heated Ethan shoveled them into a pit inside the sweat lodge and we took our clothes off and sat crosslegged in the clear, black of winter, rivulets trickling down the softness of familiar bodies. After a silence we started the Prayer Round. First we prayed out loud for others. Then we prayed out loud for ourselves. Then we prayed in silence for whatever we wanted. In between we floated through the dark...tender, disembodied voices reaching from the past into the future through the present.

When we were toweling off in the moonlight, Johnson offered

me a bed for the night. I thought of midterms, asked him to take me to the train and let him know I was giving up Nancy but not my degree. He seemed somewhat relieved. We stood in silence on the platform.

Ethan is a good kid...I said quietly then rested my hand on the small of his back. You should be proud.

I've had a lot of help...he said moving away.

Are you okay?

Fine...he said as the train announced its arrival in the station.

I'll call you...I said...when I know what I'm doing.

You better not...he said as the train pulled alongside the platform.

Johnson, don't cut me off, please. I was young. I was scared.

It isn't you. It's Elizabeth.

Elizabeth? But you don't love Elizabeth anymore than I love Nancy.

Sometimes love...

Johnson...it matters. Love matters. Look how far we've come. Both of us struggling to reconnect and we're doing it. We're really doing it.

Mol...he interrupted...you know how you don't want to be saved?

All aboard!

I'll call you tomorrow at your office...I said.

Not tomorrow...he said as I boarded the train.

Then Thursday for lunch.

I can't, Mol...she's pregnant.

Pregnant? Whose pregnant?

Elizabeth.

Elizabeth?

I grabbed onto a pole as the doors closed and the train pulled me from the lap of renewal into the black heart of the big sadness.

Now or Never

It was all I could do to pick up this pen. All I could do to open this composition book and begin in some garbage-y way to vomit forth the total blackness I've been living in...the word Pregnant driving me into the depths of this past-life apartment. I have no idea how long I've been here. No idea what time it is, what day it is or what month. I have driven myself, fully clothed, into the same old bed, between the same old sheets where it all fucking started…punishing myself for committing the sin of Having Expectations. Why didn't I leave well enough alone? What the fuck was I hoping for? Some fucked-up idea about reconciliation? Some desperate fantasy that the frozen baby would set me free? Free to do what? Something USEFUL? Whateverthefuck that means. God!…I can't believe the bullshit I have fed myself on a daily basis as if it were *pate de foie gras*…which I don't even eat let alone LIKE. Something, anything…HEEEEEEEEEEELP!!!

Sometime Later

I think the heat's been turned off. I don't hear the radiator clanging and the tip of my nose is freezing. This might be easily remedied if I paid the rent which, for some reason, I am unable to do. Last night my landlord knocked on my door. I didn't answer. I meant to…then I realized it's been weeks since I've talked out loud. I didn't want to break my silence…not for my landlord. Then for whom? Johnson? Nancy? Which one will gallop up the front stairs on a white charger, break the door down and rescue me first, right? Especially since I've ripped the phone out of the wall. Somebody called…as soon as I got here…probably J. feeling GUILTY…and I looked at the beige princess ringing away…demanding to be dealt with…then ripped the cord out…just ripped it out and never looked back.

Uh oh…what do you know…the lights just went out. Lucky for me I was a partial hippy…all those big fat dusty candles.

Even Later Than That

I keep thinking I should write (by streetlight)…you know, How I Spent My Summer Vacation. A sort of report…an update…for the person who will cull through my journals when I'm old and wizened and dehydrating in the desert like Georgia O'Keefe. I should keep all interested parties informed and the details politely up to date as if somehow or other what I do minute to minute is actually important. These details are for you whoever you are. I couldn't…in all honesty give a shit about them…but, hey, if I don't keep writing this pen will turn into a flaming sword and only God knows where it will end up...so here goes:

I stood on the corner of 31st and Third in the rain and watched the movers take the last of Hatia's stuff. When her taxi had taken her in the direction of the airport...I made my way up the old familiar stairs. I turned my keys numbly in the lock. The apartment was gray and dingy like a broken cave (what a metaphor). Nothing was as I had left it and somehow or other it was all mine. Key pictures had disappeared from the walls. There were nail holes everywhere. Hatia was big on pictures. They protected us both from the reality of a paint job. I sat on the rollaway and looked out the grimy window into the airshaft and, even though I didn't think I was going to, burst into tears. I cried for the journey that had begun there. I cried for the twisted turns it had taken. For the times I had dared to hope and the times I had festered and loathed. I went into the kitchen. The window sill was thick with soot. The refrigerator was a festival of fingerprints. I cried for the last time I'd washed it. I stared at a stack of *New York Times*. I pulled out the want-ad section and half an hour later found myself staring at the garbage can. I cried for all the waste it collected. I went to the bathroom, sat on the toilet, opened my journal and cried for the crack in the tile.... I cried for how it got there. I cried for where it went. I cried for the mornings I lay in bed listening to Johnson wash his face. I cried for the nights I listened to Nancy wash hers. I cried for my love of crying. I cried for my family's love of not crying. I cried for Johnson's fear of Intimacy. I cried for Nancy's love of Drama. I cried for my love of Drama. I took a deep breath and hurled myself in the direction of the bedroom. The bed was made with the same old sheets. Jungle animals. (Let's pause and milk the significance.) I dropped my compostion book on the neighboring pillow, hung up my coat, took off my shoes and got into bed in everything else I was wearing. I see the fact that my hands are turning white and my fingers can barely make sense of the alphabet as part of an extraordinary opportunity to open to the cold which is my mission for tonight since I have no idea where the matches are to light those ugly, fat, orange and yellow striped candles.

Chapter Twelve

Molly sees her body rocking in the warmth of her bed and as the last moments of recorded history fall through her endangered spirit, her upstairs neighbor groans and lets out a long, liberating sigh. Then all is silent. So silent Molly can see her body breathing. And she knows if she keeps moving away from it her breath will come to an absolute stop. And as the edges of her spirit begin to flutter, she tumbles from the nagging jaw of memory into the freedom of thin air. She hovers for a moment over the thickness of her nose and the bags under her eyes. Then she floats up...up...toward the ceiling, through the void and into the giant rage that spits fire. She burns and thrashes and when she is nothing more than a wisp of ash, a shadow (half-rat half-human) grabs her by the throat and pins her like a butterfly to the deadly gray of her own despair.

"Should, should, could, should, would, should, could, should... should, should, should."

This is the Mantra Maker. The Matilda-hating, Nancy-maker that thrives on the fear that rots in the secret place at the center of Molly's soul. This is the beast she forged in the chaos and buried in theories about Children, Marriage, Love, Communication, Destiny and the New Age. This is the face that has stolen her eyes and dragged them into the shadows of everyone else's fault. This is the broken biology that stuck its mantra in the hole in her belly, devoured her womanhood and sucked the marrow from her broken bones. This is everything she is not supposed to feel. This is everywhere she is not supposed to go.

The Rat Man hisses and changes its shape...smoking its way through twisted combinations of Johnson, Ethan, Nancy, Heather, Timmy...folding them into and onto and through...Conrad, Gillian, Hatia, Annie, Meimei...dazzling Molly with the evil accuracy of its wit and the truth of its twisted perceptions. And as her spirit cries out in horror, her soul, guided by everything it has come to know, takes hold of the Rat Man's feet and turns into the Wall of Sorrow. And as a tidal wave bashes Molly's spirit against the fearsome bottom of all she has ever been and never known, she opens her chest and folds the Rat Man into her heart...and when the force has subsided, finds herself in the loving arms of the Holy Nothing.

It is a while before her brain becomes aware of her reentry. It is a while before it cranks up the chatter. It is a while before her thumb finds her lips and her legs curl against her heart. It is a while before Johnson and Nancy bend over her the way her mother and father used to bend over Timmy. It is a while before they vanish only to reappear. To ooooo and ahhhh and admire her innocence. Over and over they come and go, gentle ripples in the jungle of longing. It is a while before a tear rolls from Molly's eye and lands on the color purple. It is a while before she picks an unopened envelope off the floor and pulls it into her bed.

DAVIS T. WARREN

August, 1969

Dear Molly,

I don't know how or where to begin. I have been torn between two worlds for as long as I can remember. I am only sorry they had to collide in a restaurant. How often I have begun to tell you. How often I have fled from the brink, frightened by the loss of you and a very real part of myself. I do hope you will find it in your heart to forgive me. I also hope you will call and that we can talk.

Your great friend and loyal admirer,
Davis.

1987

Dear Davis,

I'm sorry it's taken me so long to write. I met a man. I met a woman. I never had kids. I thought if I lived a conscious life I'd become a better person. I guess I'm only human. How about you?

Love, Molly

Chapter Thirteen

Davis comes to his door in a smoking jacket. He is thin and his hair is gray but his eyes still sparkle with curiosity and his lips still curl in mischief around his wit.

"I meant to straighten up," he says, waving a hand in the direction of the living room.

Molly steps across the threshold of the apartment. The air still smells of lavender and furniture polish. The walls are still hunter green. Still loaded with artwork. The couch has been recovered, though, and there is a computer, restless with potential, on the buffet. Davis takes a mohair throw off an overstuffed armchair and motions Molly to sit. Molly looks at the floor. At polished pine and frayed Oriental rugs and quietly hopes when she looks up again she will see the man she remembers.

"I know," says Davis, "I look like shit. I should have warned you."

"It's okay," says Molly, "I'm not exactly Miss America."

And together they smile and absorb the ravages of middle age.

"I see you've got a computer...says Molly, shyly. "Nancy was going to buy me one but...well...."

"Richard's," says Davis. "He said it was important to keep up. I said it was important to stay stuffy and entrenched. He won." Davis lowers his voice and, in a conspiratorial tone adds, "I liked to let him."

Molly's laugh is short and knowing and tumbles Davis silent as a feather into his newly altered world.

"Lapsang Suchong?" he says after a moment.

"What? Sure. I guess."

"Tea. Caffeine."

"You don't have to. I'm fine. Really."

Molly puts her purse on a mahogany end table and knocks over a silver framed photograph of a beautiful, tan, blond man with high cheekbones.

"Richard?"

"Early on," says Davis. "When you and I were in the throws."

"So you stayed together."

Davis nods his head, sighs silently then straightens the lace antimacassar on the arm of his chair.

"I never meant to hurt you," he says pushing back his cuticles. "I just didn't know how to tell you. I didn't know how to tell myself. It wasn't until I met Richard that I knew for certain."

"I know. I didn't then. Know. But I do now. Believe me."

Davis stands the photo upright, moves some prescription drugs to one side and pushes the plate of cookies in Molly's direction.

"Mmmmm," she says taking one, "Chocolate chip with orange rind. I used to make these for Ethan and tell him all about you. How you made a fortune playing the stock market and listened to Gregorian chants."

Davis laughs gently and reties the sash of his smoking jacket.

"So, this Johnson…did you love him?"

"I thought I did. But maybe I just loved our potential."

"You always were a romantic."

"I was?"

"I always thought that was why you fell for me," says Davis, helping himself to a cookie. "Not consciously. But you sensed a wall. And fell in love with the struggle to transform it. "

"Oh, my god," says Molly. "The Eastern Bloc. I never made the connection! I'm sorry. It's just…Walls. My parents. We aren't speaking."

"I'm sorry."

"It was time."

"Morning Thunder?"

"I'm fine…really."

"No caffeine."

"Only if you do."

Davis rises to his feet.

"Why don't I make it?" asks Molly.

"It's important to keep going," says Davis shuffling into the kitchen.

Molly gets up as Davis grabs an apron off the back of a chair, puts it over his head and smooths his fingers over hunter green lettering.

"The Leftover Queen," says Molly, reading his apron outloud.

"Oh," says Davis, "it started as a joke. We both loved to cook. Richard was the one who experimented. I was the one who made magic with leftovers."

Davis shuffles along his highly polished parquet floor, sidestepping the Orientals en route to the kitchen door. He swings it open with a sharp push. Tupperware is everywhere. Tupperware and styrofoam; huge pots and pans; an imposing pot rack, a dishwasher and two refrigerators.

"Good Lord!" says Molly. "This room's been remodeled."

"We were big on dinner parties. It was how we socialized. Then everyone started getting sick. So we started taking our dinner parties on the road."

Davis hands Molly a nicely printed menu.

"Richard used to make them up on the computer."

"Wow!"

"It was catching on…but when he died.…"

Molly turns the menu over in her hand. She can hear Davis deteriorating. Can feel the virus gnawing at his bones.

"So you and Nancy…what was that all about?" he asks.

"I don't know. Passion. Rebellion. Connection."

The Italian man in the graveyard offers Molly a rose. A child plucks it from Molly's memory and runs laughing into the shadows of the Rat Man's ruin.

"How about decaf cappuccino?" asks Davis as if he were about to do something naughty.

"How about caffeinated?" Molly counters as she circles the ruins.

Davis smiles and takes part of the espresso maker out of the dishdrainer.

"You always were a girl after my own heart."

Molly looks at a stack of bills marked "Richard." Davis was always meticulous about money. "Keep your mind open, your hands clean and trust your intuition," he would say. Then he'd tie his bathrobe a

*little tighter, put on something medieval and call his broker. Nothing
like a day in the office.*

"It must be incredible to have been with Richard for so many
years."

Davis pours the espresso beans into the coffee grinder.

"I mean...the companionship. The trust," *continues Molly.* "I always run and blame it on the other person."

*The coffee grinder turns the espresso beans to powder. Davis taps
it down and takes off the lid.*

"I fail to understand all the hoopla about coffee beans," *he says, as
the aroma makes its way up his nose.* "Which are water processed.
Which are <u>Swiss</u> water processed. We're all going to die anyway. Why
not get it over with pleasurably?"

*He opens the refrigerator closest to the sink. A curled photograph
slides, in spite of its magnet, down the refrigerator door and falls onto
the floor. Molly picks it up and finds herself looking at Richard's chiseled features as he sips champagne in a sea of flowers. An oxygen tube
is up his nose. Molly wonders if a tube is up Arthur's nose now, too.
Davis locates the half-and-half and closes the refrigerator door. Molly
hands him the snapshot.*

"AIDS?"

"What else?" *he says slipping the photo under another magnet.*

"Were you with him at the end?"

"Yes."

"Was it peaceful?"

"Suicide."

"God."

"Assisted."

"God."

*Davis pours some half-and-half in a pitcher and inserts the
steamer.*

"My turn next," *he says spooning the froth into oversized coffee
cups.*

"To do what...die or kill yourself?"

"It depends," *he says, putting the cappuccinos on a red laquered
tray.*

"I think we go on," *says Molly carefully as she opens the kitchen
door.*

"Oh," says Davis softly, "I hope so."

The cappuccino cups rattle on their saucers as Davis makes his way across the living room, the sweet smell of cinnamon penetrating lavender and furniture polish. Molly hadn't planned to share her out-of-the-body experience. It is so far from anything she's ever been through. She is afraid if she turns it into Talk it will disappear, distressed and dissected. But the combination of Davis's vulnerability and the caffeine shoot her good intentions all to hell. Her heart pounds as if each moment is her very last and, with great urgency, she tells Davis how she split in two. Looked down on herself from the ceiling. Saw herself as clearly as if she were looking in a mirror. And knew she had the power to go on. To Die. Deconstruct. But something in her wasn't finished. It was a surprisingly practical moment. No floating baby brothers. No tortured quotations about the Greater Good. Then, as quickly as she'd left, she'd reentered only to be thrown against the Wall of Sorrow. To wrestle with the Rat Man; to grab his feet and plunge him into what was left of her heart. She thinks for a moment and decides not to tell Davis about the child that has taken to playing in the aftermath. And she will definitely omit the part about sucking her thumb since she is, on occasion, still doing it. Instead, she asks Davis if he was ever sorry he never had kids. Davis flinches and moves a footstool under his leg.

"I had them," he says, "In other ways. I was a Big Brother. Worked with AIDS babies. We were going to take one in. Then Richard was diagnosed."

Davis massages his ankle and lets his slipper fall to the floor. KS has claimed part of his ankle and runs in a long nasty ribbon up the lower portion of his leg.

"Too much death," he says then winces again and before Molly knows it she is on her knees in front of him, his swollen foot between her fingers.

"Let me know if this hurts."

"It looks worse than it is," says Davis as his head falls back against his armchair.

Molly cups her hands around his heel and pulls gently.

"Your hands," he mutters, "are so warm."

On the way home, Molly passes a supermarket. A child skips ahead of her, slips through the automatic door and heads for the frozen food section. Molly follows, picks up a package of peas and waits in a cloud of subzero air for her hands to turn white. Nothing happens. She picks up another package. And another and another and another.

"May I help you?"

A young man in a red vest stands before her. Molly stares at his name tag. Sees the word Manager.

"I…uh…it's a long story. Hands. Walls. Children. Choice."

"That'll be $12.74. The White Rose, however, are on special."

When Molly returns home, she puts the peas in her freezer, pays the rest of her bills, jettisons the moldy take-out and opens Hatia's present. Please, God, not another journal. Oh, good. Letter paper. Thick. Creamy. Classy without being ostentatious. And a postcard of two girls with their arms around each other and on the backside of the card the word Write!

Molly picks up the phone. Actually gets a dialtone. Leaves a thank-you-for-the-stationery-which-I-finally-opened message on Hatia's machine then bites the bullet and calls Nancy. Leaves a time-to-return-my-key-and-pick-up-my-clothes message on hers.

Two days later, Molly opens the door to the loft and finds everything she owns in black, plastic garbage bags slumping like lost children against the kitchen counter. Her mail has been tossed into a mixing bowl. A check is on top along with a note: Please give Adella in the royalty office your new address and tell the P.O. to forward your mail ASAP!

Molly is not surprised that Nancy has chosen to be absent when she returns to deal with the remains. She can see evidence of breakfast for two and smell the honeysuckle of a new woman. Molly's heart twists then jumps, glad that friendship is out of the question. At least for the moment. She picks up her mail and stuffs it in her handbag. She has loved the loft. The tall gray windows. The tin ceiling. The wide open walls. The richness of color and texture and the ever-changing world of Nancy's art. She won't miss the toilet closet in the hall, though. Or the chaos of creation that floods every available surface with found objects, hot glue, magazine clippings, cordless drills, fabric, newspapers, ribbon, driftwood and photographs. She looks at her abandoned schoolbooks and wonders if she'll ever get her infamous degree.

When she returns to 31st Street, she throws her belongings into the center of her living room and is seized with the urge to peel the paint off the wall by the radiator. The next day she gives the garbage bags and anything else that annoys her to her neighborhood thrift store then calls the Salvation Army and surrenders the rollaway. And as the movers carry it down the stairs, Molly stands on the threshold of her naked apartment and turns forty.

To celebrate, Davis opens a bottle of his finest champagne and together Molly and Davis invent a lemony chicken-rice and mostly pea soup. Succulent, saltless and savory. On her way home, Molly delivers a container to one of Davis's friends. Inside of a week, Molly and Davis are cooking together. And by the end of the month the Leftover Queen is back in business.

Chapter Fourteen

March, 1988

Dear Nancy,

This is the first of several payments I'm planning to send you to reimburse you for my education. I have a job. Not anything I ever thought I'd be doing…but I am finally feeling useful. And, strangely enough, it's thanks to Davis. He and his longtime lover started a gourmet meals-on-wheels type thing for people with AIDS. The Leftover Queen. Maybe you've heard of it. We recently moved into the basement of a church in the village, enlisted two more cooks, a dishwasher and an endless array of volunteers to carry out deliveries. Anyway, it's a start. Hope you are well. Sorry to hear about Arthur. I called but I was too late. So be it. Love, M.

November, 1988

Dear Hatia,

They say be careful what you wish for! Lord! It's like all the years I sat around waiting for my life to happen to me…it's like I'm making up for them all at once! In addition to running the Leftover Queen, I'm also becoming a veteran of various doctors' offices, the emergency room at St. Vincent's Hospital and at least ten memorials. And, I have to say, all the MFAs in all the world could not have prepared me for the education that comes with life in the trenches.

Davis, more often than not, is my role model. In an effort to keep his illness at bay, he buries himself in the problems of his friends. Helps them decipher insurance policies; the uncertain wisdom of AZT; the politics of the FDA; Ronald Reagan, ACT UP…and who is Ed Koch, anyway? Together, we have witnessed acts of courage and kindness in the face of cruelty. Gone to clandestine meetings about black-market drugs; come face to face with quacks and saints; with compassion, dignity and tenderness in the hard, cold presence of cynicism and neglect.

Later

Dear Hatia, Cont.
I meant to send this to you last month but I haven't been able to find the time to sit down and finish it. Nancy still hasn't cashed my checks and Davis's KS has begun to spread.

Later Still

H., Promise to finish this letter tonight. When I'm not at the church or in a hospital, I'm making very pathetic stabs at remodeling my almost totally empty apartment. Am almost through scraping the living room walls. I probably shouldn't've gotten rid of as much as I did. Have sort of been living like a nun. My bed. My bathtowel. My pot. My plate. My chopsticks. God bless take-out! Shooting pains have begun to terrorize Davis's right leg and he still refuses to use a walker.

Still Later

KS has claimed the ball of Davis's left foot seriously jeopardizing his plan to "die in the act of making real key lime pie." His breathing has become labored. I am worried but prepared.

Later Than That

Good to talk to you last night. I'm still going to send this to you if, for no other reason than to let you know how much I love using the stationery you left in the refrigerator! Davis has switched doctors for the "the fourth and final time." When I question his motives, he says he's not going to let some asshole throw him in the hospital like a lab experiment. When I remind him he can't breathe he says, "This is my death and if I want to suffocate like Camille in splendid isolation then that's my right."

April

Dear Hatia...again,

Am sitting in the AIDS ward (please excuse the legal pad) waiting for someone to die so Davis can have a bed in an already over-crowded room. He fainted this morning in Jefferson's Market while standing in line for a barbecued free-range chicken and was taken to the emergency room at St. Vincent's. I found him on a gurney by the elevator talking to a disoriented teenager with hollow eyes and skin stretched against brittle bones.

"Finish this sentence," I said as soon as I saw Davis. "There are no—"

"Rooms at the inn," he said without skipping a groggy beat.

"Not funny," I said. "Not, not, not, not, not, not funny!"

Midnight

Davis finally got a room and I got a really uncomfortable orange armchair. Practically glows in the dark. Anyway, around 11 the night nurse showed up to introduce himself. Oliver something. Tall, good looking, early thirties. Exactly Davis's type. When I told him my name he said, "There's a Molly Williams who wrote a book about Tuscany." I kid you not! I was very non-commital. Said, "Oh, really?" Davis was the one who pointed the finger. Anyway, it turns out this Oliver person works with kids. Photography or video or something. He says he shows them Nancy's photographs before he even lets them look through the lens.

Glad to hear you're loving your new home and new life.

More later! But first, if it's the last thing I do, I'm finally going to send you this series of attempts at writing an actual letter! Love, M.

Chapter Fifteen

Molly can't help but notice that Oliver is big on follow-up especially when he takes to a patient and there is no question he takes to Davis. On his way to work at St. Vincent's, he drops by the apartment to make sure Davis is taking his medication, keeping his radiation appointments and honoring the time he is supposed to be resting in bed. Molly looks forward to Oliver's visits. Davis is easily bored and threatening to change his doctor yet again. Oliver knows how to reason with him. Shift his focus. Soon he and Davis are swapping detailed stories about AIDS, the FDA, Rock Hudson, the politics of choice, assisted suicide, Roe vs. Wade, the radical right, the homeless, the insane, the drugs, the greed, the violence, the infrastructure, education and, most of all, kids. Then one day, Oliver slips a video into Davis's VCR.

"This footage was shot by Letitia. She's nine. She's the one whose mother—"

"I know," says Davis, "the crack addict."

"He listens," says Oliver, "even on painkillers."

Molly turns her back to the TV and takes the covers off Davis's feet. There is no particular routine to her treatments. Nor does she demand of herself that the event be even moderately mystical. Most of the time it affords her an opportunity to talk to Davis about the Leftover Queen, the Church and all that needs to be sorted out before his death.

"So," says Oliver picking up the remote, "this is dinner at Letitia's house."

Molly looks through the bathroom door at the reflection of the TV in the full-length mirror. The camera pans over a bag of potato chips and an empty needle.

"*Look at that shot,*" *raves Oliver.* "*And she knew nothing about pacing or mood. Then all of a sudden...bang!...she's in her best friend's face by the fire hydrant. That's my car they're filling full of water. So much for being a nice guy.*"

Chapter Sixteen

June, 1989

Dear Molly,

Haven't known what to do about your offer to repay me so, as you undoubtedly have gathered, have done nothing (except talk about it in therapy). Now would feel too weird cashing them (your checks) so here they are. Please don't send anymore. You never were "an investment." Am glad you've found something to do that makes you feel useful and that I was able to contribute in whatever way to your education. You certainly contributed to mine! Congrats on the article on The Leftover Queen in the LN. I continue to recommend it to friends and friends of friends as we find our way through the plague. Hope you're well. I'm fine. Too busy. But, then, that's life. Or is it? Best, N.

Mid-July

Dear Hatia,

TB has joined the KS in Davis's lungs. His left leg has swollen to three times its normal size and through the fog of painkillers he has persuaded Oliver to care for him fulltime. I am greatly relieved. Even bought some spackle for my walls. Might even be able to find the time to fill the cracks! Am ashamed to think how long I've been living in almost total emptiness.

Davis is threatening to quit taking AZT. He says it's destroying what's left of his immune system. I go along with him because his research is meticulous, but when he gets to the part about the government using AZT to shut up AIDS activists, I try to reason with him and I always lose. Oliver, on the other hand, cuts to the chase. No AZT = No TV. Davis is totally into the videos Oliver's kids are shooting. He is convinced I am the person to help them write their narrations. I am on the verge of saying, "Boys, back off. I don't even keep a journal anymore." Am also on the verge of taking you up on your offer to come for a visit after Davis dies. I've never been to California. I've always had this image of myself driving up Big Sur in a convertible. Want to go with me? We could stand on a cliff, listen to crashing waves and remember the '60s, or, in my case, the '70s…when people were innocent and passionate and still had sex.

Heard from Nancy. She returned my checks. No mention of getting together or becoming friends. Sad. But underneath…well, you know! Love, M.

Chapter Seventeen

The kitchen in the Church is in its usual state of chaos. Three patients have died; nine more want to sign up; the fire department is due to arrive any moment to make sure conditions are sanitary and, on top of everything else, there aren't enough mushrooms for the mushroom soup. Molly chops and stirs and problem solves. Counts dinners and loads shopping bags. Washes pots and discusses tomorrow's menu and when Father Dan is outside with the homeless, packs a little something (at Davis's insistence) for Oliver's kids in Spanish Harlem.

At the end of the day, Oliver finds Molly sitting, hunched and exhausted, on the stoop. He opens his car door. She puts the bag of food on the passenger seat.

"Sure you won't come with me?"

"Oh, I know what you're thinking, Oliver," says Molly, leaning into the car, "and I'm not the person to help your kids with their videos."

"You better get in before it rains," says Oliver as Molly starts to close the door.

Molly puts the bag of food on the floor in front of the passenger seat, climbs into Oliver's car and as they lurch over potholes and around taxis, she feels green and compromised. At 30th Street Oliver stops at a red light and without thinking Molly opens the car door. Oliver looks at her as if she were about to hurl herself into oncoming traffic.

"Uh…this is where I live."

"*Oh. Okay.*"

Molly hesitates then adjusts the bag of food so it won't fall over.

"*I'll bring you back,*" *says Oliver as the light changes to green.*

"*Oliver, I'm no good with kids. It's taken me half my life to be able to even say the words.*"

"*But you're good with Davis.*"

"*That's caregiving. That's different.*"

"*Is it?*"

"*Please, Oliver, please…let me be.*"

Moments later Molly bounds up the stairs to her apartment.

'*Let me be,*' *she thinks as she opens the door.* '*It felt good to say that. Clean.*'

She turns in a slow circle, undoes her fannypack and lets it fall to the living room floor.

Chapter Eighteen

Dear Hatia,

It was all Davis could do to take air into his infected and water-logged lungs. When his oxygen tank was due for a change, he decided to return to the hospital which is where I am now. He signed all the appropriate papers without a fuss and, as soon as his doctor showed up, was put on a morphine drip.

Sometimes he confuses me with Oliver who he confuses with Richard who he is positive is hiding out in Spanish Harlem waiting for him (Davis) to die so he won't have to do the dishes. Then he becomes obsessed with going home. I tell him he's got two choices. He can either get better or jack up the morphine. Either way he is out of here. Then he becomes really lucid. Asks Oliver all about his kids. Makes sure they like the food we send them. Oliver says they do but they keep wondering why it's never pizza. And so it goes. Sometimes bad, sometimes scary, sometimes touching, sometimes mischievous, sometimes very, very funny. But never, in answer to your question, depressing. Mainly because there's no time for bullshit. Maybe that's what I mean when I say taking care of Davis has made me feel...I don't know...at home.

Later

Before I left, Davis sat bolt upright. Opened his eyes with a start. As if he were suddenly seeing God. Then he looked at me with such urgency, grabbed my wrist and said, "Take my tools." It was the last thing he ever said to me so I did.

More later. Love, M.

Chapter Nineteen

Davis never wanted a memorial. He always said there were too many of them and everyone was too burned out.

"Just open up the apartment. Serve that swordfish with capers and the carrot soufflé. But watch that Robby. He uses too much salt."

On the day, the sky is clear and the sun bakes itself into sallow cheeks and Molly and Father Dan decide to use the courtyard of the Church.

The celebration of Davis's life begins thoughtfully but, by the end of the day, it has turned into a robust gathering that spills onto the street. People who are normally housebound come in wheelchairs. Casual acquaintances. Old friends. New friends. People Molly only knows over the phone. It is a time to mull and wonder at the coming together of Davis's world. To feel grateful and disoriented. To let it all be whatever it is and to Molly (and, for all she knows, Davis), it is a relief that nobody feels the need to stand up and put it into words.

"I'll go get the car," says Oliver as Molly watches the last person leave.

Molly gets the pushbroom from the rectory and thinks about her first date with Davis. How sure she was that he was The One.

"You go home," says Father Dan.

"You have these ideas," says Molly, nudging a paper cup out of a corner, "about how your life is going to be. And then you find out your life is…none of your business."

"Yes," says Father Dan, taking the pushbroom. "Yes."

Molly gets her fannypack from its hiding place, puts it around her waist and gets in Oliver's car. They drive east in silence.

"Look at that," says Oliver pulling up in front of Molly's building, "a parking space. Thank you, Davis."

Molly sits, inert.

"It's so weird," says Oliver, turning off the ignition. "Even though you know. Even though you're there and watching. And telling him it's okay to let go. It's still so...."

"Final," says Molly, looking out the window.

Oliver takes her hand.

"You okay?" he asks.

"Just quiet. You?"

"I just wish I weren't so...used to it," says Oliver, running a hand around his steering wheel.

Molly opens the car door.

"Thanks for the ride. In fact, thanks. I don't know what I would have done without your—"

A tiny hand grips the inside of Molly's throat and in direct response her eyes begin to tear.

"Want me to walk you to your apartment?" asks Oliver.

"I don't have very far to go."

"Well, seeing as how I have this parking space, I can't let it go unappreciated."

"My place is nothing but rubble," says Molly as they climb the stairs.

"You should see where I live," says Oliver. "Furniture by Rejects."

Molly takes the keys out of her pocket.

"What will you do now?" she asks as she flips on the lights.

"Good question," says Oliver taking in the bare bones of the living room.

"I wasn't kidding," says Molly with an apologetic shrug. "For the longest time I tried to convince myself I was doing some sort of fancy penance. Then, one morning I woke up and said, 'Molly, the truth is you're hardly ever here.'"

An ambulance wails in the distance. Molly gets a couple of raspberry flavored seltzers out of the fridge as Oliver sits on the floor that once gathered dust bunnies under the rollaway and looks at Davis's tool box sitting pert and battered against the opposite wall.

"*There were bookshelves there once,*" *says Molly, entering the living room,* "*But the standards had taken to parting with the plaster.*"

"*You should expose the brick,*" *says Oliver after a moment.*

"*I've been thinking about that. Maybe put new shelves up over there. And a desk. I've always wanted my own desk. Nice and wide. With room for a computer. I've gotten spoiled with Davis's.*"

Oliver takes a swig of his raspberry seltzer, opens Davis's tool box and checks out the contents with the eyes of an expert.

"*Built-ins would make the most sense,*" *he says, looking inside a box of drill bits.*

"*Yeah. And so would a private elevator.*"

"*I'm serious.*"

"*Well, whatever you are I don't have the money so you can stop right there.*"

"*Well, I know some kids who could use a little help learning to write—*"

Molly shakes her head and tries not to smile.

"*Get out of here! I'm serious! Get out! And I thought Davis was imparting a secret wisdom from the other side! Taaaake the tooooool boooox. How long have you two been in kahoots?*"

"*Ever since the parking space.*"

"*Don't act like Mr. Innocent,*" *says Molly turning toward the airshaft.* "*You and he had it all figured out, didn't you? Even on morphine.* You *take the tool box.*"

"*Why?*"

"*I don't know. You're the carpenter. Besides…I'm tired of telling you No.*"

Molly turns her back and watches a piece of paper flutter then disappear into the mystery of the airshaft. Oliver doesn't quite know what to do. He knows what he wants to do but something always holds him back. He puts down the box of drill bits and ambles in a roundabout way toward the window, coming up quietly behind her. He stands thoughtfully looking into the airshaft. Instinctively, he reaches out his hand and runs his index finger down the bony path of Molly's spine making his way from the back of her long neck to her pelvis. Molly turns. Oliver feels awkward. Paralyzed by the confusion that widens then narrows her eyes.

"*I know,*" *he says, smiling a shy smile,* "*you think I'm gay.*"

"Oh," says Molly, "aren't you?"

"I don't know…are you?"

"I don't know."

Molly looks at the floor, all arms and legs. Oliver puts his finger under her chin and raises her face. Molly looks at Oliver's Adam's apple. Then at his strong jaw and sunken cheeks.

"You're a beautiful woman," says Oliver as Molly's eyes find his.

Molly blushes and twists away.

"What?" asks Oliver, gently.

"Nothing. Just… You're pretty beautiful, too."

Oliver's arms curve around Molly's back. They feel warm and young and full of their own agendas.

"Oliver…uh…I don't think I'm ready," says Molly, quietly.

"For what?" he asks gently.

"Oh…you know…The Talk. AIDS."

"Condoms."

"Commitment."

"Well," he says, blushing, "when you are, maybe I can help."

Molly steps back and looks at the floor.

'A man who blushes,' she thinks. 'A young man who blushes. A young man who blushes and is compassionate. A young man who blushes and is compassionate and good with tools.'

"You better go," she says putting a hand on his shoulder.

"For now?" he asks as Molly's hand travels down his arm. "Or forever?"

Chapter Twenty

Dear Ethan,

Thank you for your postcard from China. Your trip sounded amazing! What a relief you were nowhere near Tienanmen Square! I'm glad you felt a kinship with your cousins and that Elizabeth is encouraging you to explore your heritage. And that you were finally able to throw Meimei off the top of her childhood mountain. I'm also glad you have a girlfriend whose parents live in the city. I would absolutely love to meet her.

Life is pretty full these days. The Leftover Queen has a life of its own and a friend is helping me fix up my apartment. In exchange I've been helping him with some kids. I was apprehensive at first. I'm still not sure I know what I'm doing but I'm beginning to realize that maybe I'm not supposed to. The kid who really sparks me is named Letitia. She lives with her mother who is a crack addict in Spanish Harlem. When she was four, her mother began sending her alone into the streets to get her her drugs. Letitia has known physical and emotional violence and, as a result, she is tough. But she loves to write…the way you did/do. In fact, the first writing exercise I gave the kids was the answer/question game you and I made up when we wrote the poem about the Chinese moon. Letitia is particularly good with images. Her mind is scattered and immediate. Like MTV. We get together in my friend Oliver's apartment on 95th Street near the East River. There are now six kids and one fan. For the first part of class we talk about what we remember from the week before. Then we talk about creativity and why it's important to tell the truth. And when the kids can no longer stand it, Oliver has them move the furniture to one side and get physical.

"Because why?" he asks, leading them in a yoga stretch.

"Because you don't just shoot video with your eyes," they say. "You shoot with your whooooole body."

Then, after we've warmed ourselves up, we begin to write. I tell them writing is like making a quilt. All those thoughts and ideas coming together to make something—

"Pretty?"

"Yeah...sometimes," I say. "What else?"

"Warm?" asks Letitia.

"Warm!" says Raoul. "You're stupid."

"Quilts are warm," she says defiantly.

"Warm," I say. "What else?"

And much of the time I find myself speaking to them as if I were speaking to you. Not you now...but you when we were together. I'm so glad you liked getting my letter. I know I was always more of a friend than a mother. It's taken me a long time to accept that that is all that I have to give. And you, whether you wanted to be or not, were/are one of my most necessary teachers. Please give your father my love. I'm glad he's doing well. If it would fit into your plans, I'd love to see you and your girlfriend when you have your long weekend in the city.

All my love, Molly

Chapter Twenty-One

Molly puts down the level and pours a glass of lemonade.

"I've been thinking about applying for that grant," she says as Oliver drills another hole in the newly exposed brick. "We need to rent a space to teach in. I mean, it's fun using your apartment but Letitia has a friend who wants to join and there's that little boy who lives on 105th Street. We don't want to say No to them, do we? I mean, on account of space?"

"Yeah…and then there's the dilemma of the editing equipment," Oliver says arching his back and rolling his head in a circle.

"It may be old but it's free," says Molly putting her hands on his shoulders and digging into his muscles.

"Oh," he says, "that feels good."

Molly slaps him gently on the back.

"When I know you better," she says, "I'll do your feet."

In November 1989, Molly wins a raffle at an AIDS benefit. A free trip for two in a hot-air balloon. Oliver is sure she is going to invite him and is reminded how little he really understands her when she decides to take Letitia.

Letitia, however, isn't so sure she wants to go. She likes Molly but her hands are so big. You have to be careful around people with big hands. You have to be good. Letitia isn't feeling good when Molly invites her to go whereveritis. Then Molly says she'll bring the video camera and the cloud of apprehension lifts.

Molly toots the horn of Oliver's car. Letitia jumps in the front seat and turns on the radio. Rap music. Molly had hoped they'd use the time to talk although she isn't really sure about what. Finally, she makes Letitia a deal. Fifteen minutes of rap. Fifteen minutes of news. Fifteen minutes of conversation. And fifteen minutes of silence. Letitia thinks Molly is nuts, but she is also the driver.

"I never been out of New York City," *says Letitia making her poor-me eyes.*

"Sure you have," *says Molly.* "You've been to New Jersey. To the Burlington Coat Factory. Oliver and I took all you kids."

"Well, I never been up in a plane. I want to go in a plane. Will you take me?"

"Maybe one day. If you stay in school."

"You so stric."

Molly laughs.

"Strict...with a T."

"You so stric...with a T," *says Letitia.*

Molly smiles, turns a corner and pulls into a wide open field.

"Wow! Look!"

Letitia is fascinated by the fire that makes their balloon go up, up, up. And as she and Molly soar into the air, Letitia turns herself and her camera on the world.

"What's that there?"

"That's New York State and over there is New York City."

"And there?"

"That's Connecticut."

"That where you live?"

"No, that's where I grew up."

"What over there?"

"Well, the Atlantic Ocean, the Mediterranean Sea...then over there is England and Europe."

"What about where they was talkin' 'bout that wall on the radio?"

"Oh, well, that's Berlin. It's over that way...in Germany."

"What over there?"

"Well, California, then Hawaii...."

"And after that?"

"After that comes China. Then Russia."

"Wow," *says Letitia,* "it sure is big."

"Yes," says Molly quietly, "it sure is."

The balloon tilts and drifts. A young girl, crisp as summer pulls on Letitia's mind then tumbles joyfully into the shadows of a brave, new world. Letitia shrugs. Her mind is always making crazy pictures.

"I'm cold," she says after a moment.

Molly unzips her down jacket and puts Letitia inside it. Her large hands stroke Letitia's wild, unpredictable hair. Letitia doesn't know how Molly can make her hands feel so soft. So gentle. The balloon shifts away from New York, the Atlantic Ocean and Connecticut.

"Why they put it up in the first place?" asks Letitia.

"What, Honey?"

"The Germany wall."

Molly smiles.

"Good question."

"You laughin' at me?"

"No, Darling…I'm lovin' at you."

A sudden gust of wind lifts the balloon straight up. Molly laughs as Letitia squeals then lets her head fall backwards onto Molly's heart.